My Book 3/7/21

D1086676

THE TWELVE MURDERS OF CHRISTMAS

A TONI DAY MYSTERY

Also by Jane Bennett Munro

Murder under the Microscope
Too Much Blood
Grievous Bodily Harm
Death by Autopsy
The Body on the Lido Deck
A Deadly Homecoming

My book
2/2

THE TWELVE MURDERS

OF

CHRISTMAS

A TONI DAY MYSTERY

JANE BENNETT MUNRO

LitPrime
"Your story is our priority"

LitPrime Solutions™
21250 Hawthorne Blvd
Suite 500, Torrance, CA 90503
www.litprime.com
Phone: 1 (800) 980-3309

© 2020 Jane Bennett Munro. All rights reserved.

No part of this book may be reproduced, stored in
a retrieval system, or transmitted by any means
without the written permission of the author.

Published by LitPrime Solutions 09/18/2020

ISBN: 978-1-953397-05-8 (sc)
ISBN: 978-1-953397-06-5 (e)

Any people depicted in stock imagery provided
by Thinkstock are models, and such images are
being used for illustrative purposes only.

Certain stock imagery © Thinkstock.

Because of the dynamic nature of the Internet, any web
addresses or links contained in this book may have changed
since publication and may no longer be valid. The views
expressed in this work are solely those of the author and do
not necessarily reflect the views of the publisher, and the
publisher hereby disclaims any responsibility for them.

For jurors everywhere.
May this never happen to them.

PROLOGUE

By then, we were at the door to the parking garage. I pushed the door open, and Ryan Trowbridge followed me out.

"Brrr!" he said. "I think it's gotten colder, if that's even possible." He zipped up his parka and pulled his gloves out of his pocket. Something fell to the concrete floor with a dull clang.

An ice pick.

For a nanosecond, I was paralyzed with fear. All I could think was *Oh my freakin' Lord, I am so dead.*

CHAPTER 1

By the pricking of my thumbs,
Something wicked this way comes.

—Shakespeare, *Macbeth*

Is there such a thing as a poison-pen Christmas card?

I wondered about that as I went through our mail after I got home from work. It was December 1, and Christmas cards sometimes arrived that early, but this Christmas card was nothing like any Christmas card I'd ever seen.

Killer and Geraldine vied for my attention, as usual, with soft whines and wagging tails as I slit the thing open with a kitchen knife. It was in a nice white envelope with a tasteful holly and ivy decoration around the edge, but the card inside was anything but tasteful.

On the outside of the card was a crude drawing of a Christmas tree done with colored markers. Underneath the tree was a man's body drawn in black ink—or part of one. His legs were the only thing that showed, toes up. Inside the card was a verse:

On the first day of Christmas, my true love
gave to me a Partridge under a tree.

No signature.

No return address.

"Well, this is weird," I said to Hal, who was fixing me a scotch on the rocks at the bar.

"What's weird?" he asked. "The dogs have been fed, by the way, no matter what they tell you."

"Take a look at this card," I said, handing it to him. He handed me my drink before he took the card from me.

"Who's it from?" he asked before he got a good look at it.

"I don't know."

"This verse is wrong too."

"I know."

He shrugged and started to throw it into the wastebasket.

"Don't throw it away," I said.

"Why not? It's obviously a joke."

"I don't think so," I said. "I think it's a warning."

"Of what, pray tell?"

"Look," I said. "The drawing shows a body under a tree. And the word *partridge* is capitalized. It could be somebody's name."

"Yeah, right. Somebody who's dead," he said sarcastically.

"Look in the paper," I said. "See if there's a Partridge in the obituaries."

"You're serious, aren't you?"

"As a heart attack. Go ahead. Look. I dare you."

"You're on," Hal said. He picked up his beer and went on into the living room. The *Clarion* lay on the coffee table, where he'd left it that morning. He opened it to the obituaries, took a quick look, and then closed the paper and threw it back onto the coffee table. "Ha! No Partridges."

"Maybe not today," I said, "and maybe not tomorrow. But look at the card. There's a body under a Christmas tree, and if this verse is the first of twelve, it means eleven more people are going to die, unless we do something about it."

Hal sighed. "Toni, seriously? Where is it written that *we* have to do anything? And about what? So somebody's dead. Why is that our problem?"

"Because this so-called Christmas card was sent to me," I said.

Hal slung an arm around me and kissed the top of my head. "Toni, my dearest love, please tell me you're not going to blow this all out of proportion and get involved with some kind of serial killer."

My husband, Hal Shapiro, towered over my petite five-foot-three frame by a foot and outweighed me by a hundred pounds. With his blond hair, mustache, and beard, which were mostly white now; ruddy complexion; and bright blue eyes, he resembled a Viking more than the mild-mannered college professor he was. We'd been married twenty-three years.

"I'm already involved," I said. "This serial killer, if that's what he is, wants me to know about what he's doing. I can't just ignore that."

Hal threw up his hands. "Suit yourself." He went over to the fireplace and switched on the gas log before stretching out in his recliner, where he immediately turned on the TV. He was soon lost in the nightly news.

I picked up the rest of the mail and carried it into the living room. I left the bills on the stairs to be taken up to the office the next time anybody went upstairs and then settled myself on the couch with the catalogs, whereupon Geraldine, a ten-pound terrier mix, jumped into my lap. She circled around a couple times with her pointy little feet digging into my thighs before she curled up in a little black-and-brown ball with a gusty sigh. Killer, an aging German shepherd way too big to get into my lap, curled up on the floor next to me.

The cat, Spook, who was flaked out along the back of the couch, briefly opened one yellow eye and then went back to sleep.

I picked up my cell phone and dialed.

"Who are you calling?" Hal asked.

"Pete."

Pete Vincent, a homicide detective in the Twin Falls Police Department, was our son-in-law, married to Hal's daughter, Bambi.

"Seriously?"

"He might know how this guy died."

Hal sighed and muttered, "Oy vey," before turning his attention back to the news.

Hal had reason to be irritated. For the last twelve years or so, I'd gotten involved in some situations best left to law enforcement, putting my own life and sometimes the lives of my family and friends in danger. It was not a coincidence that we had a homicide detective as a son-in-law.

When Hal and I, Toni Day, first had moved to Twin Falls, Idaho, for my first job out of residency, I had become a solo pathologist at a forty-bed community hospital, Perrine Memorial. Now I was a partner in a three-pathologist group contracting with the big new 250-bed tertiary care hospital built for us by Cascade Medical Enterprises, a behemoth health-care system covering much of the Pacific Northwest. The old Perrine Memorial building was now home to county offices.

Pete was at home and off duty. When he answered, I could hear our two granddaughters, aged five and two, arguing in the background.

I told him about the card. "Was someone named Ralph Partridge murdered recently?"

"The name Partridge doesn't ring any bells, but I don't have access to the police computer here at home. Tell you what. Bernie's on duty tonight; maybe he can help."

Terrific, I thought. Bernie Kincaid, also a homicide detective, and I had a rather complicated and sometimes fraught relationship. I never knew which Bernie I'd get: the amorous one or the pissed-off one who wished I'd keep my nose out of his business. But I didn't need to mention that to Pete, so I merely thanked him and disconnected.

I had the Twin Falls Police Department and the Twin Falls County Sheriff in my contact list too, since I'd had numerous reasons to call them over the years. When I called the police station, I got the gum-smacking dispatcher. I couldn't believe she was still working there. She annoyed me so much that I thought she certainly must have annoyed everybody else as well, but evidently not.

In a bored tone, she reluctantly agreed to connect me with Lieutenant Kincaid, but it took him at least two minutes to come on the line. He seemed out of breath.

"What is it, Toni?" he asked brusquely. "Make it fast. We've had a report of a fatality in Rock Creek Park. Rollie's already there, but he can't do anything until we release the body, so I've got to go."

"Does your fatality have a name?"

"Not so far. Why?"

I told him about the Christmas card.

"Toni, I don't have time for this nonsense. I gotta go!" He hung up on me.

I called Rollie, whom I also had on speed dial.

Roland Perkins was a local mortician who'd been county

coroner as long as I'd been in Twin Falls and probably even before that. His place of business, Parkside Funeral Home, was right across the Twin Falls City Park from the old hospital. We'd known each other for more than twenty years, but he always called me either Doctor or "young lady," never Toni.

He didn't disappoint me. "Well now, young lady, I thought I'd be calling you about this, not the other way around. Heh-heh."

"Has that body been identified yet?"

"Not yet. He's lying under a big blue spruce in the snow, an apparent hit-and-run."

I knew without looking that Hal was glaring at me, because Rollie had a way of waiting until the middle of the night to call me about autopsies, and Hal really hated being awakened by phone calls in the middle of the night.

Years ago, I'd tried putting my cell phone under my pillow on vibrate and going into the bathroom to answer it, something that apparently worked for my partner Mike but not for me. Hal always woke up regardless.

So I satisfied myself with a spot of damage control. "Rollie, do me a favor. If you decide you need an autopsy, could you please wait until morning to call me about it? Hal and I would both appreciate it."

"You got it, Doc."

We rang off. Hal said, "Well?"

"They found a body in Rock Creek Park, lying under a big blue spruce in the snow, a possible hit-and-run."

"Tell me you don't want to go to the scene," Hal said.

"I don't. It's dark, it's cold, and there's snow on the ground. I'd rather be here by the fire with you and a scotch."

"Good."

The phone rang—the landline, which Hal and I had been arguing about getting rid of because the only people who called us on it were telemarketers. With a sigh, he picked up the handset next to him on the end table, answered it, and then rang off and flung the handset back onto the end table with a snort of disgust. "That same person has been calling around this time for the last three days and hanging up when I answer. It's getting old."

I had to admit I hadn't noticed. "Anytime you want to get rid of the landline, just let me know," I said.

He changed the subject. "Now that you already know there's going to be an autopsy tomorrow, are you going to do it?"

Back in the day, Hal wouldn't have had to ask that question, but now, at Cascade Perrine Regional Medical Center, I had two partners: Mike Leonard and his little brother, Brian.

"Well, Mike's on call, so he's doing frozen sections, and Brian's doing bone marrows, so yes, that leaves me."

"So then you'll know whether he's a Partridge or not," Hal said.

"Tomorrow," I replied, "I expect to find out a lot more about that guy than just his name."

CHAPTER 2

Things are seldom what they seem;
Skim milk masquerades as cream.

—Sir William Gilbert

Brian was already in his office when I arrived at the hospital the next morning. He followed me into my office and started talking before I even had a chance to take my coat off.

He greeted me in the same way Mike always did. "Hey. We got ourselves a busy day, I tell you what."

"And good morning to you too," I said. "Do we have an autopsy?"

Brian was a younger, thinner, taller, and darker-haired version of his brother. Like Mike, he wore glasses. The brothers Leonard hailed from Texas; there were five of them, and they were all pathologists. Brian was the youngest.

Deflated, he sank into my visitors' chair. "Damn. How come you already know about that? I just found out about it myself."

"Who told you?" I asked.

"Arlene—who else?"

Arlene was our senior secretary and transcriptionist. Short, with curly black hair, she was a feisty Jewish girl from the Bronx who had come here on a ski trip, fallen in love with a local boy, and decided to stay. Apparently, the lack of a synagogue in Twin Falls didn't bother her any more than it did Hal.

As if summoned by hearing her name, Arlene followed Brian into my office with papers in her hand. "It's a coroner's case," she said. "Here's the consent signed by Mr. Perkins."

I took it, glanced at the name, and exclaimed, "Ha! I knew it!"

"Knew what?" Mike appeared in my doorway.

"It's a Partridge."

"What are you talking about?" Brian asked.

I rummaged in my purse and produced the Christmas card. "This Partridge."

Mike looked at the card and then passed it to Brian.

"Looks more like a threat than a Christmas greeting, I tell you what," Brian said.

"The body's in the morgue," Arlene said, "if you want to take a look at it. Mr. Perkins wants to be called before you start so that he can be here, and so does Lieutenant Kincaid."

"Does Natalie know?" I asked, and Arlene nodded.

Natalie Scott was one of our three histotechs, and I'd trained her as a diener, or autopsy assistant. She was perfectly capable of removing the brain and the organ block all by herself, but in this case, I felt that at least one of us should be there, considering the death could be a homicide rather than vehicular manslaughter.

I also didn't expect her to move the body from the cooler to the table by herself. I intended to press Mike and Brian into service for that.

With our new electronic medical record, or EMR, we found it necessary to divide up the surgical pathology among the three of us because, far from making things easier, EMR required more hoops to jump through for each case, so everything took twice as long. The same thing was true of grossing in the surgicals, reading Paps, and doing frozen sections.

The upside was that it was far easier to look up clinical history since the patient's entire chart was there for the reading. Material from the previous system had been rolled over into the new one. We could even access information on patients in the other hospitals in the system if we needed to.

Ralph Partridge, age seventy-six, had been a longtime patient with a history of congestive heart failure, hypertension, hypercholesterolemia, and type 2 diabetes, any or all of which could have killed him if he hadn't been hit by a car first.

We decided to do the autopsy after lunch, and I called both Rollie and Bernie to let them know. I also let Natalie know. She and her colleagues would be able to get all the slides cut and stained by then.

Ralph Partridge was a heavyset elderly man with thoroughly forgettable features. He looked like someone who had sat at a desk all his life and never exercised. He looked like a heart attack waiting to happen. He didn't look like anybody I'd ever seen before.

Rollie arrived right then and stood next to me, gazing at the body. He was the personification of the jolly fat man, with the exception of his deep sepulchral voice, which was well suited to his profession.

"Notice anything?" I asked him.

"No, unless you mean there's not a mark on him."

"Yes, that's what I noticed too," I said. "This sure doesn't look like a hit-and-run to me."

Natalie was already clad in protective garb, with her long

mane of black hair stuffed under a paper head cover and her cobalt-blue eyes hidden behind a face shield.

With Rollie watching, Natalie and I examined the body and all the extremities. We found nothing, not even a needle mark. There were no broken bones. No tire marks or grille-shaped bruises. Then we turned him onto his side to examine his back.

At that point, Bernie Kincaid arrived. He was small and compact, with black hair and black eyes, and was quite good looking. At one point years ago, when Hal and I had been having marital problems, he'd expressed a desire to have an affair with me. I supposed I had been pretty tempting back then, with curly black hair, olive skin, green eyes, and a shapely figure. I still wasn't bad looking, even at fifty-two; my hair had more silver in it, and I was a few pounds heavier, but everything else was about the same.

Mutual attraction had been as far as it went back then, but from the expression in Bernie's eyes, I could tell his feelings hadn't changed. I averted my eyes hastily so as not to give him the wrong idea about my feelings.

Ralph Partridge had no marks on his back either, although it would have been difficult to make out bruises due to the postmortem lividity. His whole back and buttocks were purple. I saw no obvious stab marks or any other disruption of the skin, but there was a thin trail of blood running down from the hairline. I might have missed it completely if his hair hadn't been white.

"Where's that coming from?" I murmured, bending over to peer at the back of the neck. Sure enough, there was a small, jagged laceration just above the hairline with blood around it. "I'm going to need to cut that out and save it, so we can preserve anything that might be in there so deep we can't see it."

While I held the body in position, Natalie photographed the back of the neck. Then she held the body in position while I excised the laceration with a good margin of skin and soft tissue around it and dropped it into a jar of formalin.

I'd gone pretty deep, all the way down to bone, but I could see that the laceration had gone still deeper, between bones. There was hemorrhagic staining of the bone itself and the surrounding soft tissue. I had Natalie photograph that too.

I didn't like what I was thinking.

I straightened up. "Okay, let's get the brain out," I said.

Together we put the body back in the supine position, and Natalie propped the head back up. Deftly, she made the vertex incision, extending it down behind the ears on both sides, and peeled the scalp away from the skull, forward and back. With the Stryker saw, she removed the skullcap and lifted it away from the brain.

Bernie winced and stuck his fingers in his ears at the sound of the saw but didn't leave the room.

The cerebral cortex looked normal, but blood covered the occipital lobes and cerebellum.

"Shall I take the brain out now?" Natalie asked. "Or do you want to do it?"

"I'll do it," I said. "I don't know what we're going to find, so I want to go slow and be sure."

I had an idea of what we might find, but I didn't want to say anything until I was sure.

Gingerly, I divided the meninges and cranial nerves holding the brain in place, starting at the front with the optic nerves and working backward until I could see the brainstem, which looked like hamburger.

I took a scalpel and stuck it as far down through the foramen magnum as it would go to transect the spinal cord.

When I lifted the brain free of the skull, it became obvious what had happened.

The brainstem had been nearly transected. The segment of spinal cord dangled from it by a narrow strand of bloody, mangled tissue. It was almost as if someone had stuck a sharp object in there and wiggled it around.

"Photograph that," I said tersely, and Natalie did so. Then she looked at me. Her blue eyes widened at the expression on my face.

"Is this what I think it is?" she asked.

"Yes," I said. "This man was pithed."

CHAPTER 3

And much of Madness, and more of Sin,
And Horror the soul of the plot.

—Edgar Allan Poe

Bernie made a strangled noise and abruptly left the room. Rollie wasn't nearly as squeamish. He moved closer to see for himself. "Pithed?" he asked. "Seriously? You mean like a frog in biology class?"

"Exactly like that," I said.

"With what?" he asked.

"I don't know," I said, "but my money's on an ice pick."

"So this wasn't a hit-and-run after all."

"No. It was staged to look like a hit-and-run."

"Why would anybody do such a thing?" Rollie said.

"We won't know that," I told him, "until we know who had a reason to kill him in the first place."

I drew blood from the heart and urine from the bladder for possible toxicology. Natalie performed the Y-shaped incision, I cut the ribs, and together we lifted out the organ block and placed it on the cutting board. Other than an enlarged heart, a lot of fat in the abdomen, and a lot of plaque in the aorta, that part of the autopsy was pretty noncontributory to the cause of death.

There was no lacerated liver or spleen. The ascending aorta was not ruptured. No ribs were broken. There was no blood in any of the body cavities.

The ventilation system in the new morgue was much better than in Rollie's embalming room, where I had done most of my autopsies at the old hospital, which had had no morgue. There was little odor when we ran the bowel, but it was wasted on Bernie, who had already bailed.

We found no bowel lacerations either.

Natalie put the bucket of tissue samples in the storage cabinet and took the blood and urine samples to the lab with instructions to obtain the toxicology screen that we routinely used and on no account let anyone discard the samples.

Rollie went back to his place of business after extracting my promise to get him a copy of the preliminary findings ASAP. I thought, but did not say, the preliminary findings would probably be the same as the final findings, with the exception of possible toxicology.

Bernie, miraculously recovered from his slight gastric upset, accompanied me to my office. *Uh-oh*, I thought. *Here comes the amorous Bernie, hoping to get me alone in my office.* I resolved to leave the door open and include Mike and Brian in whatever discussion we would have.

Mike was busy doing a frozen section when we got back, but Brian was done with the bone marrows and all agog to know what I'd found.

Natalie had given me the picture card out of the camera so I could download the pictures onto my computer, and I did so, turning my monitor so that both Brian and Bernie could see.

Bernie turned away, his lips compressed.

Brian pulled the stool he occupied closer to my desk so he could see better. "Sweet Jesus," he breathed. "Is that what I think it is? Why, it looks as if he was—"

"Pithed?"

"Yes, pithed. That's exactly what it looks like. I've never seen that before."

"Except in biology class," I said.

"Oh jeez, yes. Do you know what was used?"

"I'm thinking ice pick."

"Wow. Ice Pick Man."

Mike appeared in the doorway. "Shoulda been wearing his *pith* helmet, I tell you what," he said.

All three of us burst out laughing.

Bernie abruptly rose. "Toni, I'll call you," he snapped, and he left.

"He seems pissed," Brian said.

"Better than pithed," Mike said.

I suppressed a giggle. "Okay, you guys, get out of here. I've got work to do."

Hal and I traditionally had spent our Friday evenings with Pete and Bambi, even after the birth of little Toni. But by the time little sister Shawna Renee had arrived, little Toni had been three, and Friday nights with them had become more like a rodeo than a relaxing dinner.

So by common consent, Pete and Bambi now went their own way on Friday nights, and we spent them with our next-door neighbors and best friends, Jodi and Elliott Maynard, as we had done before Bambi came into our lives and married Pete.

Bambi was Hal's daughter by his first wife, Shawna, but Shawna and Hal already had been divorced and Shawna had been remarried before Bambi was born. Hal hadn't even known of her existence until she'd shown up at the college and applied for a job as Hal's lab assistant.

Elliott was a lawyer, and Jodi owned a beauty salon. They had six children, only one of whom still lived at home. We usually ordered in pizza or went out to a restaurant.

Of course, when we wanted to talk shop, it was better to eat at home than at a restaurant, where everything one said could be overheard, and usually, our house was preferable to theirs because eleven-year-old Emily was always randomly popping in and out, with or without friends.

That was why I called Hal from work to suggest pizza at our house—because I definitely needed to talk shop.

Before I left work, I sent the pictures from my computer to my cell phone so I could show them to Elliott. I was hoping he would know who Ralph Partridge was.

Jodi and Elliott were already there when I got home, enjoying their various libations around the fire. Elliott was tall and thin, favored three-piece suits, and looked like a rabbi with his wildly curly salt-and-pepper hair and beard. Jodi, shorter and on the chunky side, favored flowing, psychedelic clothing and big, chunky jewelry and appeared to have styled her red hair with an eggbeater. It had little peaks all over it, like whipped cream.

"Finally!" Elliott exclaimed when I walked into the living room. "What took you so freakin' long?"

"He's a little impatient," Jodi said, stating the obvious.

"So am I," Hal said. "Go ahead and tell Elliott all about it while I get your drink. The usual?"

I nodded and sat down on the couch next to Jodi. I took the card out of my purse and handed it to Elliott.

"What the hell is this?" he asked, looking at the cover of the card. "Is this a joke? If so, it's not very freakin' funny. Where did it come from?"

"It came in the mail," I told him.

He picked up the envelope and examined it. "No return address. But it's postmarked Boise. Mailed two days ago. Do you know who it's from?"

"No idea," I said.

"May I?" Jodi asked.

Elliott handed the card to her. She looked at it and made a face. "This is scary."

Hal came back with my drink. "Tell them the rest of it," he said.

The phone rang. Hal swore and picked up the handset, listened for a nanosecond, and slammed it back down on the table.

"What was that all about?" Elliott asked.

Hal told him about the mysterious caller. "It's been four days now."

"Maybe you should let Toni answer it next time," Jodi said.

Hal handed me my scotch on the rocks and changed the subject. "Tell them the rest of it already."

"Do either of you know anybody named Ralph Partridge?" I asked Jodi and Elliott.

Jodi shook her head, but Elliott seemed undecided. "Hmm. Partridge. It sounds familiar, but I can't place it. Who is it?"

"His body was found last night in Rock Creek Park," I said. "It looked like a hit-and-run. The body had rolled off the road under a tree."

"A Partridge under a tree," Jodi said. "How long had he been there?"

"Overnight," I said. "He was lying in the snow under a big blue spruce."

"Do they know who hit him?" Jodi asked.

"Nobody hit him," I said. "Somebody killed him and dumped the body there so it would look like a hit-and-run."

"How do you know all this?" Elliott asked.

"I did the autopsy today," I said. "He'd been pithed."

All three of them recoiled.

"Pithed?" Elliott echoed.

"With an ice pick," I said, "or something like it."

"Oy gevalt!" Hal exclaimed.

"Like a frog in biology class," I added.

Jodi put a hand to her mouth. "Oh, that's gross."

"I have pictures right here on my phone," I said.

"I think we have the picture without seeing those," Elliott said.

"Toni thinks this means that eleven more people are going to die," Hal said.

"Oh my God," Jodi said. "Why?"

"There's no way to know," I said. "But it's obviously a parody of 'The Twelve Days of Christmas,' so I'm assuming there will be twelve verses. Will it be twelve random people or a specific group of twelve people? Maybe it's a family of twelve. Maybe this person stands to inherit if he can get these twelve out of the way. Maybe it's a tontine." I was on a roll.

"Or a jury," Elliott said.

The roll I was on came to a dead stop. "Of course!" I said. "Somebody gets out of prison on parole and kills off the jury who put him there."

"I can access court records from my office," Elliott said. "Monday I'll go into the website and look for a juror named Ralph Partridge."

"Why wait for Monday?" I asked.

"What—you want me to go do that tonight?"

"If somebody wants to kill off an entire jury and you can find

Ralph Partridge, then you'll know which jury it was, who else was on it, and who the defendant was," I said. "Then the police can arrest the person and prevent eleven more murders."

"You can't argue with that," Hal said.

"You're agreeing with her?" Elliott asked in disbelief. "You think I should go back to my freakin' office right now and look all that up?"

"No time like the present," Hal said.

"Oh, for heaven's sake, stop arguing, and go do it," Jodi said. "You know perfectly well you couldn't live with yourself if you don't and somebody else dies."

"Want me to go with you?" I asked.

Elliott did an eye roll that threatened to sprain both eyeballs.

"We'll all go," Hal said. "Pizza can wait."

CHAPTER 4

The savage in man is never quite eradicated.
—Henry David Thoreau

In Elliott's office, Jodi and I took seats on the couch against the wall while Elliott fired up his computer, and Hal pulled a chair up close so he could see the screen.

"You know what I don't get," Jodi murmured. "Why did you get that card instead of someone else?"

"I haven't the foggiest notion," I said.

"And whose true love are you supposed to be?"

I thought about that for approximately a nanosecond before it hit me. Other than Hal, there was only one person who ever had professed true love for me.

"Oh no," I moaned.

"What?" Jodi asked.

"Robbie."

"It can't be," Jodi said practically. "He's in prison."

"Or is he?" I objected. "Is it possible?"

"It's impossible," Jodi said. "It's only been eleven years, and he's supposed to be serving a life sentence."

"Well, I can't just sit here wondering," I said. "I'm going to call Pete."

Hal turned his head. "What the hell are you two yammering on about? We can't hear ourselves think."

"No worries," I told him. "I'll go out into the hall."

"Me too," Jodi said.

Out in the hall, I pulled out my cell phone, but a thought stopped me before I could dial.

"You know what? Maybe I ought to call Bernie instead," I said. "He was at the autopsy."

"Did he make it through the whole thing?" Jodi asked jokingly. Bernie's squeamishness was well known to all of us. I had done him in with a gangrenous bowel the first time we'd met, and I still was not sure he'd ever forgiven me.

"No," I said. "He bailed when I said the victim had been pithed, and that was just the brain. We hadn't even opened the body yet. Oh hell, I guess I'll just call the station and talk to whoever's on duty."

Pete was on duty, as it turned out. "Hey, Toni, what's up?"

"Please tell me Robbie is still in prison."

When we went back into Elliott's office, he and Hal were staring at the computer screen with grim expressions. Hal looked up as we came through the door.

"Well, we found Ralph Partridge," he said, "and we know which jury he was on, and you're not going to like it, sweetie."

"Only it's impossible," Elliott said.

"No, it isn't," I said. "Pete says Robbie was paroled a week ago."

"That's ridiculous," Hal said. "He had a life sentence for kidnapping and attempted murder, and they let him out after only ten years?"

"Eleven, actually," Elliott said.

"Pete said he was released for good behavior," I said. "He helped other inmates with their appeals and created a law library for their use. He was apparently a model prisoner."

"Well, I think it stinks," Hal said hotly. "He damn near killed me, and now he gets out so he can try again. What the fuck are we supposed to do now?"

Hal had good reason to be angry. Eleven years earlier, Robbie had kidnapped him and left him tied up in a crawl space in the dead of winter to die. He hadn't died in the crawl space, but the hantavirus pneumonia he'd acquired there nearly had done him in.

"At least he's not allowed to have a gun now," Elliott said. "So you don't have to worry about that."

Back in the day, Robbie had threatened to shoot Hal through the big picture window in our house with a high-powered rifle.

"Right," Hal snarled. "Now he's graduated to ice picks. Who needs a gun, when he can just go to the local hardware store?"

"He's also graduated from attempted murder to murder," I said. "He'll be back inside before you know it."

"Not so fast," Elliott said. "We don't know for sure that it's Robbie who's doing this. It may not have anything to do with Robbie."

"Then who's sending love notes to Toni?" Hal said. "This whole thing started because Robbie's in love with Toni. Who else would do that? Who else besides me is in love with Toni?"

Bernie Kincaid came to mind, but I sure as hell wasn't going to mention him to Hal in his present state of mind.

Elliott tapped a few keys. "I'm printing out the jury list for you. It'll come out on Betsy's printer. Just a minute—I'll go get it."

He went into the outer office and then returned with the list and handed it to Hal.

"Pete's coming over in the morning," I said.

Elliott powered down his computer and turned off the desk lamp. "In that case, I suggest we go home, eat pizza, and get a good night's sleep."

CHAPTER 5

She was a woman of mean understanding,
little information, and uncertain temper.

—Jane Austen

It had snowed during the night, and there were three inches in the front yard Saturday morning when Hal went out to get the paper.

Pete didn't show up until we'd had breakfast and cleaned up the kitchen, and I had gone upstairs to pay some bills and check email. Hal hollered at me from the bottom of the stairs to come down and bring the Christmas card.

My son-in-law was as tall as Hal but not as husky. His sandy hair, blue eyes, and freckles made him look like the all-American boy, and his easygoing personality was the perfect foil for Bernie's uptightness. He'd graduated from our community college, and Hal had been one of his professors. Hal had also arranged for him to watch me do autopsies while he was still a college kid. As a policeman and later a detective, Pete never hesitated to ask me or Hal for help with medical issues related to his cases, so he was at our house frequently.

He was helping himself to a cup of coffee when I got downstairs. He seemed preoccupied and barely acknowledged my presence when I went into the kitchen to get my own coffee. The reason became obvious when I went back to the living room and heard what he was telling Hal.

"There's been a bit of a shake-up at the station," he said. "Bernie's been promoted. He's not going to be my partner anymore."

Bernie and Pete had been partners forever. Well, actually, about fifteen years, but it seemed like forever. Bernie had been a detective lieutenant since I'd first known him, but Pete had been a detective sergeant until a few years ago, when he'd passed the lieutenant exam. Now both of them were lieutenants, and maybe that was the problem.

I sat on the couch next to Pete. "What happened?"

"Well," Pete said, "after the commander retired, it left a vacancy at the top, and our captain was promoted to fill it. That left another vacancy, which has remained unfilled because there was no one qualified to replace him. Yesterday they announced that Bernie passed his captain's exam, so he got promoted to captain in charge of detectives. So now he's my boss instead of my partner." He paused, as if unsure what to say next.

"Okay," I said. "Why do I have the feeling that's not all there is to it?"

"It isn't," Pete said. "When I made lieutenant, it left a vacancy for detective sergeant, and after all this time, they've decided to fill it."

"So who did they promote?"

"Unfortunately, there's nobody qualified to replace me, so they had to recruit from outside."

"So you're going to have a new partner?"

"Correction. I *have* a new partner. Her name is Adriana Sinclair, and she's from Boise."

"So she's already here?" Hal asked.

"She's on duty as we speak. So what about this Christmas card?"

Pete was clearly anxious to get off the subject of his new partner, so I handed him the card and the envelope it had come in.

"This is bizarre," Pete said, waving the card. "No return address and no signature, and why send it to you? What have you got to do with Ralph Partridge?"

"It's postmarked Boise," Hal said.

"All our mail is postmarked Boise," I said. "That's the processing center now."

The US Postal Service had recently changed the way our mail was processed, so instead of being postmarked Twin Falls, all our outgoing mail went to Boise to be sorted and then was sent on to its final destination. It might have saved money to do it that way, but it added another day to the transit time. That was especially annoying when sending something to someone else in Twin, because it still had to go to Boise first.

"She's right," Pete said. "Even if it was mailed in Twin Falls, it's gonna be postmarked Boise."

"Well, that's no help," Hal grumbled.

Pete put the card and the envelope in an evidence bag. "I wanted to take a look at that jury list," he said. "Have you gotten any more of these Christmas cards?"

Hal looked out the living room window. "Not so far. There's the mail now. I'll go get it." He rose and went out the front door into the snow.

"I don't see how Robbie can murder someone in Twin Falls," Pete said. "He's supposed to be in a halfway house in Boise, with a job, and he has no car."

"Have you heard of Uber?" I asked. "Or, for that matter, Greyhound?"

Hal came back in, stomping the snow off his shoes; sat back down in his recliner; put the pile of mail on the coffee table; and started to sort it.

Pete stopped him. "Here—let me. There might be fingerprints." He pulled a pair of nitrile gloves out of his pocket and put them on.

"Sorry about that," I said. "By the time we realized what the first one was, we'd both handled it."

"No problem," Pete said. "We can eliminate your prints."

Our fingerprints were on file because Hal taught at the college, and I had a state license to practice medicine.

Pete and I spotted the envelope at the same time. Like the other one, it was tastefully decorated with holly and ivy around the edges. Pete picked it up, carefully slit it open, and extracted the card. On the cover was a drawing in black ink of a dead bird lying on its back, with a splotch of red covering its chest and spilling into the white space. The verse on the inside read,

> On the second day of Christmas, my true
> love gave to me one Robin redbreast.

"Hal," I said, "where's that list of jurors Elliott gave you?"

"Right here," he said, pulling it out of his pocket. He handed it to Pete. "You can keep that. Elliott made an extra copy."

Pete unfolded it and scanned it, with me reading over his shoulder.

I saw it first. "There! Fourth one down."

"Robin Renee Jones. Teacher at Lincoln Elementary School, Twin Falls."

"If my theory is right," I said, "she'll be the next to die."

"Unless we get to her first," he said grimly. "There's an address and phone number here."

"You do realize that was her address eleven years ago," I said.

"Then let's hope she's still there." He pulled out his cell phone and dialed. He let it ring for a full minute before he ended the call. "No answer. I'd better get someone over to her house ASAP."

But before he could dial again, his phone rang. He answered it. "Bernie? What's up? Oh no. I'll meet you there." He hung up and turned to me, his face stony. "We're too late."

"Where?" I asked.

"Her house. Stabbed in the chest."

"Oh no."

"Oh yes. I gotta go."

"Can I go with you?"

"Sure," said Pete.

"No," said my husband.

"Hal—"

"Last night you said you'd rather be here by the fire with me and a scotch."

"That was at night, and the body was under a tree in the snow in Rock Creek Park. This is daylight, much too early for a scotch, and indoors. I can do this and come back, and then it won't be too early for a scotch, and plus, I won't sulk all afternoon."

Hal threw up his hands and rolled his eyes at the ceiling. "Oy gevalt! So go already!"

Robin Renee Jones had been tall, slender, and fiftyish and had long blonde hair. In life, she had probably looked like a model. Now she just looked dead.

She lay in the middle of her living room floor on her back. A kitchen knife protruded from the left side of her chest at about the level of the fifth rib, right through her nightgown. A couple of crime-scene investigators moved around the room, taking pictures and collecting evidence. Bernie and Rollie stood looking down at the body. A gurney stood by the door with a body bag open and spread out on it.

Next to Rollie was a female plainclothes detective I had never seen before. She stood, I estimated, close to six feet tall in four-inch heels and probably weighed less than I did. I deduced that she was the illustrious Adriana Sinclair, and I waited for Pete to introduce us.

When we entered, she turned to look and frowned. "Excuse me. This is a crime scene. You need to leave."

Rollie was a little more polite. "Well, good afternoon, Doctor and Lieutenant. Notice anything funny about this body?"

"Like there's no blood?" I said.

"Exactly. What do you think that means, Doctor?"

"That she was already dead when she was stabbed," I said.

"Mr. Perkins," the female detective said, "who are these people?" Her expression suggested she really didn't want to know.

Pete extended his hand. "I'm your partner, Detective Lieutenant Pete Vincent, and this is Dr. Toni Day."

She shook Pete's hand while looking down at me as if I were something under a dissecting scope. "Are you the medical examiner?"

Rollie saved me the trouble of answering, which was a good thing since I was rapidly developing an aversion to Detective Sergeant Adriana Sinclair. "She's the next best thing," he said jocularly. "Doctor, this is—"

Adriana didn't let him finish. "Detective Sergeant Adriana Sinclair," she said, extending her hand. "Happy to meet you. Our medical examiner in Boise has mentioned you often." Judging from her expression, her medical examiner had not been complimentary, and she wasn't really happy to meet me.

At that point, the feeling was mutual. "How do you do?" I said noncommittally.

Adriana's flowing auburn hair fell to the middle of her back, and she might have been pretty if she ever smiled. Her eyes were a cold, icy gray. Her complexion was fair and lightly freckled. I could not decide if she was simply arrogant or if she was doing an excellent job of covering up an inferiority complex. She was, after all, at least twenty years younger than I and probably ten years younger than Pete, so maybe a modicum of defensiveness would not have been out of place under the circumstances.

"So, Lieutenant, you think she's the second victim?" Rollie said.

"She is on the jury list," Pete said. "We just now received the Christmas card about her when you called."

"What are you talking about?" Adriana said. "What jury list? What Christmas card?"

Pete pulled his copy out of his pocket and handed it to her. "This jury list," he said. "This is the jury that put Toni's old boyfriend in prison ten years ago."

"Eleven," I said, correcting him. "And now he's out on parole."

Adriana glanced briefly at the list and then back at me. "Your old boyfriend? Oh, now let me guess," she said sarcastically. "You think your old boyfriend—uh, does he have a name?"

"Robbie," Pete and I said in chorus.

"Robbie?" Adriana looked skeptical. "What kind of name is that for a grown man?"

"His name is Robert Simpson," I said.

"And you think Robbie is going to kill off the entire jury who put him away? Is that the idea?"

"This is the second member of that jury to be killed," I said. "The first was Ralph Partridge."

Adriana looked again. "Humph."

Rollie peered over her shoulder. "Doctor, you said something about speculating that this young lady would be next. How?"

"Someone's been sending Toni Christmas cards," Pete said.

"The first one said, 'On the first day of Christmas, my true love sent to me a Partridge under a tree,'" I said. "Then today I got one that said, 'On the second day of Christmas, my true love sent to me one Robin redbreast.'"

"Since you're so smart," Adriana said, still in sarcastic mode, "who do you think the next one's gonna be?"

I shrugged. "I won't know until I get the next card."

"The scary thing is," Pete said, "by the time Toni gets the card, the victim is already dead."

"Then I'd say we have a problem," Rollie said. "Is there any reason I can't take the body back to the mortuary now?"

Pete signaled to one of the CSIs, who came over to us. "Are you guys done with the body yet?" Pete asked.

"Yep. We got all the photographs we need. Only problem is, how did the killer get in? We've found no evidence of a break-in."

Pete shrugged. "Maybe it was somebody she knew, and she let him in."

Rollie rolled his gurney over next to the body and collapsed it. "Can one of you guys give me a hand?"

"Sure," Pete said, and he grabbed the body by the shoulders. Rollie grabbed the feet, and they swung the body easily onto the gurney. The arms and legs were already stiff with rigor mortis, suggesting the victim had been dead for several hours.

Rollie started to zip the body bag closed, but I stopped him. "Wait," I said. "Before you zip that bag up, can you roll her onto her side and let me see if she's been pithed?"

Adriana's gray eyes widened. "What did you say?"

"Ralph Partridge appeared to be the victim of a hit-and-run," I told her, "but he'd been pithed and staged to look like that."

"Pithed," Adriana repeated uncomprehendingly.

"Pithing is done by inserting a sharp instrument into the base of the brain," I explained, "and scrambling the brainstem." I indicated the spot on the back of Adriana's slender neck, and she jerked away angrily.

"I know what pithing is!"

I shrugged. "Sorry. You didn't look like you did." I turned away and approached the gurney. "Gentlemen, can you give me a hand here?"

Pete handed me a pair of gloves without saying anything. I donned them and pushed Robin's hair up out of the way to reveal the now-familiar laceration at the back of her neck.

Adriana hung back. I beckoned to her, and she reluctantly stepped over to me so I could show her the laceration. "There it is."

She looked briefly and stepped back. Her face was white, but she stood her ground. I wondered how she would react if she had to attend an autopsy. Did we have another Bernie on our hands?

I stepped back. Rollie zipped up the body bag, and he and Pete returned the gurney to its original upright position and wheeled the gurney out of the room.

There was no bloodstain on the carpet where her head had been.

"So why wasn't there any blood on the carpet?" Adriana asked.

"Because the blood was already dried before the killer put her there."

"You're saying she wasn't killed here?" Adriana said.

"I don't think she was," I said.

Pete came back in just in time to catch my remark. "Was what?"

I repeated my assessment. "See? There was dried blood on

the back of her neck but no blood on the carpet. There's enough rigor mortis for her to have been dead for hours, like maybe since early this morning. And the CSI said they hadn't found any evidence of a break-in. So I'm thinking maybe she went out to get the paper right after she got up, and the killer grabbed her and pithed her and then carried her into the house."

Pete shook his head. "In front of God and everybody?" he asked.

"It probably was still dark," I said.

"She goes out in the snow in her nightgown?" Bernie asked.

"So maybe she put on a coat and boots, and the killer removed them when he staged the body," I said. "Or maybe he came into the house with her and pithed her after he closed the door."

"Then there'd be blood near the front door, and the CSIs didn't find any," Adriana said.

"If he'd pithed her while she had a coat on, the blood would be on the coat, not the floor," I said.

Adriana turned her palms up. "So where's the coat?"

"Well," I said, "maybe he took it with him and threw it into a dumpster somewhere, or maybe he just hung it up in the hall closet. Did the CSIs look there? Or maybe she just put on a robe instead of a coat. Did the CSIs look for one?"

"I don't know," Pete said. "They've all left. I'll have to ask them when we get back to the station." He looked at his watch. "Wow, it's getting late. I'd better get you home before Hal starts worrying."

"Who's Hal?" Adriana asked.

"My husband," I said.

"Huh," Adriana said. "You're married. How about that?"

I had no idea how to answer that, and apparently, neither did Pete, so we just said our goodbyes and left.

CHAPTER 6

Revenge, at first though sweet,
Bitter ere long back on itself recoils.

—John Milton, *Paradise Lost*

"How'd it go?" Hal asked when I got home.

"Fine," I said as I took off my coat and hung it in the closet. "She'd been pithed, so there was no blood. And Adriana was there."

Hal got up, went to the bar, and began fixing me a drink. "Really? What's she like?"

"Kind of snarky," I said, "and really cold. She doesn't like me—that's for sure."

"Maybe she's afraid of you," he said.

He always said that, and I still couldn't fathom why anybody should have been afraid of me, even if I had twenty or thirty years of experience on him or her. "I suppose that's possible," I said. "But I'd prefer to think I command respect, and I get the feeling that with her, I command contempt."

Hal nodded. "There you go. A good offense is the best defense. Once she gets to know you better, she'll come around."

"I don't think she wants to know me better," I said, "and I'm not sure I want to know her better either, but I think something's bothering her, and unless I can find out what it is, that won't be an issue."

"Good," Hal said. "Now all you have to worry about is the cat being out of the proverbial bag. I don't think there's anything you can do about that either."

He meant people finding out about Robbie, I knew. "Everybody's going to be talking about it at work," I said in exasperation. "It'll be a bloody nightmare. Christ on a crutch. Maybe I should just go on vacation until this all blows over."

"Well," he said, "you do have one coming up in a couple weeks when Fiona and Nigel are here."

In all the excitement, I'd completely forgotten Mum and Nigel were coming. "I need to call them and let them know what's going on. They may not want to come under the circumstances."

Hal hooted. "You don't believe that for a second. Nigel will be champing at the bit for a chance to sink his teeth into a juicy mystery like this."

My stepfather, Nigel Gray, was retired from Scotland Yard. Hal was right.

"In that case," I said, "I need to call and get his agile brain working on this so he can hit the ground running when they get here."

I knew Mum would be upset to find out that I was mixed up in another murder, so I was glad it was Nigel who answered the phone.

"Robbie is out on parole?" he said. "You don't say. Fiona won't like that, I'll wager."

I told him about the two Christmas cards and the matching murders. "Those people were on the jury at his trial," I told him, "and I'm afraid he's going to kill the rest of them if he isn't stopped."

"Sounds to me as if he's challenging you to do just that," he said. "What does your son-in-law think about it?"

"He and Bernie are both working on it," I said. "And now there's a new detective, and she's working on it too."

"Really," Nigel said. "How'd that happen?"

I told him about the shake-up at the station.

"You don't sound happy about it," Nigel said. "I should think you'd like working with a female detective."

"Not this one," I said. "And she doesn't like me either."

"Give it time," Nigel said. "She'll warm up to you once she gets to know you. And speaking of that, how much time passed between the first and second murders?"

"Two days."

"You know, if he sticks to this twelve-days-of-Christmas schedule and kills them in order, p'r'aps you could predict which juror will be next. It might be possible for the police to warn him or her, take protective measures, and p'r'aps set a trap for the killer. Is there any way to match the names to the remaining verses?"

"That's a terrific idea!" I exclaimed. "I'll get right on it. Thanks, Nigel!"

"What was that all about?" Hal asked after I hung up.

"He just gave me an idea for figuring out who's next." I told him what Nigel had said.

"Of course," Hal said. "I'm sure you would have come up with it, given time."

"Time is what we don't have," I said. "Hand me that jury list, would you?"

"Why don't we take it over on the couch so we can both look at it at the same time?" he said, so we moved over to the couch and put the jury list on the coffee table, which we pulled close enough for both of us to write on it.

"Okay," he said, "we already know about the partridge in the pear tree." He put a 1 next to Ralph Partridge.

"And then, the next day, we got the two turtle doves," I said, and I put a 2 by Robin Renee Jones.

"You notice he also changed the number from two to one," Hal said, "so he'll probably also change the other numbers, three through twelve, to one."

"Unless he's planning to kill two people at once."

"I don't think so," Hal said. "That would screw up the sequence."

"If Robbie keeps up the pace, we should get the third card tomorrow," I said. "That doesn't leave much time to save the next victim, does it?"

"Next we have three French hens." Hal said. "We need a bird name. We have George Starling and Jonathan Swann."

"We should save Jonathan Swann for the seven swans a-swimming," I said.

"Oh yeah, you're right. So that leaves George Starling." He started to put a 3 after George's name, but I stopped him.

"If you do that, what are you going to use for the four calling birds?"

"We're out of bird names," Hal said.

"How about a French name for the three French hens?" I said. "Here's one. Penelope Leroux."

"Okay," Hal said, and he put a 3 next to her name and a 4 next to George's.

"We need to call the station," I said. "We need to let them know who's next." I started to get up to fetch my cell phone, which I'd left by my recliner, but Hal stopped me.

"Are you sure about this?" he asked. "Sure enough to have

the cops scare the hell out of a couple random people for possibly no good reason?"

I threw up my hands. "I'm not sure of anything," I said. "But what if we don't do it and someone gets killed tomorrow?"

"Or today," Hal said. "So far, we aren't getting the cards until after the victim is already dead. We may already be too late."

"Only one way to find out," I said.

Bernie answered when I called the station. "What now, Toni?" he said.

"The next victim is Penelope Leroux," I told him.

"Seriously?" he said with sarcasm dripping from his voice. "What—are you clairvoyant now?"

I explained what Hal and I had been doing.

"Whose bright idea was that? Oh, now, let me guess. Yours."

"Sorry to disappoint. It was Nigel's."

That apparently took Bernie aback. After a moment of silence, he said, "Oh."

"Bernie, there's no time to lose. We're due to get the next Christmas card tomorrow. That means she's either already dead or due to be killed sometime today."

He sighed. "Okay, I'll see what I can do."

"Congratulations, by the way."

"Thank you. It was about time."

Leave it to Bernie to gripe about a promotion, I thought as I disconnected.

"What did he say?" Hal asked.

"He'll see what he can do," I said.

Hal snorted. "I'm gonna call Pete. I don't trust that guy, even if he is a captain now." He pulled his cell phone out of his back pocket and dialed.

While Hal was talking to Pete, I continued with our project.

39

Next were the five golden rings. There was a Stan Goldman. It had to be. I put a 5 next to his name.

Next were six geese a-laying. *Birds again! Now what?* We were out of bird names. I moved on to the seven swans a-swimming and put a 7 next to Jonathan Swann.

The eight maids a-milking gave me pause once again. I didn't see any names suggesting maids or milk. There was a Marian Chandler, though. Hadn't Robin Hood had a Maid Marian?

I put an 8 with a question mark next to her name.

That made me wonder, and not for the first time, where were the cows those maids were supposed to be milking? There wasn't any verse about cows. Maybe the cows were implicit.

My luck was no better with the nine ladies dancing. I looked in vain for a name with any reference to ladies or dancing and gave up.

That left me with ten lords a-leaping, eleven pipers piping, and twelve drummers drumming. Dead easy. In quick succession, I put a 10 next to David Lord, 11 next to Piper Briscoe, and 12 next to Jeffrey Drummond.

That left the six geese a-laying and nine ladies dancing without matching jurors and Eleanor Morehouse and Melinda Roper without matching verses, assuming Maid Marian was really number 8.

I sincerely hoped Robbie would be caught before we had to find out.

I showed Hal what I had worked out. "Any ideas for six geese a-laying and nine ladies dancing?"

He studied the list and finally shook his head. "Not a clue."

"They both have a noun in their names," I said. "Morehouse has *house* in it, and Roper—"

"Has *rope*," Hal said. "As in hanging."

"One lady hanging? Okay, let's put a 9 with a question mark

next to Melinda Roper. That leaves Eleanor Morehouse. One house a-whatting?"

"Burning?" Hal said. "I'll put 6 with a question mark next to her. Maybe she's supposed to die in a house fire."

"Yes, and maybe Melinda Roper is supposed to hang herself. But they'll all be pithed."

At that point, Pete came in through the garage door into the kitchen just in time to hear my last remark. "Who'll be pissed?" he asked.

"Not pissed, pithed," I said.

"All these prospective murder victims," Hal told him.

"So I talked to Bernie," Pete said, "and I think you were right to be concerned."

"Aha!" Hal said. "I knew it."

"Bernie has a tendency to not want to do anything Toni suggests just because she suggests it," Pete said, "even more so now that he's a captain, so I reminded him—again—that you've been right more often than not, and how would he feel if that lady turned up dead today?"

"Good," I said.

"There's another thing," Hal said. "Toni doesn't want a lot of gossip about her and Robbie going around."

"It may not be Robbie, you know," Pete said. "It could be anybody."

"It's Robbie," I said firmly. "We all know it's Robbie. I don't want a lot of publicity about there being any kind of link between me and the serial killer, no matter who he is."

"Because it's gonna turn out to be Robbie," Hal said with a wink in my direction.

"We may be too late to save Penelope Leroux, but the next victim is George Starling. It's not too late to save him."

Pete sighed.

"I'm just saying," I said.

"I know," he said. "I'll get right on it."

Later, as we lay in bed, Hal asked, "Are you going to do the autopsy tomorrow?"

"No, thank God," I said. "Brian's on call, so he'll be doing it."

"Don't you want to be there?"

"No need," I said. "Pete or Bernie will be there, Rollie will be there, and Natalie will be assisting. They all know about the pithing detail. What could possibly go wrong?"

CHAPTER 7

It was a pity he couldna be hatched
o'er again, and hatched different.

—George Eliot

On Sunday morning, I found out what could go wrong. "Serial Killer Threatens Jurors" was the headline that blared from the front page of the Sunday *Clarion*. The article beneath, written by one Ryan Trowbridge, announced to subscribers that a serial killer was threatening all members of a Twin Falls jury that had put a kidnapper in prison eleven years earlier.

> This reporter has discovered that two members of this jury have already been murdered. Ralph Partridge, 76, a retired local banker, was found dead in Rock Creek Park Friday, an apparent hit-and-run. Robin Renee Jones, 55, an elementary school teacher, was found dead in her home yesterday, an apparent stabbing.
>
> According to Dr. Brian Leonard, pathologist at Cascade Perrine Regional Medical Center, autopsies done on the victims showed that both were actually

> killed by a sharp instrument, possibly an ice pick,
> inserted into the base of the brain, a procedure known
> as pithing. The bodies were then arranged to look like
> a hit-and-run and a stabbing, respectively.

"Oh brother," Hal said. "The police won't like that. This could start a panic."

"Not only that, but I'll bet they wanted to keep the pithing detail confidential," I said. "Now the murderer may change his MO. And that's not the worst of it. Listen to this."

> The murderer sent homemade Christmas cards
> depicting the murders to Dr. Leonard's partner,
> pathologist Dr. Toni Day. It was Dr. Day who connected
> the cards to the murders.

Hal put an elbow on the table and dropped his head into his hand. "Oh boy."

"I don't like it," I said. "Blabbermouth Brian. I should have told him not to talk to reporters. I never even thought of it. Who the hell alerted the fourth estate anyway?"

"Probably the police," Hal said. "They have to report all murders. They have to report autopsy results. This reporter took it a step further and interviewed the pathologist."

"Who was all too eager to talk about it," I said bitterly. "Now I'm going to get all kinds of phone calls about it. How long will it be before someone puts two and twelve together and comes up with Robbie?"

Robbie Simpson had been a year ahead of me in high school. We'd met at a party and dated all through high school and nearly all the way through college. He'd gone away to Harvard while I was still in high school but had come home at Christmas and for the summer.

I'd stayed at home and attended Long Beach State, majoring in biology. While Robbie was away, I'd dated other boys, but I never had stopped loving Robbie.

Then I'd met Hal.

He had been tall, blond, blue-eyed, gorgeous, and married. He also had been my chemistry professor. To my astonishment, he had been as smitten with me as I was with him.

Robbie, in comparison, had been tall but not as tall as Hal and thin, with dark hair he wore in a crew cut, glasses, and buck teeth. Obviously, I'd known an affair with a married professor could go nowhere, and Robbie had been a huge part of my life for years, so I'd continued to do what I'd always done: date other boys until Robbie came home.

When Robbie had come home after graduating from Harvard and being accepted to Harvard Law School, I'd tried to be glad to see him, but in truth, I'd felt slightly repelled. He'd noticed. He'd gotten mad. He'd beaten me up and raped me.

That had been the end for me but not for him. He'd continued to call. Mum would answer the phone and tell him I wasn't there. When I'd gone off to medical school, he'd continued to call her. She'd never told him where I was.

That had gone on until she told him I was married. By that time, I'd been in my first year of pathology residency at St. Mary's in Long Beach.

Four years later, Hal and I had moved to Twin Falls, and Robbie had faded into the misty past. Then, eleven years ago, he'd shown up in Twin Falls, and the stalking had started all over again, culminating in his kidnapping of my husband.

Robbie had a real problem with the fact that I'd married a Jew. He thought I deserved better.

Now he was back.

He'd already killed two people, and if not stopped, he would kill ten more. When he finished with the jury, I had no doubt he'd come after Hal and me.

Unless somebody stopped him first.

My fear now was that once the persistent Ryan Trowbridge found out who the killer was, he'd find out what he'd done to go to prison in the first place and to whom he'd done it. From there, it was only a hop, skip, and jump to all the sordid details about Robbie's and my past relationship.

I could see the headline now: "Local Pathologist's Love Affair with Serial Killer Revealed!"

Hal told me I was being silly. "So far, nobody knows who the killer is," he said. "Just because your name was mentioned—"

"It's not just that he mentioned my name," I said. "It's that he mentioned it in conjunction with the killer sending me Christmas cards."

"Does either Brian or Mike know about Robbie?"

"No, I've never mentioned it. I didn't say anything about Robbie on Friday either."

"If I remember rightly," Hal said, "you didn't know it was Robbie yourself until Friday night. All you have to do is not mention him to anyone but me and Elliott and Jodi—"

"And Pete and Bernie," I said, "and Adriana. Which means the whole police department will know, and one of them will be bound to let it slip to a reporter. Not only that, but Elliott will no doubt mention it to Stan Snow."

Stan Snow was one of Elliott's law partners, and it was his crawl space Hal had been found in. In the dead of winter. With hantavirus pneumonia.

The phone rang. I remembered Elliott saying I should answer it next time, so I picked up the handset. I looked at the number. It had an Idaho area code, but I didn't recognize it. "Hello?"

"Finally!" said Robbie's voice. "I've been calling every

night for a week, and I really didn't want to talk to Grizzly Abramowitz."

Back in the day, that had been Robbie's less-than-flattering nickname for Hal.

"What do you want, Robbie?" I said, marveling that my voice was not as shaky as I felt.

"My darling Toni," Robbie murmured seductively, "you know perfectly well what I want."

I thought I might throw up but managed not to by gritting my teeth. "Don't you ever call me again, you damn murderer," I said evenly, and I rang off.

Hal took one look at my face. "Toni! What?"

The phone, still in my hand, rang again. I looked at the screen. "It's the same number," I said.

Hal snatched it out of my hand and answered it. "Look here, you son of a bitch—" He stopped. "He hung up." He put his arms around me. "You're shaking."

I clung to him. I felt as if I'd been transported back in time to the last time Robbie had stalked me, eleven years ago. It wasn't a place I ever wanted to be again. "It was Robbie," I murmured into his shirtfront.

"That does it," Hal muttered into my hair. "We're getting rid of the goddamn landline."

Pete arrived shortly after that to find Hal with a face like a thundercloud and me on the couch, shivering in an afghan and sipping scotch neat from a shot glass.

He looked from me to Hal and back again. "Scotch at ten in the morning?"

"Robbie called, and Toni answered it," Hal said tersely.

"No way!" Pete exclaimed in disbelief. "Are you serious?"

"As a heart attack," Hal said.

"We're getting rid of the landline," I said inanely.

"What number did he call from?" Pete asked.

Hal handed him a sticky note. "I wrote it down."

Pete stuck it in his shirt pocket. "I'll check it out."

His cell phone rang. He took it out of his pocket and looked at the screen. "Uh-oh. It's Adriana. Hello? Yes, I'm over at their house. Where? The library? I'm on my way." He disconnected. "Did you get the gist of that?"

"Somebody got killed in the library," I said. "Who was it?"

"Penelope Leroux. She works there. When they opened up this morning, there she was. Dead as a doornail. So I gotta go."

"Can I go with you?" I asked.

Hal gave me his professorial glare over the top of his glasses. "Now, Toni—"

"Better not," Pete said. "You guys need to stay put."

With a backhanded wave, he was out the door.

I looked at the jury list. There she was, sixth on the list: Penelope Leroux, age fifty-nine, librarian.

I swung my feet off the couch and stood up. "I'm feeling a lot better now. Does anybody besides me feel like taking a nice walk in the snow? In the city park maybe? To look at the Christmas lights?"

"Oh no you don't," Hal said. "Christmas lights, my ass. You want to go to the murder scene."

I went over to the coat closet and got out my black peacoat. "You don't have to go," I said. "I can go by myself."

Hal sighed and brought his recliner upright. "Hand me my coat, would you?"

I held out his coat. He took it, put it on, and sat down to put his boots on. I put on my peacoat, shoved my feet into boots, pulled a wool cap down over my curls, and wound a scarf around my neck. "Ready?"

"Aren't you going to wear gloves?" he asked.

I pulled a pair out of the pocket of my pea coat and put them on. "Aren't you going to wear a hat?" I asked.

"Nah."

I took my cell phone out of my purse and put it in my coat pocket. "Better take your phone," I told him. "Pete might call you instead of me."

Killer and Geraldine were already by the door, jockeying for position to be the first one out, but Hal shook his head. "Not this time, guys. Sit. Stay."

Grudgingly, they did so.

Finally, we got ourselves out the door and onto the street. As we crossed Montana Street and walked down Hansen Street toward the library, we could see the flashing lights.

The snow, which was still falling, was about four inches deep on the ground, but on the sidewalk, it had been flattened by other pedestrians and refrozen as ice. Hal took my hand. "Tiny baby steps," he said. "We don't need to rush."

As we got closer, we saw that the police, the fire department, and an ambulance had been deployed. Even as we approached, the ambulance pulled away without lights or siren, and Rollie's hearse nosed into view on the far side of the city park.

"Let's cross the street," Hal said. "We're supposed to be taking a walk in the park, so let's get into the park. We can see everything from there, and maybe they won't notice us."

Twin Falls City Park was just as pretty as I'd thought it would be. The Christmas lights on the tall firs and spruces had been put up in November and lit on the first of December.

No sooner had we entered the park and found a good place to watch than we heard Pete's voice. "Hey! What part of 'Stay put' did you guys not understand?"

Startled, we turned to see Pete coming across the grass toward us. "What if I'd tried to call you?" he said.

We both held up our phones. "Not notice us, huh?" I muttered in Hal's direction. He didn't answer me.

Across the street, Rollie pulled a gurney out of the back of the hearse. A uniformed policeman helped him unfold it. Instead of carrying it up the steep stairs to the library's front door, they rolled it along the sidewalk to the parking lot in back, where we could no longer see them.

Pete answered my unspoken question. "They need to use the elevator."

"Was she pithed?"

"No," Pete said. "She was shot."

"Shot!" Hal exclaimed.

"Yes, and the body was arranged to look like a suicide. She had the gun in her left hand."

"I wonder," I said. "Is it possible she really did commit suicide, and it's just a coincidence that she did it today?"

"Possibly, if she's left-handed," Pete said.

At that moment, his phone rang, and he answered it. "Rollie, what's up?"

Rollie's reply was inaudible.

Pete said, "Yeah, she's here. I'm sure she will be. We'll be right there." He disconnected. "Rollie wants you at the crime scene. Let's go."

Hal threw up his hands and muttered, "Oy gevalt," but he followed Pete and me up the stairs without further comment.

One of the CSIs opened the door as we neared the top. "She was using her computer," he said. "He must have snuck up behind her and shot her point-blank before she even knew he was there. He blew her right out of her chair." He held the door open for us. "Watch where you step. There's stuff everywhere."

The smell of blood was pervasive enough to make me grimace with distaste. When I looked down at the pale gray carpet, I saw bits of brain tissue, next to which the crime-scene techs had thoughtfully placed markers, making it easier to navigate without stepping on them.

What I did not see was a pool of blood under her head or, indeed, much blood anywhere.

Penelope Leroux wore a gray tweed skirt, a crisp white blouse, and sensible shoes. Her gray hair, originally in a bun on top of her head, was in disarray. I recognized her as soon as I saw her. I'd seen her there every time I had occasion to use the library, and I had never even known her name.

She lay on her back with her head turned to the right, so the bullet hole was clearly visible in her left temple, with powder burns around it. Her arms were flung up over her head, and the gun lay just beyond her left hand. Little yellow numbered markers stood next to her head, her hands, her feet, and the gun, and a photographer circled her body, taking pictures from every possible angle.

She'd been using the computer at her station. The chair lay on its side on the floor in front of it. The shattered screen was plastered with bits of tissue but not much blood. The bullet had torn right through her head and into the computer.

Carefully, I tiptoed around the computer station, trying not to step on anything squishy. The computer had an exit wound too. "Where was the bullet?"

The tech pointed. "Right there, in the middle of *Uncle Tom's Cabin*. The perp must've come in yesterday and camped out in here. We found a blanket and a backpack way back behind the stacks."

"Why would he leave his backpack?" Hal said.

"What was in it?" I asked. "Did he have an ice pick?"

"The backpack was empty," the tech said. "He probably carried the blanket in it."

"Well," Pete said, "you know what to do. You'll have to take up all that carpet too."

The tech grimaced and said, "Don't I know it."

A second CSI emerged from between the stacks and addressed his colleague. "You almost done?" he asked.

The photographer shot one last picture and said, "I am now."

"Good," said the other, brandishing an evidence bag, into which he dropped the gun. "She's all yours, Mr. Perkins," he said, and they both left.

"Let's get her into the body bag," Pete said. "I'll give you a hand."

"Me too," Hal said.

Rollie went back to where he'd left the gurney, rolled it up close to the body, and collapsed it. He laid the body bag out flat on the gurney and unzipped it. Hal grabbed Penelope's ankles, Pete grasped her under the arms, and together they lifted her onto the open body bag. Her head rolled to the left, allowing me to see the exit wound on the other side of her head. It was pretty spectacular.

"She's still warm," Hal said.

"No rigor mortis?" I asked.

"Not that I could tell."

"Jeez," Pete said. "If we'd moved a little faster, we might actually have caught the dirtbag."

Rollie started to zip up the body bag, but I stopped him. "I just want to check something," I said.

"What? Surely you don't think she was pithed as well as shot?" he said.

"Why not? The others were," I said.

"Why bother to pith her," Rollie said, "if you're just going to shoot her? Seems like a waste of time."

I shrugged. "Next time Robbie calls me, I'll ask him."

"What!" Rollie said. "He called you?"

I told him about the phone call.

"We're getting rid of the landline," Hal added.

Rollie and Pete turned the body onto its side. I grabbed the hair and lifted it up off the neck. The familiar-looking jagged laceration was there, with dried blood around it. A black hair was embedded in it. I called Pete's attention to it.

"Isn't that hers?" he asked.

"I don't think so," I said. "It's black. She doesn't have any black hair, at least not anymore."

Pete signaled to a CSI, who came over with an evidence bag and carefully tweezed the hair into it.

I stepped back. Rollie zipped up the body bag and headed toward the elevator with the gurney, while Pete, Hal, and I went out the front door. The snow had stopped falling when we got back outside.

"No wonder there was such a mess," I said. "Did you see that exit wound?"

Hal made a face.

"That would be a yes," I said.

"No matter how hard I tried not to," he said.

Pete unlocked his SUV and opened the door. "You guys want a ride home?"

The Twin Falls police had recently replaced their cruisers with Ford Interceptors. *About time the police have four-wheel drive like everybody else around here, especially in the winter,* I thought.

I said, "No, we can walk."

At the same time, Hal said, "Yes. My ears are cold."

"You should have worn a hat," I told him.

"Will you be doing the autopsy?" Pete asked.

"No," I said. "It's Mike's turn. Brian did the one yesterday, and I did the one Friday."

After Pete dropped us off and we were back in the warmth of our house, Hal asked, "Now what?"

"Now," I said firmly, "we put up the Christmas tree. Maybe it'll take our minds off all this gruesomeness."

CHAPTER 8

I didn't want to harm the man.
I thought he was a very nice gentleman.
Soft-spoken.
I thought so right up to the moment I cut his throat.

—Truman Capote

"That was some nasty autopsy y'all stuck me with yesterday, I tell you what," Mike said on Monday morning. "Why the hell are we getting so many autopsies all of a sudden? We go for months without one, and now we get three in one weekend?"

"Yeah, and they're all pithed," Brian said. "Toni, do you know something we don't know?"

"Why would you ask me that?" I asked innocently.

"You got that Christmas card," Brian said. "Then we got an autopsy. Did you get another card? Or two?"

"Yes," I said, "I did get another one Saturday." I described it.

"That explains the stabbing I got on Saturday," Brian said. "Then this reporter buttonholed me the minute I stepped outside the morgue and peppered me with questions."

"Yes, now that you mention it, Brian, don't talk to reporters anymore," I said. "Just tell them you can't comment on an ongoing investigation, because that's what this is."

"Toni, does this have anything to do with that Christmas card you got?" Mike asked.

"Probably," I said evasively. I was loath to tell them what I really thought was going on, because I didn't want to talk about Robbie.

But my partners weren't willing to drop the subject. "Toni, is there something you aren't telling us?" Brian said.

I shrugged and tried to look casual. "I don't know any more than you do," I said.

At that point, Arlene stuck her head in the door and informed us that there was a frozen, saving me from further questioning.

That was just the beginning. I spent the day with my head buried in the cryostat, or grossing surgicals.

When I finally got home at six o'clock after a day on call and several late frozen sections, Pete was there.

Killer and Geraldine met me at the kitchen door with whines and wagging tails, as always. Spook was again draped over the back of the couch. The pile of mail sat on the coffee table. Hal was in his recliner but got up to fix me a drink. Pete was on the couch, holding an envelope in his nitrile-gloved hand.

"Ah, there you are, just in time," he said, slitting the envelope ceremoniously.

I put my purse on the coffee table, took out my cell phone, and sat down next to Pete.

Hal came back in with my drink, Bloody Mary mix because I was on call, and handed it to me. "We were just waiting for you."

He'd stuck a stalk of pickled asparagus in it. While Pete took the card out of the envelope, I pulled out the asparagus, took a bite, and then licked my fingers.

"By the way," Hal said, "Robbie called before you got home. He hung up on me, as usual."

"Didn't you get rid of the landline?"

"I called," Hal said, "and made arrangements, but it won't take effect until Wednesday."

"Oh," I said.

Pete showed us the card. On the cover was a sketch of an elongated object with a fountain pen nib on one end and a pistol grip with a trigger on the other. On the inside was a verse:

> On the third day of Christmas, my true
> love gave to me one French pen.

I took a picture of it with my cell phone.

"What's that for?" Hal asked.

"I had to tell Mike and Brian what was going on today," I said. "I want to be able to show this to them since I know you're going to take it for evidence."

"Oh, good idea," Hal said.

"Were you able to get hold of George Starling?" I asked Pete.

"We did," Pete said. "Bernie arranged for him to stay at the Holiday Inn for a few days while we stake out his house. He's been instructed to lay low. Order room service instead of going out to eat. Do business over his cell phone and not tell anyone where he is."

"Is there a cop staying with him?" I asked.

Pete shook his head. "We don't have manpower for that. We just have to hope he does what he's told."

"So did you stake out his house last night?" I asked.

"No. We start tonight."

I looked at Hal and shook my head slightly. Hal sighed.

Pete noticed. "What?"

I shrugged. "I just think you should have started last night. Is he already at the Holiday Inn?"

"Bernie said he checked in last night." Pete had no sooner finished the sentence than his phone rang. He looked at the screen. "It's Bernie," he said. "I'd better take this."

"Go ahead," Hal said.

As Pete listened, his expression changed from shock to disbelief to anger. "Okay, I'll meet you there." He disconnected and turned to me. "We've got a jumper."

"At the Holiday Inn?" I asked.

Pete pounded his fist on the top of the coffee table so hard that my glass jumped. "Why the hell can't we get ahead of this guy?"

"It may not be George Starling," Hal said. "It could be someone else."

"Well, whoever it is, I've gotta go," Pete said.

"Can I go with you?" I asked.

Hal said, "Toni—"

"I'm going to get the autopsy tomorrow anyway," I said. "It's my turn. I may as well know what I'm getting into."

"You'd better follow me in your car," Pete said. "It's really cold, and you don't want to stay any longer than you have to."

Hal looked out the window. "It's also really dark."

"I'll be okay," I said.

"Okay, sweetie, have it your way," Hal said with a sigh. "But don't stay too long. How about picking up some burgers or something for supper while you're out?"

The Holiday Inn was on Blue Lakes Boulevard, at the north end of Twin Falls. I followed Pete as he turned into the hotel parking lot.

One couldn't miss where the action was. The scene was brightly lit and surrounded by vehicles. A police SUV I assumed was Bernie's, a police van, an ambulance, and Rollie's hearse were among them. Pete parked right up close, but I went on through and parked on the street. I locked my car and went back to join Pete.

Pete had been right about the cold. The wind was blowing too. The parking lot had been cleared of snow, but there were still icy spots, so I picked my way carefully until I reached the circle of light. Rollie was the first to see me.

"Good evening, Doctor," he said, greeting me in his sepulchral voice.

"Hi, Rollie," I responded.

Pete said, "Watch where you step. There's broken glass all over the place."

Bernie, who was squatting next to the body, looked up, and annoyance crossed his face. "Toni, what are you doing here?"

The person squatting next to him looked up too, and I recognized Adriana, even with her auburn hair hidden under a wool cap. The lighting was perfectly adequate to illuminate the eye roll she gave upon seeing me.

Before I could say anything, another voice said, "Toni? Toni who?"

I turned to see who'd spoken, and I found myself nearly blinded by a bright light right in my face. I raised a hand to shield my eyes and saw a young man holding a video camera on his shoulder and a microphone in his hand. Then I heard Bernie, that traitor, say, "This is Dr. Toni Day."

"The pathologist?" the young man asked. "Dr. Day, I'm Greg Holloman from KMVT. Would you mind answering a few questions?"

"Yes, I would," I said as politely as I could, considering I really wanted to shove the camera right in his face and tell him to bugger off. "I'm sorry, but I can't really comment. Why don't you talk to these nice police detectives? I'm sure they know much more than I do."

With that, I backed away and went around on the other side of Rollie's hearse, out of camera range.

It was the wrong thing to do.

Another man stepped into my path—a larger man in a parka with a fur-lined hood that shadowed his face. He held a notebook in one gloved hand. "Dr. Day, I'm Ryan Trowbridge from the *Clarion*. Can you answer a few questions for me?"

Ryan Trowbridge! The same reporter who'd interviewed Brian. Well, I knew better than to talk to him, and I'd make sure he knew it too.

"I'm sorry, but I really can't comment. Why don't you ask Captain Kincaid over there? I don't even know who that is," I said, pointing toward the crumpled shape lying on the ground under a sheet.

"Then why are you here?" he asked slyly.

"Because I don't know who that is," I replied. "I'm probably going to have to autopsy him—or her—tomorrow."

Ryan Trowbridge shoved his notebook into his pocket with an air of finality. "Well then, Dr. Day, I will see you after the autopsy tomorrow. Good night." He touched the edge of his hood in farewell and walked away.

Damn. I didn't have to tell him that. Why did I?

No matter. What I'd actually come for was to find out if the decedent was George Starling and if he had been pithed.

However, I wasn't willing to do that while Greg What's-His-Name was still filming the doings, so I huddled up next to the hearse, trying to stay out of the wind as much as I could. Rollie took pity on me and offered to let me climb inside the hearse to get warm, an offer I accepted with alacrity.

Through the windshield, I watched two CSIs examine the

corpse while Pete and Bernie held up the sheet in such a way as to shield the body from the avid gaze of the TV camera. A police photographer snapped pictures from every angle he could. One of the CSIs handed a wallet to Pete, who brought it over to Rollie. Together they perused its contents. Rollie tapped on the window, and I rolled it down.

"It's George Starling," Pete told me. "Good thing he was carrying this, because his face is smashed beyond recognition. Funny thing, though. He doesn't seem to have bled much."

"Was he pithed?"

"I don't know. Why don't you come out and look?"

"Because I don't want to be on the ten o'clock news," I said.

Here in the mountain time zone, the eleven o'clock news was on at ten.

Pete looked over his shoulder. "They're leaving. I think you're okay."

I climbed out and went over to the body, which was now on Rollie's gurney in a body bag. I cast a glance at the ground where the body had lain, where the CSIs carefully picked their way around inside the taped-off area where the body had been, using their ALSs—alternate light sources—under which blood would fluoresce bright blue. Bernie and Adriana stood and watched.

Rather than a big pool of blood, I saw only a few small smears localized to one end of the taped-off area, undoubtedly from his face, which had been smashed flat when it hit the asphalt.

Rollie unzipped the body bag enough to expose the head. Pete offered me a pair of nitrile gloves. They both assisted me in turning the body onto its side, a procedure made more difficult by the gelatinous quality of a body in which practically every bone was broken. Even so, I was able to see a jagged puncture wound with blood around it on the back of the neck.

"It's there," I said. "He was pithed. He was dead before he fell.

The killer might have left some clues in his room. What room was he in anyway?"

Bernie and Adriana had come up behind me as I spoke. "He was on the fifth floor," Bernie said, pointing upward. "See the broken window?"

"We already spoke with the night manager," Adriana said. "We're way ahead of you."

Of course you are. "Well, if the killer thought this puncture mark would be obscured by the damage resulting from a sixty-foot fall onto asphalt," I said, "he was sadly mistaken."

The police photographer took pictures of the puncture wound. Rollie and Pete laid the body flat again, and Rollie zipped up the body bag.

I stripped off the nitrile gloves and replaced them with my own warmer ones. "Well," I said, "I got what I came for, and now I think I'll go home. Will I see you at the autopsy tomorrow, Adriana?"

She tossed her head. "I wouldn't miss it."

"Good," I said. "See you tomorrow."

"Don't forget to pick up takeout," Pete called after me as I walked to my car.

I stopped at McDonald's on my way home. When I walked into the kitchen with the takeout sack, Hal practically pounced on it, informing me that he was starving. Then he felt my hands.

"You must be freezing," he said. "Here—I'll take care of that. You go sit by the fire."

For once, I was more than happy to do what I was told. I sat on the hearth with my back to the fire while Killer and Geraldine greeted me by licking my hands and trying to lick my face. Geraldine climbed into my lap.

Hal came back in with a plate on which he'd placed my Big Mac and fries. He'd cut the Big Mac in half and salted my fries, just the way I liked them. He ordered the dogs away, put the plate down on the hearth, and handed me a fresh Virgin Mary.

I thanked him. He went back to his recliner. "The news said it was gonna be down to ten degrees, with the wind chill making it minus five," he said.

"I think it's already there," I mumbled around a mouthful of Big Mac.

"So was it George Starling?"

I swallowed. "It was, and he fell from the fifth floor. And yes, he was pithed. And by the way, you may see me on the ten o'clock news."

Hal muted the TV. "Do tell."

"It's all Bernie's fault," I said. "When he saw me, he said, 'Toni, what are you doing here?' and this guy behind me said, 'Toni who?' and Bernie told him who I was, and it was a guy from KMVT."

"So what did you tell him?"

"I said I couldn't comment."

"That's it?"

"That's it, and then I walked away and went around behind Rollie's hearse, out of the wind, and ran straight into Ryan Trowbridge."

"Who's that?"

"The guy from the *Clarion* who interviewed Brian."

"And you told him you couldn't comment?"

"Not until after the autopsy, and he said he'd see me then and walked away. Oh, and by the way, Adriana was there too. She gave me the eye roll."

"I see what you mean about commanding contempt," Hal said. "You need to do something about that."

"I would if she worked for me," I said, "but she doesn't."

"So what are you going to tell the reporter?"

"The same thing I told Brian and Mike to do. I'm going to say I can't comment on an ongoing investigation."

By then, I'd finished my supper and was warm. I took my plate out to the kitchen and my Virgin Mary over to the couch.

Suddenly, my cell phone rang. It was Pete. "Can you give me a copy of that jury list with the numbers on it?" he asked. "We need to try to get ahead of this guy. He's killing jurors faster than we're getting the Christmas cards."

"I know," I said. "We won't get a card for George Starling until Wednesday. By that time, he could have killed two more people."

"Why has he sped up?" Pete said, thinking aloud. "Has something happened to cause him to accelerate his kill rate?"

"I don't think he's sped up," I said. "He's killed one a day from the beginning, and besides, if he's read the Sunday *Clarion*, he knows you're onto him. Maybe he's in a hurry to get them all killed before he's caught."

"Can I come over and get that tonight? We need to alert the rest of those jurors and get them into protective custody."

"Sure," I said. "I'll run upstairs and make you a copy right now." I disconnected and picked up the jury list from the coffee table. "Pete's coming over for a copy of this," I told Hal, and I went upstairs to the office, where the combination printer, copier, fax, and scanner was hooked up to the computer.

Pete arrived just as I got back downstairs with his copy. "The next one is Stan Goldman," I told him.

"Stan Goldman the jeweler?"

"Yes, why?"

"His wife reported him missing yesterday. I just found out today."

"Are you serious?"

"As a heart attack. She said his assistant saw him leave Friday night. She remembers it particularly because he left early, before it got dark."

"For the Sabbath," Hal said. "It starts at sundown Friday night and ends at sundown Saturday. If he's an observant Jew, he wouldn't want to still be at work after sundown."

"Yeah, I know. Bambi told me. But his wife says he never came home."

"Why didn't she call then?" Hal asked.

"She did but got told she had to wait forty-eight hours."

"Christ on a crutch," I said. "No wonder you feel left behind. That makes five since Thursday."

"Don't I know it," Pete said.

CHAPTER 9

No one is such a liar as the indignant man.
—Friedrich Wilhelm Nietzsche

The Tuesday *Clarion* had a short story on the front page about the suicide of George Starling, a real estate broker at Magic Valley Realty, but it wasn't written by Ryan Trowbridge, and it didn't mention me, only that an autopsy was pending.

Apparently, my partners had read it, because they converged on me when I walked into my office.

"Toni, you've got to tell us what you know," Mike said earnestly. "Now we've got that jumper in the morgue. What's next? Are we gonna keep getting more autopsies? This is playing hell with our workflow."

I sighed. I didn't want to tell them about Robbie, but I didn't see how I could keep it from them, considering the situation.

"Yes," I said, "we're going to keep getting more unless somebody stops the killer." I got up and closed the door. "I'm about to tell you guys something about myself that not very many people know about me, and you're not to tell anybody outside this room. Anybody! Got it?"

They chorused assent.

I told them about Robbie. I told them about the rape, the stalking, the kidnapping and near death of my husband, and the prison sentence.

"Holy shit, Toni," Mike said. "What a horrible story, I tell you what. So how is he doing this from prison, and why?"

"He's out on parole now, and he's taking out the jury that put him in prison," I said. "One by one. Ralph Partridge, Robin Jones, and Penelope Leroux were on that jury. If he's not stopped, we will get nine more autopsies, and then I'm very much afraid he'll come after Hal and then me."

"And he's sending you those cards to let you know he's going to kill somebody else?" Brian said. "That's really creepy."

"No, by the time I get the card, the person's already dead," I told him.

There was a knock on the door, and Arlene stuck her head in. "Sorry to disturb you guys, but there's a frozen."

That broke up the speculation. Since Mike was on call, he took care of the frozen section. After that, we got too busy for any more storytelling.

For starters, there was the autopsy.

I arranged with Natalie to do it at one o'clock, which would give her a chance to get all the slides cut, and I notified Pete and Rollie. Then I turned to my own stack of surgicals to get through first.

I presented myself in the morgue at the stroke of one o'clock to find Rollie and Adriana already there. The body was already on the table.

Natalie, already swathed in personal protective gear, was laying out my instruments.

"Why do we have to autopsy this guy?" she asked. "Isn't it perfectly obvious what killed him?"

"Because the cause of death isn't obvious," I told her. "He's been pithed just like the others. All we need to do is document it. Isn't that right, Rollie?"

"That's correct, young lady," Rollie said. "Just the brain—that's all I need."

As autopsies went, that one was rather anticlimactic, especially for Natalie, who had assisted with three of them now.

But not so much for Adriana. I wondered how many autopsies she'd seen in Boise. In a city of a hundred thousand with its own medical examiner, I would have thought she'd seen a lot more autopsies there than she would see in Twin Falls, along with a greater variety of pathology, but she seemed to have a real approach-avoidance conflict about it. She wanted to know what we found but didn't really want to look at it. Maybe she was just grossed out by the pithing. Time would tell.

I wondered how she'd been at the other autopsies over the weekend. I'd have to ask Pete next time I talked to him.

I had Natalie photograph the puncture wound on the back of the neck, and then I removed the brain and part of the spinal cord and had her photograph the mangled brainstem. Then we put the brain in a bucket of formalin, and that was about it.

Rollie waited while Natalie sewed up the scalp, and then he took the body away. Adriana left too, without a word to me.

Natalie jerked a thumb in her direction as the door closed behind her. "What's with her?"

"Your guess is as good as mine," I said.

She began washing down the autopsy table. "Dr. Day, what's going on? Are we going to keep getting these autopsies?"

I answered her question with a question. "Did you see Sunday's paper?"

"We don't take the paper," she said. "We go online. Why?"

I picked up the instruments I'd used, put them in the sink, and turned on the water to get it hot. "There's a serial killer who's out on parole and going around killing the members of the jury who put him in prison. He's gotten to four of them so far, and a fifth is missing."

Natalie stopped scrubbing and looked at me in disbelief. "They let a serial killer out of prison?"

"He was actually in prison for kidnapping and attempted murder," I said. "He didn't become a serial killer until he was out on parole."

"Who'd he kidnap? Anyone we know?"

"My husband," I said. "Eleven years ago."

"Oh my God!" Natalie exclaimed, dropping the sponge in her agitation. "Is that the creep who was hanging around your office and bringing you flowers in the middle of the night?"

Natalie had started working at the old hospital just about the same time Robbie had done that, so I shouldn't have been surprised she remembered him, but I was startled to find out that she had actually seen him.

"When did you see him?" I asked.

"One night when I was on call in the lab," she said. "I saw this guy coming out of your office. He was dressed all in black with a hood pulled down over his face. I asked him what he was doing, but he just ran out of the lab and didn't answer me. So I went back and looked in your office to make sure everything was all right, and there was this big bouquet of yellow roses."

The water was hot. I plugged the drain and added disinfectant soap. "I remember," I said. "I thought they were from Hal. When I found out they weren't, I felt violated. It was like being raped all over again."

Natalie stopped in the act of picking up the sponge she had dropped. "Raped? This guy raped you?"

Apparently, I'd never shared that detail with her. Actually,

69

outside of Hal, Jodi and Elliott, Mum and Nigel, Pete and Bambi, and now Mike and Brian, nobody knew. "When I was in college. That's the reason I broke up with him in the first place."

She shuddered. "I should think so. He should have gone to jail for that. Did you press charges?"

"No."

"Why not? I would have!"

I sighed. "This is now, and that was then. Back then, women who reported rape got blamed for it, and their marriages broke up, and their reputations were ruined. Mum wanted me to, but I was scared to."

That was an understatement. Mum had been absolutely livid with me and would have cheerfully killed Robbie herself if it had been legal.

"Are you scared he'll come after you?" Natalie asked.

I removed the blade from the scalpel and put it in the sharps container. "Yes," I told her. "I think that once he's done with the jury, he'll come after Hal and then me."

"Can't the police protect you?"

"Not any more than they could then," I replied. "They still haven't got the manpower."

"So that means they don't have the manpower to protect the other jurors either," Natalie said.

I began scrubbing the instruments, using a toothbrush to get blood out of all the cracks. "I think the plan is to alert the remaining jurors and put them up in hotels until the killer is caught," I told her, "but that sure didn't do this guy any good. Maybe they'll all have to leave town."

"What about their jobs?" Natalie asked. "People can't just walk out on their jobs and expect to come back and have those jobs waiting for them."

"Especially since it would be for an indefinite period," I said.

"Hal and I could maybe, because Mike and Brian can cover me, and Hal's out for Christmas break at the college. But we've got my mother and stepfather coming for Christmas."

"Won't that be putting them in danger too?"

I rinsed off the instruments and laid them out on paper towels to dry. "Maybe," I said. "On the other hand, there's safety in numbers. Besides, it's possible he might be caught before they even get here. They're not coming until a week from Saturday."

"I hope you're right," Natalie said. She gave a final rinse to the autopsy table and began wiping it down with paper towels.

I stripped off my Tyvek jumpsuit, head cover, shoe covers, and gloves; threw them into the biohazard trash; and wiped down my face shield. "I'm done here. How about you?"

"In a minute."

I left her there and went back to my office. Ryan Trowbridge was waiting for me, lounging comfortably in my visitors' chair, playing a game on his tablet with his booted feet up on my desk.

I instantly morphed into my mother. "Get your feet off my desk this instant! Who the bloody hell do you think you are?"

Trowbridge's boots hit the floor, and he was on his feet before I even finished the sentence. "I'm so sorry, Doctor. Where are my manners?" He used his coat sleeve to wipe the mud and melted snow off my desk and then extended his hand.

I didn't take it. "Make it fast," I told him. "I don't have a lot of time." I walked around him and sat at my desk.

He sat back down and consulted his tablet. With his parka unzipped and his hood flung back, I could actually see what he looked like. He was probably in his forties, with a shock of unruly dark brown hair that badly needed a trim; bushy eyebrows; a big, bulbous nose; and a beer belly. "I've done a little checking around," he said, "and I already know that the deceased was one

George Starling, real estate broker at Magic Valley Realty. I also know he was on the same jury as the other three victims. He lives here in Twin. Why was he at the Holiday Inn?"

"You should ask the police about that," I said.

"I have. For protection. Didn't do him much good, did it?"

"Nope. Can we move this along?"

"Was he pithed?"

"Yes."

"So he didn't die from the fall."

"No."

"So that's it?"

I indicated the pile of slide trays on my desk. "I hope so. I've got a lot of work to do."

I expected him to get up and leave at that point, but he remained firmly wedged in my visitors' chair, intently studying his tablet. Finally, he looked up.

"Does the name Robert Simpson mean anything to you?"

I supposed I could have lied and said no, but I was a terrible liar, as Mum could attest.

"Should it?" I asked carefully. How much did he know? I wondered. I wasn't about to add to it if I could help it.

"Well, I should think so since the jurors getting killed now put him in prison back in 2005 for the kidnapping and attempted murder of one Dr. Hal Shapiro. Do I need to ask if that name means anything to you?"

"That's my husband," I said.

"And why would Robert Simpson want to do away with Dr. Shapiro?"

For once, I was ready with an answer. "He's anti-Semitic," I said.

Trowbridge laughed. "Oh, come on, Doctor. There's got to be more to it than that!"

"Perhaps," I said, rising to my feet. "But that's all I'm going to tell you. Now I really must ask you to leave and let me get back to work. Patients are waiting." I folded my arms defiantly, waiting for him to take the hint.

He took it, and I sank back into my chair, heart pounding and hands shaking, wondering what on earth I had just done.

I had a terrible time trying to concentrate on my surgicals and everything else I had to get done before I came home, and I was still pretty agitated when I walked through the kitchen door to find Pete stretched out in my recliner, enjoying a beer with Hal while they watched the news on TV.

I greeted the dogs, fixed myself a scotch on the rocks, and took a huge swig right there and then, hoping it would settle me down, but all it did was make me choke on the fumes.

Hal turned to look at me. "Hey, take it easy, sweetie. You don't have to drink it all in one gulp, you know."

I was too busy coughing to answer him. I simply topped off my glass and went on into the living room, where I gave my husband a kiss and then curled up on the couch with my scotch and Geraldine.

"Any news?" I asked when I could trust myself to speak without coughing. Of course there was news, because Pete was there, and it wasn't Friday.

"Well, for starters, we got another Christmas card," Hal said. "It's there on the coffee table."

I looked. The card was already in its transparent evidence bag. On the cover was a sketch of another dead bird, with feet in the air, one wing draped across the body, and the other flung out to the side. I turned it over to read the verse.

On the fourth day of Christmas, my true
love gave to me one falling bird.

"You know," Hal said to Pete, "you've already got three other cards in evidence, so you should know whose fingerprints are on it already, shouldn't you?"

"Not necessarily," Pete said. "So far, there haven't been any, except yours and Toni's on the first card. Whoever's doing this must have worn gloves."

I put the card back on the coffee table. "So what went wrong with your plan to hide George Starling at the Holiday Inn?" I asked Pete.

"We're still playing catch-up," Pete said. "We just got started a day too late. We interviewed his girlfriend, and she said she stayed at George's house the night before last, and she thought she saw someone in the backyard, but by the time George got out there to look, nobody was there. We figure Robbie, or whoever it is, was staking out the house and followed George to the Holiday Inn."

"You might as well just call him Robbie and be done with it," Hal said with a wink in my direction. "Toni won't hear of it being anybody else." Then he turned to me. "By the way, did you tell your partners about Robbie?"

"Yes, and I swore them to secrecy. I figured they had a right to know why we were getting an autopsy every day all of a sudden, when we hadn't had one for months."

Pete cleared his throat. "When the CSU guys went up to the room, there was a room service cart all set up for dinner. The dishes still had lids on them. Only the bottle of wine had been opened, and it was lying on the carpet with its contents spilled all over, and snow was blowing in through the broken window."

A scene was forming in my brain. "So Robbie followed George to the Holiday Inn. Once there, it would be easy to call for room service to George Starling's room and then follow the cart to the room, slip inside behind it, hide somewhere until the room service guy left, and then take George by surprise, pith him, and push him out the window."

"I hope you're staking out Stan Goldman's house," Hal said.

"That won't do any good," I said. "He's already missing. What you should do is get all the rest of the jurors out of their houses, put them all in different hotels, and stake out all their houses at once. He can't follow all of them, can he?"

"God, I hope not," Hal said.

I wasn't sure. Robbie was beginning to assume an almost supernatural quality, seeming like a ninja in his ability to move about without being seen. The Robbie I remembered hadn't been the athletic type, but he might have buffed up in prison. God only knew what he was capable of now.

I shivered. Hal noticed. "Sweetie, what's going on with you? You're as nervous as a cat in a room full of rocking chairs."

I told them about my conversation with Ryan Trowbridge. Pete listened impassively, while Hal's expression went from outrage to shock. But they both laughed at the anti-Semitic reference.

"It's the absolute truth, you know," I said.

"That's what makes it so funny," Hal said. "It's true, but there's so much more to it that Trowbridge doesn't know."

"That's not necessarily a good thing," Pete said. "That's not going to stop Trowbridge from filling in the blanks with what he suspects and putting that in the paper."

"Oh jeez," I moaned, putting my face in my hands. "I need another scotch."

The phone rang. Nobody moved. Then Pete said, "Is there an extension?"

"It's upstairs in the office on the desk," I said.

Pete got up and started for the stairs. "You answer it, Toni, and I'll listen in."

His suggestion had a ring of familiarity because we'd done

the same thing eleven years ago, only it had been Elliott listening in instead of Pete.

I waited until he got to the top of the stairs, and then I picked up the handset. "Hello?"

"I'm not a murderer," said Robbie's voice. "Your husband didn't die."

"What about the four jurors you killed?"

"What the hell are you talking about?"

"Four of the jurors on the jury that convicted you have been murdered," I told him. "And you claim you didn't do it?"

"I didn't know anything about it," he said, and he sounded sincere.

"Where are you calling from?" I asked him.

"The halfway house where I'm staying," he said. "I'm there for the next six months, and I'm not allowed to leave except to go to my job."

"In Boise?"

"Yes, in Boise," he snapped. "So how could I kill four people in Twin Falls?"

"Pete, did you get all that?" I asked.

"I got it," he said. "You hang up now."

I did so. Pete came downstairs. We stared at each other in silence.

"Well?" Hal said. "What did he say?"

"He says he didn't do it," I said.

"Then who did?"

CHAPTER 10

Reputation, reputation, reputation! Oh, I have
lost my reputation! I have lost the immortal
part of myself, and what remains is bestial.

—Shakespeare, *Othello*

Ryan Trowbridge didn't lose any time in getting his story
into the *Clarion*. "Jury Killer Count Mounts" was the
headline that graced the front page of Wednesday's
Clarion, under Ryan Trowbridge's byline.

"Well, that doesn't look so bad," Hal said over breakfast. He
handed me the A section. "Here—see for yourself."

I had to admit the title didn't look so bad, but I knew something
might be lurking in the body of the article that could blow my
privacy to kingdom come.

"Go ahead. Read it," Hal said. "It won't bite."

That's what you think, bub, I thought, but he was right. The
article was out there whether I read it or not, so I figured I might
as well read it and be prepared for all the questions coming my
way. I read it out loud to Hal.

The mysterious Jury Killer has claimed a fourth victim. George Starling, 66, was found dead in the parking lot of the Holiday Inn Monday night after having fallen to his death from a fifth-floor window, an apparent suicide.

An autopsy revealed that the victim was already dead when his body hit the ground. Dr. Toni Day, chief pathologist at Cascade Perrine Regional Medical Center, confirmed to this reporter yesterday that the victim had been pithed.

Starling, a local Realtor, had been sequestered at the Holiday Inn so the police could stake out his house. However, police investigation found evidence that the killer had gotten into the victim's room by way of a food service cart.

I stopped and looked up at Hal, who nodded encouragingly and said, "That's not so bad, now, is it?"

"Not so far," I said.

Further investigation has revealed that members of this jury deliberated and returned a guilty verdict in the case of one Robert Simpson, convicted and sentenced to life in prison for kidnapping and attempted murder in 2005. Simpson was recently paroled for good behavior.

Uh-oh. I stopped.

Hal, who had gotten up to refill his coffee cup, said, "Well?"

"Here it comes," I said.

Simpson's victim, Dr. Hal Shapiro, is a professor at Canyon Community College and also the husband of pathologist Dr. Toni Day.

Hal came back and sat down. "I don't think I like this," he said.

"I know I don't," I said. "This is exactly what I was afraid of."

"You may as well finish it," he said resignedly.

"Okay."

> Dr. Day has been the recipient of gruesome Christmas cards announcing each murder but not until the victim is already dead. Twin Falls Police Captain Bernard Kincaid admits they have been unable to get ahead of this killer.
>
> Will they be able to prevent this killer from claiming a fifth victim? And what is the connection between Simpson and Dr. Toni Day?

Hal sighed. "Oh brother."

I handed the paper back to him with disgust. "Damn. He sounds like a sleazy gossip columnist. I think I'll unplug the phone and stay home today."

"You'll do no such thing," Hal said with finality, "and neither will I. We're going to hold our heads up high and persevere."

Persevere, my ass, I thought, but I stood up, rinsed out my coffee cup, and went upstairs to get dressed.

The pathology office was abuzz when I got to work. Histotechs Lucille and Natalie huddled in a group with the lab manager and our other transcriptionist, Linda. Arlene buttonholed me the minute I walked in the door. "Dr. Day! Did you see the paper this morning? There's a big article—"

I held up a hand. "I saw it," I told her, "and I can't tell you anything you don't already know."

At that point, Charlie Nelson walked in the door, and my heart sank to my toes.

Charlie Nelson was short, plump, and fiftyish and favored

three-piece suits with a pocket watch on a chain. He had been assistant administrator at the old hospital and was a renowned repository of gossip. If there was anything juicy floating around, Charlie was sure to know about it and would gladly provide details. If you wanted something spread around, Charlie was your man.

Put another way, the man had a mouth like a sieve. If you wanted to keep something under wraps, you didn't tell Charlie.

Unfortunately for me, the *Clarion* had done that for me, and Charlie's eyes lit up when he spotted me.

"Hey, Doc! I saw that article in the paper about you! Wasn't that—"

"Charlie! I haven't seen you in ages! Get in here!" I grabbed his arm, hustled him into my office, and shut the door before he had a chance to utter the fatal words "your old boyfriend" in front of the entire department.

"Toni, what's this all about?" Charlie said while extricating himself from my grasp.

"Charlie, if you don't stop talking about that article, I'm going to sic my cousin Vito on you," I hissed.

"Toni, you don't have a cousin Vito," Charlie said.

"I'll find one. I'm serious, Charlie. I don't want anybody talking about me and the Jury Killer around here. I don't want to be inundated with reporters and phone calls about it; it'll interfere with my work, and that'll interfere with patient care. And it's not just me. Other people are going to be bothered by reporters asking about me. You don't want that, do you?"

"Well, no, but I'm not the only gossip around here," he said. "You can't shut them all up."

"I don't plan to. That's your job."

Charlie raised his eyebrows. "My job?"

"Yes. You're an administrator. So go administrate already."

There was a knock at the door, and Mike put his head in. "Everything all right in here? I heard raised voices."

"We're done," I told him. "Aren't we, Charlie?"

"Whatever you say, Doc," Charlie replied shortly, and he left.

"What was that all about?" Mike asked.

"The article in the *Clarion* about the Jury Killer," I told him. "The reporter hinted at a relationship between me and the killer. That's what I was afraid of. So I told Charlie to shut everybody up about it."

"Good luck with that," Mike said. "Charlie can't even shut himself up."

"Well, he's been warned," I said. "If reporters start bothering other employees or, God forbid, other doctors, he's going to get a raft of shit from lots more than just me."

Out in the office, the huddle had dissipated. Arlene stopped typing when we came out. "What's going on? Is it about the article?"

"Yes," I told her. "You may get calls from reporters and others wanting details. If you do, transfer them right to Mr. Nelson. You too, Linda."

"Oh, good idea," Mike said. "I'll go tell histology and the lab. That should take care of us. The others are on their own."

Lucille came in with a stack of paperwork and slide trays and began distributing them. I'd known Lucille ever since I came to Twin Falls, and I knew she was almost as big a gossip as Charlie, so I took her aside.

Lucille was a large lady with bleached blonde hair piled on top of her head, a voice like a foghorn, and the vocabulary of a sailor. Most gossips tended to spread news in low voices, but not Lucille. One could hear her for miles.

"I assume you've heard about the article in the paper," I said.

"I sure did," she said. "I bet you're going to ask me not to talk about it, aren't you?"

"Yes, I am," I said.

"Don't worry, Doctor," she said with a little pat on my shoulder. "I remember what you were going through back then, and I figured you wouldn't want me to drag all that out again."

"Good. Now Dr. Mike is going to go back to histology with you and tell all of you what to do if you get any phone calls from reporters."

Lucille's eyes widened. "Reporters?"

"That's who writes articles in newspapers," I said. "Then there's TV and radio and magazines and the internet—"

Lucille put her hands over her ears. "Stop! I get it."

"You never know who's going to put it out there, so please don't talk to anybody. Anybody! Got it?"

"Got it."

"And that goes for everybody you work with."

"Okay."

"Now, don't keep Dr. Mike waiting!"

No sooner had they left than Brian came in, having just arrived. "You're late," I said.

Brian dropped into my visitors' chair and stretched out his long legs. "There was a traffic jam on Pole Line Road," he said. "Three fire trucks, a couple of ambulances, and I don't know how many cop cars. Everybody had to pull over and wait till they all went by."

"Where were they going?" I asked.

"I don't know," he said. "By the time I got to the turnoff for the hospital, they were out of sight."

"Oh well, can't be helped, I guess. You missed all the fun."

"What fun?"

"Didn't you read the paper this morning?" I asked.

"Not yet. Why?"

"Remember me telling you about Robbie the other day?"

"Yes. Has he killed someone else?"

I hesitated, debating the wisdom of revealing my conversation with Robbie the night before. I decided not to mention it for now.

"Yes," I said, tapping on my cell screen to bring up the picture I'd taken of the last Christmas card. I showed it to Brian. "His name was George Starling, and he was pushed out of a fifth-story window at the Holiday Inn."

"What was he doing there?" Brian asked.

"The police put him there for protection."

"Didn't do him much good, did it?"

I shook my head. "No. They didn't do it soon enough. The killer followed him and got into the room by pretending to be room service."

"Is that what's got everyone all excited?" Brian asked.

"No, but the reporter has found out which jury the victims were on, identified Robbie and who he kidnapped, and is speculating on what the connection might be between him and me. That's what's got everybody all excited."

Brian groaned. "Oh no. How many people around here besides us know about Robbie?"

"Lucille and Natalie do because they were here then, and maybe a few of the doctors from the old hospital. Charlie Nelson was here just a few minutes ago and nearly blew my cover, but I stopped him just in time."

"So what are you going to do?"

"I've told Arlene and Linda not to talk about it and to refer any calls from reporters to Charlie, and Mike is doing the same thing in histology and the lab as we speak."

Brian sighed and rose to his feet. "I hope it works."

"Not half as much as I do," I told him.

Mike came back just as Brian was leaving my office and stopped him. "Did Toni tell you what's going on here?"

Brian nodded. "You don't need to worry about me," he said. "I won't say anything."

They returned to their offices, and we all got down to the day's workload. I struggled to put Robbie out of my mind and concentrate on my work, and I had nearly succeeded, when it was time to go home. I didn't give the fire trucks, ambulances, and police cars another thought until I got home.

"Guess what we got?" Hal sang out from his recliner as I entered the kitchen from the garage, trying unsuccessfully to circumnavigate the dogs.

"Another Christmas card from the Jury Killer?" I said as I kicked off my boots.

Hal came over, helped me off with my coat, and gave me a kiss. "I guess this means Stan Goldman is officially dead."

I hung my coat in the closet and closed the door. "For at least two days anyway. I don't suppose they've found him yet, have they?"

"Not that I know of," Hal said.

The card lay on the coffee table. A crude drawing in black ink depicted a snowbank with a head and the business end of a shovel poking up out of it. The head had no features and wore a knitted winter cap with a pompom.

With the tip of a pen, I carefully lifted the cover. The verse on the inside read,

On the fifth day of Christmas, my true
love gave to me one golden chill.

"Let me guess," I said. "They're going to find him buried in a snowbank."

Hal gestured at the card. "Pete's coming over to get this. Maybe he'll know."

As if the mention of his name had conjured him up out of thin air, Pete came in through the kitchen door from the garage. "Have I got news for you," he said as he pulled off his boots by the door. He grabbed a beer from the refrigerator; sat on the couch; pulled an evidence bag out of his pocket; and, with small forceps, put the card into it.

Hal went to the bar to fix my scotch on the rocks. I sat next to Pete on the couch. "Did you find Stan Goldman?" I asked.

"No, the fire department did," he answered. "There was a big house fire on West Pole Line Road this morning."

"Oh yes, Brian mentioned that this morning at work," I said. "He was late because he had to pull off the road to let all the emergency vehicles go by. Whose house was it?"

"The house belonged to Thomas and Eleanor Morehouse," Pete said. "It was a total loss."

Hal came back with my scotch. "Eleanor Morehouse? Isn't she—"

"One of the jurors," I said excitedly. "Hal, you were right! Instead of six geese a-laying, it was one house a-burning. Did both of them die in the fire?"

Pete grinned. "No, they didn't, because they weren't there. Actually, Thomas passed on sometime last year. We sent Eleanor to visit the grandkids in Boise."

Hal applauded. "Good for you! Does that mean you're finally getting ahead of the killer?"

I was less elated than worried. "She's in Boise? Robbie's in Boise. Isn't that a little too close for comfort?"

"I don't think so," Pete said. "How would he know where she is? And besides, he says he didn't do it."

"And you believe him?"

Pete shrugged. "Until we can prove he wasn't where he said he was, I have to."

"Whoever he was, he knew the same way he knew where George Starling would be," I said. "He could have followed her."

"Toni, my dearest love," Hal said with a sigh, "don't go borrowing trouble."

"Besides," Pete said, "don't you want to know about Stan Goldman?"

"Oh yes, what about him?" I asked.

"That fire was so hot that it melted all the snowdrifts the plows kept piling up, and there he was."

"Pithed?" Hal said.

"Oh yes."

"Is there any way to know how long he'd been there?" Hal asked.

"After being frozen and then thawed?" I said. "I should think that would just hasten decomposition. We already know he's been missing since Friday, and this is Wednesday."

"But we don't know he's been dead all that time," Hal said.

"I'll bet he was," I said. "Why would Robbie, or whoever, want to encumber himself with a live victim? It would be too dangerous. I'll bet he caught Stan in the alley out back of his shop, pithed him, and then put him in the trunk of his car, drove him out to Eleanor Morehead's, and put him in the snowdrift."

"You're probably right, Toni," Pete said. "He could have done that Friday night, and then we had that big snowstorm on Saturday morning. That body could have been there until the spring thaw."

A thought occurred to me. "When did Eleanor leave for Boise?"

Pete frowned. "I don't know. Maybe Bernie does. What are you getting at, Toni?"

"What if she left for Boise Friday night? What if he saw her leave? He could have followed her then. He could have burned down the house she went to."

"Then why burn down her house here?" Pete said. "What would be the point?"

"To throw us off the track," I said. "We'd be congratulating ourselves for getting her out of her house before the fire and never think to check on a fire that may have happened in Boise any time since last Friday night. Do you know the address?"

Pete stared at me with a deer-in-the-headlights look.

Hal said, "Here we go."

"How the hell does she think these things up?" Pete asked Hal.

Hal shrugged. "I have no idea. Thing is, she's right more often than not. So what are you waiting for already?"

Pete said, "On it," and he left.

CHAPTER 11

Where the telescope ends, the microscope begins.
Which of the two has the grander view?

—Victor Hugo

On Thursday morning, we found out what had happened to Eleanor Morehouse.

I had just poured my coffee, when my phone rang. I picked it up.

"Thought you might like to know," Pete said, "that Eleanor Morehouse did leave for Boise Friday night, and her daughter says she never got there."

"Uh-oh," I said.

"What?" Hal asked.

"Pete says Eleanor Morehouse never got to Boise," I told him.

"Well then, you're gonna want to read this," Hal said.

I sat down opposite him at the kitchen table. "Read what?" I asked.

Pete said, "What are you two talking about?"

Hal pushed the paper over to me, and I picked it up. He had

folded it into fourths so the headline that greeted me was "Victim of Burning Car Identified."

"There's an article in the paper about a burning car," I told Pete. "Do you know anything about that?"

"No. What does it say?"

"Here—I'll let you talk to Hal," I said, "since he's actually read it." I handed Hal my phone and began to read the article.

Hal said, "It says the victim of the burning car was identified. You know that car that was found just off the interstate between Glenn's Ferry and Mountain Home on Saturday?"

Pete's answer was inaudible. "Put it on speaker," I said.

Hal did so. At that moment, I saw the name of the victim and exclaimed, "Oh my God!"

Pete said, "What, Toni?"

"The victim was Eleanor Morehouse!"

"No way!"

"Oh, yes way," Hal told him. "There was an article in Sunday's paper about it that said the state police found the car on Saturday, burned to a crisp. There was a body in it, also burned to a crisp. It said it was a lucky thing there was snow on the ground, or it would have caused a hell of a range fire."

On I-84, there was a long segment between Glenn's Ferry and Mountain Home that passed through BLM land. At night, with little traffic, a car could have gone off the freeway anywhere along there and burned without anyone seeing it, even in the dark. Unless, of course, it touched off a range fire.

"It says here," I said, "that they were able to recover the license plates and the VIN, and they were registered to Eleanor Morehouse."

"Good thing," Pete said, "because they sure couldn't get any usable DNA from her if she was a crispy critter."

"I suppose they couldn't tell if she was pithed either," I said.

Hal threw his hands toward the ceiling and said, "Oy gevalt!"

"Toni, what are you suggesting?" Pete asked. "It was probably just an accident."

"Maybe, but don't you think it's a hell of a coincidence for it to happen to Eleanor Morehouse just as she's in the process of escaping the Jury Killer? If he followed her from her house, he could have forced her off the road anytime he wanted to. You know what the commander used to say about coincidences."

"But he couldn't be sure the car would burst into flames," Pete said.

"He could if he torched it," I argued.

"So you think he forced her off the road and torched her car?" Pete said skeptically.

"Here's what I think," I said.

Hal said, "Here we go."

"I think he forced her off the road, stopped to offer assistance, pithed her, doused her and the car with gasoline, lit a match, and got the hell out of there."

"And came back here and burned her house," Pete said.

"Exactly."

"Jeez. I'm gonna have to talk to the state police."

"When you do," I said, "ask them where the body went."

"Why?"

"So we can find out if she was pithed."

Hal interrupted. "Toni, they won't be able to tell that if she's all burned."

"Maybe not, but surely there's a bone expert who might be able to identify marks on the bones," I said. "My friend Patti Magruder at the LA County coroner's office has a bone expert there, if there isn't one closer than that. I could call her if you want."

Pete heaved a huge sigh. "First things first. Let me talk to the staties, and I'll get back to you."

"How come you didn't mention the burning car before now?" I asked Hal.

"As I recall," Hal said dryly, "we were a trifle busy on Sunday, what with Robbie calling and going to the library to view a body and putting up the Christmas tree. It must have slipped my mind."

"Fair enough," I said.

"Besides, why would I think it had anything to do with this case?"

He had a point.

I could hardly wait to get to work to tell Mike and Brian all about it, but when I got there, Arlene informed me I had an autopsy.

"Stan Goldman?" I asked.

She nodded and handed me the chart. "Mr. Perkins wants to be notified, and so does a Detective Sergeant Adriana Sinclair. Who's that? I never heard of her."

"A newbie," I said. "Does Natalie know?"

Arlene nodded again. "When are you going to do it?"

"After I check with the boys," I said. "It's going to be a stinker. He's been dead five days and buried in a snowbank."

"Ew, gross," she said. "Sucks to be you."

I arranged with Mike and Brian that I would do the autopsy in the afternoon, because I'd have to go right home and shower afterward, as I'd be too fragrant to show myself anywhere there were other people, in spite of having been covered head to toe in protective gear. Then I notified Natalie, Rollie, and Pete. He could pass the message on to Adriana.

At precisely 2:30, I presented myself at the morgue. The body was already on the table with a sheet over it, and the fan was going full blast. Even so, the smell of putrefaction was strong.

Rollie and Pete were present, but Adriana was nowhere to be seen. "She didn't want to come," Pete said, "and she wouldn't tell me why."

"Oh well," I said, and I donned my protective gear. Natalie had thoughtfully provided a jar of Vicks VapoRub, and we all put some under our noses.

"After you told me what this body was going to be like, I ran out to the drugstore on my lunch break," she said.

Once we removed the sheet from the body, the smell made my eyes water and my throat hurt. "We'd better make this fast," I said. "We could suffer permanent lung damage. This must be what mustard gas was like in World War I. The Vicks isn't cutting it."

"It's going to be worse when you open the belly," Rollie said. "It's distended with gas. I suggest we procure some respirators."

"Let's get out of here," I said. "Close up the room, and slap some Do Not Enter signs on the doors. I'm sure the safety officer will have some respirators on hand for formalin spills and such."

Rather than remove my protective gear and go back to my office, I opted to use the phone in the morgue waiting room. From the hospital safety officer, I obtained four respirators and biohazard signs for the morgue doors. Thus armed, Natalie and I were able to take our time to remove and photograph the brain, examine the organs and take samples, and remove blood clots from the great vessels and heart for toxicology.

Stan Goldman was short and fat, with a fatty liver and abundant fat in his abdomen, which was not distended with gas, just with fat. His coronary arteries were crunchy but not occluded, and he had an incipient aortic aneurysm. His heart showed scarring from a previous myocardial infarction, or heart attack.

And of course, he had been pithed.

"I'm going to keep these respirators and signs down here for now," I said. "This may not be the last decomposed body we get from this killer."

The others murmured assent. Pete left, but Rollie waited for Natalie to sew the body up before we transferred it back to the body bag on the gurney and zipped it up. Nobody wanted to stay around and chat. I couldn't wait to get out of my clothes and shower, and I was sure Natalie felt the same.

I cleaned instruments while Natalie washed the autopsy table. We left the morgue with the signs on the doors and the fan running. Natalie's shift was over by then, so she could go home and shower, but I went back to my office to dictate the gross description and preliminary diagnoses before I went home.

I wasn't expecting to find Ryan Trowbridge waiting in my office, but there he was.

"You shouldn't be here," I told him. "You should be talking to Mr. Nelson in administration."

"He's the one who sent me here," he said smugly. "You got another Christmas card, didn't you?"

"Not yet," I said. "I expect one tonight."

"You didn't get one for Stan Goldman yet?" he asked. "Or are you talking about somebody else?"

Uh-oh. "Maybe you'd better tell me what you already know," I said.

"Oh, we're going to play that game, are we?"

I folded my arms. "Your move."

"I know that Stan Goldman's body was found in a snowdrift at the site of a house fire," he said. "I also know that the house belonged to Eleanor Morehouse, another juror, but she wasn't in it. Where was she?"

"The police sent her somewhere she'd be safe," I said. "You'll have to ask them where."

He sniffed. "Did you just do another autopsy?"

"Yes. Stan Goldman. And yes, he was pithed."

"There's nothing more you can tell me?" he asked. "Seriously?"

"I don't know anything more," I said. "What I have is a lot of conjecture but no facts. You really need to talk to the police."

Mike came in with a slide tray in his hand but stopped short when he saw Trowbridge. "Oh, sorry. Didn't know you had company," he said, and he turned to go, but I stopped him.

"This is Ryan Trowbridge from the *Clarion*, who wrote the article that got everybody all excited yesterday," I said.

Mike frowned. "You don't say."

"As you can see, we're busy," I told Trowbridge. "So perhaps you'd better go now."

Mike put the slide tray down next to my microscope and sat down on the other side of my desk. He adjusted the eyepieces on his side and then fixed Ryan Trowbridge with a beady eye. "You heard the lady," he said, and he didn't sound particularly friendly.

Trowbridge took the hint.

Mike put a slide on the microscope stage. "Prostate case," he said.

"It's cancer," I said.

"I know. What Gleason grade would you give that?"

"Seven."

"Three-plus-four or four-plus-three?"

I moved the slide around and looked at more of the tissue on it. "I think I'd call it three-plus-four."

It made a difference because in the grading of prostate cancer, Gleason patterns three-plus-four, score seven, had a better prognosis than Gleason four-plus-three, score seven. In other words, the more of the cancer that was pattern four, the worse it was.

"Good," Mike said. "That's what I thought too. What was that guy doing here? He's supposed to go to Charlie."

"He did. Charlie sent him here."

Mike put the slide back in the tray and stood up. "I think it's time I had a word with Charlie."

"I'll go with you," I said.

Charlie was in his office, but he wasn't alone. Through the glass wall of his office, we could see a man sitting in one of his visitors' chairs. He wore jeans, dirty work boots, a plaid flannel shirt over what appeared to be long underwear, and an orange knit winter cap on his head. A disreputable brown parka hung over the back of the chair.

When Charlie saw us, he motioned for us to come in, so we did. The man stood up. He was tall and thin and stood ramrod straight. That was when I recognized him.

"Monty!" I exclaimed. "What are you doing here?"

Bruce Montgomery had been the administrator at the old hospital, Perrine Memorial. He had also been a Mormon bishop. Charlie had been assistant administrator under him. When we'd moved to the new hospital, he had retired and gone on a mission. Mike and I hadn't seen him in three years. Brian had never met him.

Mike shook Monty's hand. "Good to see you, sir. How are you?"

I shook his hand too. Usually, I hugged people when I was glad to see them, but one didn't hug Monty. His austere demeanor didn't encourage it.

"What are you doing here?" I asked again.

"I just had to have a little blood work," he said. "I'm having surgery soon. Prostate."

Uh-oh, I thought. *Cancer? Or benign hyperplasia?* "Good luck with that," I said. "How come you're dressed like a farmer?"

Monty almost smiled. "I am a farmer," he said. "I always was a farmer. You didn't know that?"

I was ashamed to admit I hadn't. But Monty never had talked about himself much.

"Now that I'm retired, I can go out and get my hands dirty once in a while."

"Why don't you all sit down?" Charlie said. "What can I do for you two?" He sniffed. "Did you just do an autopsy?"

I sighed. "Yes, I did, and I'm sorry about the smell. I was planning to go home right after dictating the gross. I wasn't planning to be here."

Mike and I took chairs, but Monty remained standing. "You have business to discuss. I should go," he said.

"No, stay," I said. "You might be able to help."

Monty sat down.

Charlie said, "What's this all about?"

"Ryan Trowbridge," I said. "Why did you send him to me? You were supposed to get rid of him."

Charlie looked mystified. "Who's Ryan Trowbridge?"

"He's the reporter from the *Clarion* who wrote that article about the Jury Killer," I said.

Charlie turned his palms up. "I never saw him."

I turned to Mike in consternation. "Then he was lying! He just walked into my office without coming here first."

"Then we've got a problem, I tell you what," Mike said. "What are y'all gonna do about it?" The question was directed at Charlie. "We can't have reporters barging in here and harassing Toni. He's interfering with patient care is what he's doing."

Monty looked interested. "What's going on here? Doctor, have you gotten yourself involved in another mystery?"

"I'm afraid so," I said. "Monty, do you remember when my husband got kidnapped and almost died from hantavirus pneumonia?"

"I do," Monty said. "What's that got to do with this?"

"The kidnapper is out on parole," I told him, "and somebody's killing off the jury that put him away. He claims he didn't do it, but I don't know."

"You've talked to him?" Mike asked in disbelief.

"My wife mentioned something about that to me last night," Monty said. "She said there was some kind of connection between you and the killer, but I can't believe that. It isn't true, is it?"

"Well, it kind of is, in that the killer has been sending me these gruesome Christmas cards with crude drawings and verses from 'The Twelve Days of Christmas' altered to suit the presumed murder scene."

"What do you mean 'presumed'?"

"So far, the victims have been pithed and then arranged to look like some other method of murder."

"Except for one," Mike said. "One of them was shot."

"She was pithed first," I said, "and then shot and arranged to look like a suicide."

Monty made a face of severe distaste. "And the cards don't help the police catch him?"

"Not when I don't get them until two days after the murder," I said. "He's killed six of the twelve so far, and we still haven't gotten the card for the sixth one yet."

"Why does the killer send the cards to you?" Monty asked.

"That's what that reporter wants to know," Mike said. "That's why he keeps pestering her."

"What do you say when he asks you?" Charlie asked.

"He's never asked me that particular question," I said. "What he asked was why the kidnapper would want to do away with my husband."

"And?" Monty seemed to be losing patience.

"I said it was because he was anti-Semitic."

Monty looked mystified.

"My husband is Jewish," I added.

"We know that," Charlie said.

"I didn't," Monty said.

"What I don't want reporters to know," I told them, "is that the kidnapper, who might also be the Jury Killer, is an old boyfriend who never got over losing me and has a real problem with the fact that I married a Jew."

"It's the old 'If I can't have her, nobody can' scenario," Mike said.

"Doctor, do you feel that you are in any danger from this killer?" Monty asked.

"Yes, I do," I said. "If it's my old boyfriend, I'm afraid that when he's done killing off the jury, he'll come after Hal and me."

Mike nodded sagely. "Natalie mentioned that yesterday when I was in histology."

"It's all this speculation about what the relationship is between me and the Jury Killer that's making the situation so juicy," I said, "and Ryan Trowbridge is playing that for all it's worth."

"I gave instructions in both the lab and histology to have all calls from reporters transferred to Charlie," Mike said. "I don't know what to do about reporters coming into the hospital and pestering Toni or pestering other employees about Toni."

"And I asked Charlie to make sure none of the employees talk to reporters or even among themselves about this subject," I said.

"Asked me, my ass," Charlie said. "You practically ordered me. And I did it. I met with all department heads and asked them to pass it on to everybody in their departments."

"It's still going to interfere with patient care," Monty said. "Have you considered putting Dr. Day on administrative leave?"

"How's that going to help?" I said.

"Maybe the gossip will die down if you're not here," Monty

said. "At least this Trowbridge character won't be able to pester you."

"Who says? He'll just pester me at home."

"Not if he doesn't know where you live," Charlie said.

I snorted. "Really? All he needs to do is follow me home from here. Or he can google me and find out. For all I know, he followed me home from the Holiday Inn the night George Starling was killed."

"What about your personal safety, Doctor?" Charlie asked. "Maybe you should let us put you on administrative leave, and then you can get out of town. Do you have plans for Christmas?"

"Yes. My parents are coming to visit."

"When?"

"Week after next, and they're staying until the end of the year. That way, they can celebrate both Christmas and Hanukkah with us."

"How do you celebrate Hanukkah?" Monty asked.

I explained that Hanukkah was the Festival of Lights, to commemorate the rededication of the temple after the Maccabean revolt in the second century BC, wherein a one-night supply of oil miraculously burned for eight days and nights. I also told them about the menorah and the dreidel game.

"Is that all?" Charlie asked. "Aren't there gifts involved?"

"Some people do that," I said, "but since we also celebrate Christmas, the kids get gifts anyway. We also put a lighted Star of David on top of the Christmas tree."

"How does your mother feel about that?" Charlie asked.

"She's fine with it. It's Hal's mother who hates it. She thinks we're making a mockery of it."

"Does this killer know where you live?" Monty asked, clearly having had enough of Hanukkah 101. "I suppose all he has to do is look for a menorah in the window."

"We're not the only Jews in Twin," I said, thinking of Arlene. "But he was here in 2005, remember, and we're still in the same house."

"Then maybe you should go to your parents instead of having then come here," Charlie said. "Why put them in danger?"

I laughed shortly. "He knows where they live too. Don't forget: he was my boyfriend in high school and college, when I lived at home. Besides, if they don't come here, they won't get to see the grandkids."

"She's got you there," Mike said. "I suggest you don't do anything, and let Toni take the two weeks' vacation she's got coming. I think the gossip's going to continue as long as this guy keeps writing articles about the Jury Killer, whether she's here or not."

That was where we left it. I went back to my office, did my dictation, and went home.

CHAPTER 12

Simply by being compelled to keep constantly
on his guard, a man may grow so weak
as to be unable to defend himself.
—Friedrich Wilhelm Nietzsche

When I walked in the door, Hal was feeding the dogs in the kitchen. He sniffed. "You had an autopsy, didn't you?"

"What was your first clue?" I asked. "I'm going to go take a shower before I do another thing."

When I came back downstairs all clean and comfy in my old black sweats, Hal had already poured me a scotch on the rocks. "There's something here for you," he said. He reached out and picked up the folded newspaper on the coffee table. Underneath it was a familiar-looking envelope. "I haven't opened it; I'm waiting for Pete to get here."

I picked up my drink and settled on the couch with Geraldine, who sniffed me suspiciously. I must have left a few molecules of putrefaction behind on my person. "That's okay. We both know it's about Eleanor Morehouse."

The sound of feet stomping snow off in the garage was followed by the kitchen door opening. "Here he is now," Hal said.

Pete went directly to the refrigerator, snagged a beer, and then came into the living room. "You finally got it, huh?"

"Right here," Hal said, pointing.

Pete pulled on gloves and took an evidence bag out of his pocket. "Did Toni tell you about the autopsy yet?"

"Not yet," Hal said. "Who was it?"

Pete slit the envelope and pulled out the card. "It was Stan Goldman, and he was so badly decomposed that we all needed respirators."

"Jesus," Hal said. "You've never had to do that before, have you?"

"No," I said, "but this was much worse than anything I've ever encountered. It made me think of what mustard gas must have been like in World War I."

Pete turned the card around so we could see it.

"What the hell?" Hal said. "That's not a house burning."

On the front of the card was a crude drawing of a bathtub with a long arm sticking up out of it. The hand showed three fingers in the air.

"Definitely not Eleanor Morehouse," I said.

Pete opened the card and read the verse on the inside:

> On the seventh day of Christmas, my true
> love sent to me one swan a-drowning.

"It's Jonathan Swann," I said. "I thought you guys were going to sequester the rest of the jury."

"We did," Pete said with exasperation. "They're all in different hotels. We had Swann at the Comfort Inn."

"Is he still there?" I asked. "Did he order room service?"

"What the hell's going on here?" Hal said. "We still don't have a card for Eleanor Morehouse, who we know is dead, but we have one for Jonathan Swann already? That means he's already been dead for two days."

"Beats me," I said. "I thought maybe you guys were beginning to get a handle on this case, but now the killer seems to have stepped up the pace."

"Well," Pete said, "he probably reads the papers too and knows we're catching up with him. He's probably just rushing to finish off the entire jury before he gets caught."

"And in all the excitement, he omitted to send the card for Eleanor Morehouse," I said. "You know what this means, don't you? The sooner he finishes with the jury, the sooner he'll come after us."

Pete sighed and pulled out his cell phone. "I'll get Adriana on it."

"Oh, speaking of Adriana," I said, "how are you two getting along? How did she do watching those autopsies over the weekend?"

Pete scratched his head. "She did okay, but she's hard to figure. She doesn't talk about herself much. She doesn't talk much at all. It's almost like she's afraid to say anything in case it's wrong and we'll laugh at her or something."

"That's the feeling I got too," I said. "Something's bothering her, and I wish I knew what. She doesn't seem to like me much—I know that."

"Well, now that you mention it, there was something she said the other day. She asked me why I let you push me around so much."

"*Moi*? Push you around?" I asked in mock disbelief. "I don't really push you around, do I?"

"You kind of do, sweetie," Hal said. "You can't help yourself."

He was right, of course. "Sorry about that," I said to Pete. "I'll try not to. What did you say to her?"

"Well, the way she said it, it sounded like she was accusing me of being a wuss, so I was offended, but I just laughed and said, 'Of course she does; she's my mother-in-law,' and that was all there was to it."

Hal and I both laughed. "Glad we could help," Hal said.

"Another thing," Pete said, looking somewhat uncomfortable. "Would it be okay if I told Adriana about you and Robbie? I've been trying to respect your privacy, so I watch what I say, but I think she needs to know as much about this case as Bernie and I do."

"I agree," I said. "Tell her anything you need to."

After Pete left, I told Hal about the conversation in Charlie's office. "They wanted to put me on administrative leave so the gossip going around about me would stop. They find it disruptive to have reporters pestering people while they're trying to work."

"Why would they think having you leave would change anything?" Hal asked. "As long as that reporter writes about the Jury Killer, there's going to be gossip, whether you're there or not."

"That's what Mike said. They also suggested we go to Mum and Nigel's instead of having them come here, so we don't put them in danger, but I reminded them that since Robbie was my boyfriend in high school, he knows where they live too."

"Look, I get that you don't want to put your parents in danger by going down to Long Beach for Christmas," Hal said with a worried expression, "but do you think it's wise to have them come up here? I mean, I know you and I might be in danger, but we have Pete and Bernie, and we can take care of ourselves."

"How about we let them make that decision?" I said, picking up my cell phone. "I should call Nigel anyway to let him know how his suggestion turned out."

Mum answered the phone when I called, sounding worried. "Kitten, I was intending to call tonight, but you beat me to it. Nigel says you're involved in some kind of serial murder case having to do with a jury and 'The Twelve Days of Christmas,' but he didn't go into much detail. Are you all right? Do you need us to come sooner than we planned?"

Mum and I had emigrated from England when I was three years old and lived with my father's parents until they both passed on while I was in high school. Mum and Nigel still lived there.

Even after nearly fifty years, she still sounded as British as she had then, while my accent was all but gone.

I put my phone on speaker. "That's what I wanted to talk to you about," I said. "Did Nigel mention which jury it is?"

"No, dear. What's that to do with our visit?"

"It's the jury that put Robbie in prison," I said, "and Robbie's out on parole. So far, he's killed six of the twelve, although he says he didn't."

Mum gasped. "You've actually talked to him?"

"I'm afraid so. He started calling us as soon as he got out. He'd hang up if Hal answered, but he talked to me, and he said he didn't do it. He claimed he didn't even know about it."

"I never liked that boy," Mum said, "but I never expected him to become a murderer."

"Well, he was a kidnapper," I said, "and Hal could have died. That's attempted murder right there."

"That's true, kitten," Mum said. "It's just a hop, skip, and a jump from one to the other. Are you sure it's not him who's killing those people?"

I laughed shortly. "I'm not sure of anything anymore. When I thought it was Robbie, I was afraid that after he finished with the jury, he'd come after us, but now I don't know."

Mum gasped again, but I didn't give her a chance to say anything before I rushed on. "We're concerned that you and Nigel might be in danger too if you come up here."

"Nonsense, kitten. Wild horses wouldn't stop us. Safety in numbers and all that. Are you sure you don't want us to come sooner?"

"There wouldn't be much point, Mum. I have to work next week."

"Well, all right, kitten, but if you change your mind—"

"You'll be the first person I call," I promised. "Is Nigel home? I need to talk to him about the case."

"He's gone to the grocery store, but he should be home any minute. Do you want him to call you, or can I give him a message?"

"Tell him his theory seems to be panning out, but I'd like to talk to him about it."

"Very well, kitten. Take care now. I love you."

"Love you too," I said, and I rang off. I looked at Hal. "Well, there you have it."

Nigel didn't call until after we'd had dinner and cleared away the dishes. "Fiona says that bloke has killed off six of the twelve," he said. "Did he do it in order?"

"He did for the first five," I told him, and I gave him a rundown on the first five Christmas cards. "We haven't gotten the sixth yet, but we did get the seventh today, so we don't know if he still is."

"Sounds like he's picked up the pace a bit, eh, what? Those police johnnies ought to sequester that jury for their own safety. Put 'em in hotel rooms or something of the sort."

"They have," I said. "Number four was killed in his room at the Holiday Inn, and number seven was at the Comfort Inn."

"Was he also killed in his room?"

"We don't know yet," I said. "Number six was on her way to Boise, when she was forced off the road and set on fire. This killer seems to be everywhere at once. It's almost as if there's more than one person doing this."

"Spot on, my girl," Nigel said. "I'll wager that's precisely what's happening. I'm surprised those police blokes haven't caught on by now."

"Well, if they haven't before, they will now," I said. "At this rate, they'll finish up the jury by the middle of next week. Then, if Robbie has anything to do with it, they'll come after us."

"That's torn it," Nigel said. "We'll be there Saturday."

"But Nigel—"

He'd already rung off.

"What was that all about?" Hal asked. "Did he hang up on you?"

"Sort of. They're coming Saturday."

"This Saturday?" he asked in disbelief.

"Yes. The next time we wake up and it's Saturday, that Saturday. The day after tomorrow."

"All right already," Hal growled. "I get it. Is the guest room ready?"

"It should be. Nobody's used it since they were here last. I suppose it could do with a dusting, though."

Hal snorted. "After six months? Ya think?"

After we got in bed and I was deep into the latest Dick Francis mystery, Hal said, "I think maybe Pete just put his finger on what's bothering Adriana. She feels left out of the loop."

"I hope you're right," I said. "It can't hurt for her to know my story."

I thought that was true when I said it, but you know what they say about famous last words.

CHAPTER 13

The newspapers! Sir, they are the most
villainous, licentious, abominable, infernal …
Not that I ever read them! No, I make it a
rule never to look into a newspaper.

—Richard Brinsley Sheridan

Ryan Trowbridge was on the ball, as usual.

"More Jury Killer Victims Identified" was the headline gracing the front page of Friday's *Clarion*.

Hal was already up and drinking coffee when I came downstairs for breakfast. I toasted myself an English muffin and poured myself a cup of coffee before sitting down to eat.

Hal folded the paper and handed it to me. "Your buddy Ryan Trowbridge has done it again."

> Two more victims of the Jury Killer have been identified as a result of a house fire on West Pole Line Road.
>
> A house belonging to Eleanor Morehouse burned to the ground the morning of Tuesday, December 7. As a result of the fire, a body was found in a melted

snowbank and identified as Stanley Goldman, a local jeweler who went missing the evening of Friday, December 2.

The autopsy performed yesterday by Dr. Toni Day, chief pathologist at Cascade Perrine Regional Medical Center, confirmed that the victim had been pithed.

Eleanor Morehouse was not in the house at the time of the fire but had gone to Boise to visit her daughter, who reported that her mother never arrived.

A burned car was found Saturday morning, December 3, on I-84. It had gone off the road between Glenn's Ferry and Mountain Home. The license plate and VIN identified it as belonging to Eleanor Morehouse.

The body inside was burned beyond recognition, and the Ada County medical examiner, Dr. Frank Robertson, confirmed that it was too badly burned to determine if it had been pithed.

This brings the Jury Killer count to six. The Twin Falls Police Department has sequestered the remaining members of the jury in local hotels for their own safety. However, victim number four, George Starling, was killed in his hotel room.

So far, Dr. Day has refused to divulge what her connection is to the recently paroled Robert Simpson and indeed has even refused to tell this reporter whether or not she has received Christmas cards about these latest two victims.

What is she hiding?

I read the article while munching on my marmalade-slathered English muffin. When I was finished, I handed the paper back to Hal. "More fodder for the gossip mill," I said.

"Maybe they'll have another go at putting you on administrative leave," he said.

"I may accept."

Well, they didn't put me on administrative leave, but when I got to work Friday morning and told Mike and Brian what had happened, they insisted I take the next week off as well as the two weeks I already had, which was the same thing as administrative leave, only with pay.

"Are you sure?" I asked. "I mean, that's awfully nice of you guys, but really? You know how brutal it can get this time of year with everybody trying to get their surgeries done on this year's deductible."

"Tell you what," Mike said. "You take your three weeks off but help us out with the autopsies."

"Deal," I said. "We'll probably be getting another one soon. I received a card for juror number seven yesterday."

"Yesterday?" Mike echoed. "That means he's already been dead three days."

"What happened to number six?" Brian asked.

"She went to Boise," I said.

"So she's not dead?"

I realized I hadn't yet told the boys what had happened to Eleanor Morehouse, so I rectified that. "Since her body was recovered in Elmore County, it was taken to the Ada County medical examiner in Boise."

"Thank God," Mike said. "Do they know if she was pithed?"

I shook my head. "I don't know. I asked Pete if he could find out, but I haven't heard anything yet."

At that moment, my phone rang. I reached over and picked it up.

"Good morning, young lady." Rollie's sepulchral voice greeted me. "We've got another one for you."

I put the phone on speaker for the benefit of my partners. "Jonathan Swann?" I asked.

"The very same. Drowned in the bathtub of his room at the Comfort Inn. The chambermaid found him this morning."

"This morning?" I asked in amazement. "I got the card about him yesterday. Usually, the victims have been dead for two days by the time I get a card. How come nobody found him sooner?"

"I don't know," Rollie said. "You'd better ask your son-in-law about that. We'll be delivering the body to you shortly."

"Okay," I said. I hung up and then called histology to let Natalie know the body was coming. Then I turned to Mike and Brian and asked, "Who's up?"

"You are," they chorused.

I'd told both Pete and Rollie that I'd be doing the autopsy on Jonathan Swann around one o'clock, right after lunch, so it was no surprise to find them both present in the morgue when I got there.

The body lay on the autopsy table, partially covered by a sheet. Natalie, already clad in her Tyvek jumpsuit, gloves, booties, and face shield, bustled about, getting my cutting board and instruments laid out.

"Your gear is right over there, Doctor," she said, pointing to the counter next to the sink.

"Thanks," I said, and I started donning my personal protective equipment. While I did so, I asked Pete the same question I'd asked Rollie earlier. "Why didn't anyone find him before this morning?"

"He's had his Do Not Disturb sign out for the last three days. The hotel has a policy that after three days, housekeeping can go in and check to make sure everything is all right."

"That must have been quite a shock," I said.

"The chambermaid screamed and fainted," Pete said. "Luckily, she had one of the security guards with her, and he called 911."

"Did Swann order room service?"

"He did the first night he was there," Pete said. "He'd been instructed to do so, remember?"

"Seriously?" I asked while struggling to get a surgical bootie on over my shoe. "After what happened to George Starling?"

Pete turned up his palms. "What else can we do? If he left his room to go eat, somebody could get in and lie in wait for him. We're damned if we do and damned if we don't."

I saw his point. After snapping my face shield into place, I stepped over to the autopsy table and removed the sheet.

Jonathan Swann was a tall, thin man with salt-and-pepper hair and a mustache. In life, he had probably been quite good looking, but nobody ever looked good in the morgue. His skin was wrinkled and pruny-looking from prolonged immersion.

The faint smell of putrefaction I'd noted when I removed the sheet was getting stronger by the minute.

"First, we need to turn him over and see if he was pithed. Natalie? Want to give me a hand?"

Natalie was already pulling the left arm across the body before I finished the sentence. Pete and Rollie moved up behind me to get a closer look.

He'd been pithed all right. While I held the body in place, Natalie photographed the laceration.

Postmortem lividity covered the back and shoulders but ended at the buttocks. "Did you find him flat on his back with his knees bent?" I asked.

"That's exactly how he was found," Rollie said. "With his face underwater."

"Here's a loose hair stuck to his back," I said. "It's black."

"He has black hair," Pete said. "It's probably his."

"It's too long," I said.

Pete put it in an evidence bag. "I'll need some of his hair, though, to compare it to." He yanked a few hairs out of the decedent's head, put them in another bag, and labeled both bags.

"There's some skin slippage here," I said, indicating a spot on the left shoulder where I'd pushed to turn the body. "And there's no rigor. This is all consistent with his having been dead at least three days."

Pete made a face. "He smells like it too. Are we going to need those respirators again?"

"I don't know. At least we've got them if we need them. Let's start with the Vicks and go from there."

Next, we removed the brain with its scrambled brainstem, and Natalie photographed that too before lowering it into a bucket of formalin.

There were no surprises in the body cavity. Since he'd been pithed, he would have already been dead when he was put in the bathtub, so I didn't expect to find water in the lungs, and I didn't. Aside from a couple of colon polyps, Jonathan Swann had been perfectly healthy.

We finished up as fast as possible because the stench in the morgue was getting to all of us, even me, although it wasn't nearly as bad as Stan Goldman's had been. The Vicks helped, and we didn't need the respirators.

Ryan Trowbridge was waiting for me in my office when I got back. I supposed I shouldn't have been surprised.

I sighed. "How did you know?" I asked.

"I was there when they found him," he said.

"What were you doing there?"

"I saw the police cars and the hearse there when I was driving by, so I stopped to see what was what."

I didn't bother to ask why he'd just happened to be driving by. The Comfort Inn was right on Blue Lakes, and in the early morning rush-hour traffic, countless people constantly drove by.

"Did you see the crime scene?" I asked instead.

He shook his head. "Didn't need to. I interviewed the desk clerk and the security guard. I suppose he was pithed, and there was no water in his lungs."

"You suppose correctly."

"Anything else?"

"Nope. The man was the picture of health."

"Except he was dead."

"Right."

I was keeping my answers short in hopes he would give up and go away, but nothing doing.

"Can I ask you a personal question?" he said.

"No."

He ignored me. "What's the relationship between you and Robert Simpson?"

"There isn't one."

"But there was one, wasn't there?"

I remained silent.

He shrugged. "Tell me, or don't tell me; it doesn't matter. I can find out."

I folded my arms. "Knock yourself out."

He stood, zipped up his parka, and gave me a mock salute. "Until next time."

I wished I could have said there wouldn't be a next time, but I knew there would be.

CHAPTER 14

The supreme happiness of life is the
conviction that we are loved.

—Victor Hugo

Mum and Nigel's flight was due to arrive in Twin at noon,
which gave Hal and me plenty of time to sleep in, eat
breakfast, and read the morning paper.

"Jury Killer Count Now Seven" was the headline that
screamed from the front page of the Saturday *Clarion*. Ryan
Trowbridge had let no grass grow under his feet in getting the
story out.

> Early yesterday morning, a body was discovered in
> a room at the Comfort Inn on Blue Lakes Boulevard.
> The victim was Jonathan Swann, a local insurance
> broker. The body was found in the bathtub, apparently
> a victim of drowning.
>
> However, an autopsy performed yesterday by Dr.
> Toni Day showed that the victim, like all the others,
> had been pithed, and the body had been arranged to
> simulate a bathtub drowning.

Swann was the seventh victim of the Jury Killer, whose identity remains unknown. He, like the other remaining jurors, had been sequestered at the Comfort Inn since Tuesday.

The hotel manager, the desk clerk, and a member of the kitchen staff were interviewed by this reporter. The victim checked in Tuesday afternoon and ordered room service at approximately six o'clock. The kitchen staffer who delivered the evening meal was apparently the last to see the victim alive, as the Do Not Disturb sign remained on the doorknob afterward.

According to hotel policy, housekeeping staff is authorized to enter the room to check on the occupant after the Do Not Disturb sign has been out for three days. The body was found by housekeeping staffer Consuelo Barrera and security guard Eric Schmidt, who called 911.

Dr. Toni Day was said to have received a Christmas card depicting the bathtub drowning of victim number seven on Wednesday. If this killing follows the pattern of all the others, Swann must have been killed Tuesday night. However, neither the police nor Dr. Day have yet confirmed that.

Dr. Toni Day still refuses to divulge what her relationship is to Robert Simpson. Stay tuned.

"He could have gone all day without putting in that last bit," I grumbled. "Now everybody at work will be gossiping about it again."

"Luckily, you won't be there to hear it," Hal said practically. "Look, it's almost eleven thirty. Let's go to the airport."

The flight from Salt Lake City was right on time. Mum and Nigel were nearly the last to deplane. They descended the ramp, loaded down with gaily colored shopping bags.

"Jesus," Hal muttered. "How'd they get all that through security?"

Mum breezed through the door first, dropped her packages onto the floor, and threw her arms around me. "Oh, kitten, it's so good to see you!"

Nigel came next and nearly came to grief as his feet encountered Mum's shopping bags. "Blimey," he said. "Fiona, did you have to drop that lot right in the doorway?"

Mum let go of me and turned to look. "Oh dear," she said. "I'm so sorry."

Hal and I hastily gathered up the offending bags and moved them out of the doorway. People lining up behind Nigel were clearly not pleased to be kept out in the cold when they couldn't get past him and Mum's shopping bags.

"I couldn't see my feet because of those bloody things," he complained as we made our way to the baggage claim area at the other end of the building.

"So how was your flight?" I asked.

Mum sank into a chair in the waiting area and sighed. "It was terribly crowded, and they stuck us way in the very back row, and we couldn't even sit together. We were on opposite sides, in window seats."

My mother was shorter than I was and slightly heavier. Back in the day, she'd been a dead ringer for Susan Hayward, a gorgeous actress from the 1950s with a mop of curly red hair. Mum's hair was generously streaked with white, but she still wore it the same way.

Nigel dropped his shopping bags and wrapped me in a bear hug. He planted a mustachioed kiss on my cheek. "Toni, old girl, what a sight for sore eyes!"

I kissed him back. "It's good to see you too. You both look terrific."

My stepfather resembled the actor Bernard Fox, who had played Dr. Bombay in the 1960s sitcom *Bewitched*: somewhat stocky, with wavy gray hair and a rather remarkable mustache. He liked to wear sweater vests over his shirts unless it was too hot.

He dropped into the chair next to Mum. "It wasn't a bad flight as flights go, but it took forever to get through security."

"I can imagine," Hal said.

At that moment, the doors opened, and suitcases and other baggage began to slide down the chute into the claim area. Hal got up to retrieve Mum and Nigel's bags, which were the first off. Nigel got up too, but Hal shook his head. "I've got this."

Mum and I got up, gathered all the shopping bags, and followed Hal and Nigel out the door. Hal had parked his Jeep Cherokee nearby, so it was a short walk, but it was icy in places, and Hal cautioned us to be careful where we stepped. We reached the car without incident.

I helped Mum into the front passenger seat and got in the backseat with Nigel, while Hal stowed the luggage and all the shopping bags in the cargo area in the back. It was completely full, and I was glad we'd brought the Grand Cherokee instead of my Subaru Outback.

"We thought we were being smart to bring the presents with us instead of trying to get everything here," Mum said, "but nobody told us not to wrap the packages. They made us unwrap and open every single one."

"Oh dear," I said. "If I'd known you were going to do that, I would have warned you."

"I was afraid we were going to miss our flight," Mum said. "That's probably why they stuck us in the back."

Nigel harrumphed. "Now, Fiona, we had plenty of time."

"That's not why you were in the back," Hal said. "It's because you moved your reservations up a week, and those were the only seats left."

"Oh," Mum said. "Well, in any case, all those presents need to be rewrapped before we put them under the tree."

"No worries," I said. "There's still two weeks before Christmas."

When we got back to the house, Killer and Geraldine greeted my parents with soft whines and wagging tails. Killer stood on his hind legs and put his front paws on Nigel's shoulders, and Nigel had time to give him a hug before Hal saw him and ordered him down.

Nigel and Hal took the luggage upstairs while I deposited the shopping bags under the Christmas tree. They would be out of the way there until we got them all wrapped. I hoped Mum and Nigel would remember who got what when the time came.

While Mum used the bathroom, Spook slithered down off the couch and ambled over to investigate. When she came out, she was greeted by the sight of a shopping bag on its side with a black tail protruding from it.

She took umbrage. "What's that cat doing? Get him out of there!"

"He can't hurt anything," I told her. "He's declawed."

She wasn't reassured. "Do you hear that? He's tearing the paper! We were hoping to reuse the same wrapping paper, and it's in the bag too."

"Oh, I didn't realize." I went over, grabbed Spook by the tail, and hauled him out of the bag. He had a fragment of red-and-gold paper in his teeth.

"See that?" Mum said.

I put my hands on her shoulders. "Mum, you're cranky. You need a nap."

Hal came back downstairs in time to hear me. "Good idea," he said. "Nigel's already asleep up there."

"Right then," Mum said. "I believe I'll join him."

Once Mum was upstairs, I got Hal a beer and fixed myself a scotch on the rocks. "I think that flight was harder on them than they were letting on."

"I think so too," Hal said. "How old are they now?"

"They're both in their seventies," I said. "Maybe we ought to start going down there for Christmas from now on."

"I don't know," Hal said. "If we go to them for Christmas, they'll feel they have to entertain us as well as fix Christmas dinner, and that might be harder on them than flying up here, not to mention they wouldn't get to see the grandkids."

"Maybe you're right," I said. "Maybe if they hadn't had to wrestle with all those bags, they wouldn't be so tired."

"They'll feel better after a nap," Hal said.

"I hope so," I said, "because this year, they also have to deal with a serial killer who may be trying to kill us."

CHAPTER 15

Accidents will occur in the best-regulated families.
—Charles Dickens

W e'd invited Pete and Bambi and the girls for dinner, and I hoped Mum and Nigel would feel good enough after their naps to cope with a five-year-old and a two-year-old.

When I voiced my concern to Hal during a commercial, he said, "Don't worry about it. Little Toni's pretty good at keeping Shawna Renee occupied."

"That works as long as Shawna wants to be occupied," I said. Judging from what I'd heard over the phone while talking to Pete, little Shawna frequently objected to being bossed around by her big sister. "I suspect she'll spend most of the time on Mum's lap."

Hal chuckled. "I doubt Fiona will object."

Mum and Nigel slept for two hours, and both said they felt much better afterward. Nigel went straight to the bar. "Anyone care for a libation?"

That was one of the things I loved about my stepfather. "We're way ahead of you," I said, brandishing my scotch, which looked rather depleted. "But you can give me a refill."

Mum came over to the sink, where I was cutting up carrots and potatoes. "What are we having for dinner, kitten?"

"A pot roast," I told her. "Pete and Bambi and the girls are coming."

"Is there anything I can do to help?" Mum asked.

"No, thanks," I told her. "I've got this."

Nigel brought me my scotch, and he and Mum went into the living room. I put the cut-up vegetables into water, added some ice, and joined them.

"Now then," Nigel said, "how about a peek at that jury list?"

I fetched it from Hal's end table and joined Nigel on the couch. "Your theory seems to be working," I told him. "The first one, Ralph Partridge, was found under a big blue spruce in the snow, and the second one, Robin Jones, appeared to have been stabbed. But they were both pithed, and their bodies were posed to look like a hit-and-run and a stabbing."

"What about number three, Penelope Leroux?"

"She was pithed and then shot and arranged to simulate a suicide, and number four, George Starling, was pushed out of a fifth-floor window at the Holiday Inn after he was pithed."

"How the devil did this bloke manage to get the jury list?"

"That's a good question. Maybe someone on the inside could have hacked into court records, but he would have had to know where to look. I doubt someone could just google it. Elliott had to use his work computer, and he needed a username, password, and PIN."

"Next time you talk to Robbie, you might ask him," Nigel said.

"I could, but he's not going to be calling me anymore because we got rid of the landline," I said, "and besides, he says he didn't do it."

"So much for that then. What was number four doing at the Holiday Inn?"

"The police sequestered him there while they staked out his house."

"Didn't do him much good, did it?"

"Not really. Nor did it protect number seven, Jonathan Swann. He appeared to have drowned in his bathtub at the Comfort Inn, but he was pithed first."

"How did the killer get into their hotel rooms?"

"By way of a food service cart. They were all instructed to order room service instead of leaving their rooms to go eat, because someone could get in while they were gone and lie in wait."

Nigel shook his head. "Damned if they do, and damned if they don't."

"That's what Pete said. Number five, Stanley Goldman, disappeared last Friday night and was found in a snowdrift at the site of a house fire on Monday. The snowdrift melted, and there he was."

"Pithed?"

"Yes. The house that burned belonged to number six, Eleanor Morehouse, who had gone to Boise to visit her grandkids. Her car was forced off the road and torched with her in it."

"Blimey. Was she pithed?"

"I don't know. Her body went to the medical examiner in Boise. Pete was going to try to find out, but according to the paper, the medical examiner said she was too badly burned to tell."

"Have you gotten today's mail yet?"

"Not yet, but we should have it by now," I said, getting to my feet. "I'll go see."

"I'll get it, honey," Hal said. "There's a commercial on right now, and I'm still wearing my boots." He went out the front door into the snow and returned with a handful of mail, which he put down on the coffee table in front of us. "Have at it."

I began to sort through the mail carefully with the tip of a pen, and sure enough, there was another tastefully decorated envelope. "There it is! This must be the one for number six. We'll let Pete open it, just in case there's a fingerprint."

"Do you still have the other Christmas cards?"

"No, because Pete took them for evidence, but so far, there are no fingerprints. I did take pictures of the last four, however." I picked up my cell phone, found the pictures, and let Nigel look through them.

"One French pen," he said. "One falling bird. One golden chill. One swan a-drowning. What were the verses for numbers one and two?"

"A Partridge under a tree and one Robin redbreast."

"Clever bloke, eh, what? Quite ingenious, actually." Nigel gestured at the envelope. "Can't wait to see what this one says."

"Hal thought it might say 'one house a-burning,'" I said.

"Kitten," said my mother, "speaking of burning, shouldn't you be getting that roast into the oven?"

I looked at my watch. "Oh dear, I lost track of time. The roast is going to be rare."

"Good," said Hal. "That's how I like it. Mooing."

Pete and family arrived around five thirty. I heard them stamping snow off their boots in the garage before they burst into the kitchen. Little Toni jumped into my arms before Killer and Geraldine had time to greet the newcomers. Little Shawna ignored me and ran into the living room, where I knew she would jump into Hal's lap, coat, boots, and all.

"Girls!" Bambi said in a tone that brooked no refusal. "Come back here, and take your coats and boots off. Honestly!"

I hugged my elder granddaughter and set her back down on the floor. Somehow, in the ensuing melee of dogs and children, the coats and boots got put in their proper place, and everyone went into the living room. Spook was nowhere to be seen.

Smart cat. I hoped he wasn't inside a shopping bag.

By that time, with Mum's help, the roast was done, the vegetables were done, and the gravy was made. I took the roast out of the oven and set it on a platter to rest before it could be sliced. Then I turned to see both dogs hungrily eyeing it, so I hastily moved it to the microwave, where they couldn't get at it.

I'd already fed them, but with the delectable fragrance of roast beef in the air, they'd hardly touched their food. They were holding out for table scraps.

Mum had already set the table, and the high chair and booster seat were in place. In the living room, little Shawna snuggled in Mum's lap, and little Toni cuddled with Hal. Pete and Bambi sat on the hearth to warm themselves by the fire. I fetched beers for both of them and refreshed my scotch.

The Beach Boys song "Surfer Girl" could have been written for Bambi. Standing six feet in her stocking feet, she was the personification of the California beach bunny. Her platinum-blonde hair used to be waist-length but was now cut to a more serviceable length just past her shoulders, and her eyes were as blue as Hal's. In the summer, her creamy skin acquired a gorgeous tan.

Little Toni would grow up to be the image of her mother. At five, she was tall for her age, and her thick, wavy white-blonde hair hung halfway down her back. Little Shawna, however, took after Pete. Her hair was red gold, completely straight, and cut in a bob with bangs. Both girls had bright blue eyes, but little Shawna also had freckles on her pert little nose.

As Hal had predicted, little Shawna spent more time on

Mum's lap than she did in her high chair, and Mum didn't mind a bit. Once Shawna's belly was full, it wasn't long before she began yawning, and Bambi took her upstairs to the crib in the guest room for a nap. While Mum and Bambi entertained little Toni in the living room, Hal, Pete, Nigel, and I cleared the table and gave the dogs their long-awaited table scraps.

Then the four of us returned to the dining table so Pete could update us on recent developments. I had put the mail and the jury list on top of the refrigerator to keep it away from the girls, and I retrieved it so Pete could extract and open the latest Christmas card.

He put on nitrile gloves, carefully slit open the envelope, removed the card, and opened it out on the table so we could all see it.

"Blimey!" exclaimed Nigel.

"What the hell?" Hal said. "That's not Eleanor Morehouse. Who is that?"

The front of the card showed the figure of a woman hanging with a noose around her neck. Inside the card, the verse said,

> On the ninth day of Christmas, my true
> love sent to me one lady hanging.

"Christ on a crutch," I said. "He's not even sticking to the order anymore. He's completely skipped number eight and gone straight to number nine. This is Melinda Roper."

"Here," Pete said. "Let me see that jury list."

I handed it to him.

He pulled out his cell phone and dialed. "Bernie? Somebody needs to check on Melinda Roper. I'll text you the address and phone number." He paused briefly. "Yes. Toni just got another Christmas card." He rang off. "Bernie will let us know."

The dogs, sated by their generous portions of roast beef scraps, returned from the kitchen and stretched out under the table.

"What I want to know," Hal said, "is what about Robbie? Does he have an alibi or not?"

"I called the number you gave me, the one Robbie called from," Pete said. "It's not the halfway house. It's a cell phone."

"Are parolees allowed to have cell phones?" I asked.

"Yes, they are. So I had the computer geeks trace it, and it's a burner phone."

"Uh-oh," I said. A burner phone, I knew, was a cheap phone that one loaded with enough minutes to make one call and then threw away. They were impossible to trace. "Why would Robbie have a burner phone?" I wondered.

Pete said, "The only reason to have a burner phone is if you don't want anyone to know where you are."

"So if Robbie has one, it means he doesn't want anyone to know where he is?" I asked. "Isn't he at the halfway house?"

Killer came out from under the table and went over to the french doors. After a few seconds, he began to growl, and the fur stood up along his back. Geraldine stood next to him and barked.

"So I got the number of the halfway house," Pete said, "and he wasn't there."

"Where was he?" Nigel asked.

Hal got up, opened the french doors to let the dogs out, and turned on the outside lights.

"Nobody knows," Pete said. "He didn't go back there last night after work, and nobody's seen him since."

"So Robbie's in the wind," I said. "Can I see that envelope?"

Pete pushed it over to me.

I looked at it and pushed it back. The hair rose on the back of my neck. "Does anybody else see what's different about this envelope?" I asked the group.

Nigel was the first to notice what had sent a frisson of fear down my spine. "Well, I'll be jiggered. Don't the rest of you see it?"

Hal and Pete looked at each other and then back at me.

"No stamp," I said, "and no postmark."

"Holy shit," Pete said. "That means—"

"That means it was hand delivered," Hal said as his eyes met mine, and I saw my fear mirrored in them.

"Robbie is here," I said hollowly. "He could be right outside this house."

As if they had heard me, the dogs started barking outside.

Hal opened the french doors again. "Killer! Get in here!"

Killer's reply consisted of a savage growl followed by a very human yell.

CHAPTER 16

Some circumstantial evidence is very strong,
such as when you find a trout in the milk.

—Henry David Thoreau

Pete wasted no time. He picked up his cell phone, got up from his chair, and dialed all in one fluid motion. "I'm calling for backup," he said tersely. "Stay away from the windows."

Hal, for once, didn't argue. He and Nigel went into the living room, and I heard them exhorting Mum and Bambi to get a move on if they didn't want to be killed, and I saw Hal turn on the front porch light.

I got up, turned off the lights in the dining area, and pulled the drapes. Hal went into the kitchen and did the same. I could still hear Killer barking, and the sound seemed to be coming from the backyard.

Pete and Hal went out to investigate, and I surreptitiously followed them, even though I knew both of them would chew my ass for not staying inside and safe. Killer was barking ferociously at the back fence, and little Geraldine was right behind him, doing the same. A scrap of dark blue cloth was caught between two slats of the fence.

While Pete and Hal conferred over the clue, I went back into the house and called the dogs. Killer came charging in, nearly knocking me over, and Geraldine followed right on Killer's heels.

We never had to worry about Geraldine. She did whatever Killer did. We joked that Killer even had housebroken her. It had been hilarious to watch her try to squat and hike her leg at the same time.

When Hal and Pete came back in, Pete had the scrap in an evidence bag and was on the phone, requesting backup to search the neighborhood for an escaped parolee who could be armed and dangerous.

"That piece of cloth has blood on it," Hal told me. "I'm not sure if that's because of the fence or Killer, and he's not talking."

"Good," I said. "Maybe the DNA will match Robbie."

The others were sitting near the top of the stairs in a huddle in the dark. When Shawna saw Pete, she screamed, "Daddy!" and held her arms out.

Bambi shushed her, and Pete said, "It's okay. He's gone." He took her from Bambi and cuddled her.

Nigel and Hal went to look out the front window in the office, followed by the dogs, and then came back to report. "Our backup is here," Hal said.

Pete gave Shawna back to Bambi. "I have to go. I'll be back as soon as I can."

At that point, my cell phone rang. To my astonishment, it was Adriana. "I'm trying to reach Pete, but he's not answering his phone."

"He's right here," I said, and I handed Pete my phone. "It's Adriana for you," I told him.

Pete took it. "I turned my phone off," he said. "Toni and Hal had a prowler. What's up?" He listened for a moment and then said, "She's right here. Why don't you tell her that?" He handed the phone back to me.

"I suppose you'll find out soon enough, but there's no need to rush," Adriana said. "We found Melinda Roper hanging in her garage. She's frozen solid."

Did I detect a note of glee in her voice as she told me that?

No, I decided. It was just my overheated imagination.

"Okay," I said. "Do me a favor. Would you ask Rollie to please wait until tomorrow to call me about the autopsy? Hal and I would both appreciate it."

CHAPTER 17

Like one that on a lonesome road
Doth walk in fear and dread,
And having once turned round walks on,
And turns no more his head;
Because he knows a frightful fiend
Doth close behind him tread.

—Samuel Taylor Coleridge

Rollie called me early Sunday morning to tell me he was about to deliver Melinda Roper's body to the hospital morgue and to ask me what I wanted done with her, as she was still mostly frozen.

"How frozen is she?" I asked.

"Her skin and subcutaneous fat feel pretty soft," he said, "but under that, she's still hard as a rock. I stuck a needle into her, and it only went in about half an inch."

"I think she can go into the cooler," I said, "because we don't want her to decompose too much on the outside while she thaws on the inside. Does that make sense to you?"

Rollie said it did. "When do you think you'll do the autopsy?"

"I'll check her tomorrow to see if she's thawed enough and then let you know."

"Okay."

"That's a relief," I told Hal after we rang off. "I don't have to do this autopsy until tomorrow because she's still frozen. I'll run down to Jim Bob's and get us some doughnuts, okay?"

Hal assented.

I took my phone with me in case somebody else called about Melinda Roper, and it rang as I was giving Jim Bob my doughnut order.

First, it was Natalie. "Dr. Day, the lab just called and said we have another coroner's case. Are you going to do it today?"

"No," I replied, "it's still frozen solid. Maybe tomorrow. I'll let you know."

"Okay," she said, and she hung up.

Next, it was Bernie. I told him the same thing.

I hoped Jim Bob and the other customers would think we were talking about a Christmas turkey and not a dead body, which would have freaked everybody out.

Nobody else called. I took the doughnuts home, and we were able to have a leisurely breakfast and plan what to do with the rest of Sunday.

Mum wanted to get her presents rewrapped, and I gave her the dining room table to work on. Hal and Nigel wanted to watch football, although Nigel still complained about how American football didn't make any sense to him.

I went upstairs to the office and left them to it. I was still grappling with the concept of two killers, so I fired up the computer and tried to reconstruct the time line of the murders so far.

I found that of the first seven murders, one had been killed on December 1; two on December 2; and one each on December 3, 4, 5, 6, and 7. He must have been a busy boy on December 2, kidnapping a jeweler as he closed up shop for the night, delivering the body to the home of the next victim, and then chasing her on the interstate to run her off the road and set her on fire, all on the same day.

No, all on the same *evening*.

Stan Goldman had been abducted as he closed his shop early for the Sabbath. It got dark early in December, so sundown would probably have been around four thirty. Then the killer had had to take the body to Eleanor Morehouse's house, bury it in a snowbank, follow Eleanor as she drove to Boise, and force her off the road somewhere between Glenn's Ferry and Mountain Home.

At that point, I heard voices, and Hal yelled up the stairs that Jodi and Elliott were there, so I powered off the computer and went downstairs. Jodi and Elliott were on the couch, having already helped themselves to coffee and doughnuts. I was glad I'd bought a whole dozen.

"What was going on around here last night?" Jodi asked. "Did Robbie try to get in the house and attack you?"

"Somebody was in the backyard," Hal said, "and Killer bit him."

"Good for him," Elliott said. "Did the police catch the guy?"

"No," I said. "He went over the fence."

"He ripped his pants too," Hal said.

Mum came into the living room with an armload of freshly wrapped presents and began arranging them under the tree. Spook was on the back of the couch, watching her intently.

"Is that all of them?" I asked.

Mum straightened up and turned to face me. "All but the last two. What were you working on up there, kitten?"

"I was trying to figure out whether or not one person could have done all the murders."

"And could he have?"

"It's possible. They were all done on different days except for two, and given the time line, those could have easily been done by one person."

"So that awful Robbie could have done them all," she said.

"Which he denied," Hal said.

"If one chooses to believe him," Nigel said from my recliner, where he was sipping tea and enjoying another doughnut.

"Which I do not," Mum said tartly as she went back to the dining room table. "Keep that cat away from those presents!"

The sound of booted feet stamping off snow announced Pete's arrival in the garage.

"Oh boy, doughnuts!" he said upon entering the kitchen.

"Help yourself," I told him. "If there are any left."

Pete poured himself a cup of coffee, as usual; greeted Mum and Nigel; and sat on the couch with the cup in one hand and a doughnut in the other.

"So what's new?" Hal asked.

"Adriana's been busy," Pete said. "Way I look at it, she saved you at least three autopsies."

"How do you figure?" I asked.

"She's contacted the remaining four jurors, and they're all alive and well."

"Well, yeah," Hal said. "We haven't gotten cards for any of them."

"All that means is that if any of them are dead, it would be for less than two days," I said.

"But they're not," Hal argued. "They're alive and well as of today."

Pete intervened. "All right, you two, quit arguing, and listen up. Marian Chandler is on vacation from the hospital and left yesterday for Miami to visit her daughter and grandkids. She's due home on the thirtieth, by which time I hope we've caught this bastard."

"Did she get there?" I asked.

"I assume so. What are you getting at, Toni?"

"Eleanor Morehouse was on her way to Boise, and she never got there. Did Marian board the plane? Did she even make it to the airport? Could she have been killed in her home before she even left? Has anyone spoken to her since she left? Did Adriana actually talk to her, or did she just check with the hospital?"

Pete was getting that deer-in-the-headlights look again. "Whoa, whoa, whoa, one question at a time!"

"She's got a point, you know," Nigel said.

"You don't know, do you?" I said.

Pete sighed. "No, I don't. I just took Adriana at her word. Do you want to know about the others or not?"

I opened my mouth, but Hal quelled me with a look. "Yes, she does. Please go ahead."

"David Lord made plans to take his family on one of those Disney cruises in the Caribbean. It doesn't leave until the twentieth, so we were going to put him at the Best Western, but he decided to fly to Fort Lauderdale early and spend the week there instead of here. He said he wouldn't feel safe in any of the hotels here."

"Smart man," Hal said. "And since he owns his own business, he can make sure nobody in his office tells anyone where he's going."

"He does?" Mum asked. "How do you know that?"

"He's an accountant, according to the jury list," Pete said, "but we'll check that out too. Jeffrey Drummond has left to go fishing off the coast of Baja. His computer repair shop is closed until the end of the year. We tried to put Piper Briscoe up somewhere too, but she refused because she didn't think she'd be safe in any of the local hotels. She said she'd stay with a coworker instead."

"That doesn't sound very safe," I said.

"I know," Pete said, "but we can't force her."

"I guess not," I said. "But all the same questions apply. Did they all get to their destinations? Do they have cell phones that Adriana can call?"

"Only one way to find out," Pete said, taking out his cell phone.

"And here's another thing," I said. "What if our killer decides to follow them to those places? Robbie's already violated his parole, hasn't he, by leaving the halfway house?"

Pete nodded. "Just how obsessed do you think he is?"

"Is there anything stopping him from getting on a plane?" I asked. "Because I think he is that obsessed."

"Nobody knows that better than Toni," Hal said.

"There's nothing stopping him if he can afford the fare," Pete said, "unless he gets caught by the police. They don't put parolees on the no-fly list, if that's what you're getting at."

"But how would he know where they went?" Nigel asked. "Who would tell him?"

"As far as Marian is concerned, he could go to the hospital and inquire," I said. "He could pretend to be a friend or a relative who just happened to be in town and thought he'd look her up. Any one of her coworkers might tell him where she was going."

"It might be somewhat difficult to reach Jeffrey Drummond on a fishing boat off the coast of Baja California," Nigel said, "but surely one could contact David Lord in Fort Lauderdale. Did he tell Adriana what hotel he was going to?"

Pete picked up his cell phone and dialed. "I know when I'm beat. Adriana? Can you find out if Robbie booked a flight to Miami or Fort Lauderdale, either out of Twin or Boise? Of course it was Toni. What if she's right? Just do it, okay? And another thing: Did you actually speak to any of them personally? Because you need to, and you need to follow up on them to make sure they got to their destinations. It's called being thorough, okay? Thanks again." He rang off and looked up at me. "Satisfied?"

I nodded. "Thank you. Did she give you a hard time?"

"She's got a lot to learn," Pete said shortly. "When are you doing the autopsy on Melinda Roper?"

"Tomorrow if she's thawed enough," I said. "I'll let you know."

CHAPTER 18

What other dungeon is as dark as one's own heart?
What jailer is so inexorable as one's self!
—Nathaniel Hawthorne

By Monday morning, Melinda Roper was thawed enough. Natalie and I checked out the body while she was still in the cooler by sticking a needle into her thigh. It went in all the way to the bone.

Melinda Roper was black and wore her hair in a short, neat Afro.

We got Natalie's husband, Dale, and another tech to help us get her onto the autopsy table, and then I called Rollie and Pete.

Rollie and Bernie showed up, and so did Adriana. It was the first time I'd seen her since the abbreviated autopsy on George Starling. Pete was not there, Bernie said, because he was busy making sure that both David Lord and Jeffrey Drummond had gotten safely to their destinations.

"I spent all day," he told me, "trying to find out if Robbie booked a flight. It was like pulling teeth. They don't want to give out passenger information, but I told them it was a police matter and that he was a possible serial killer, and then airport security got involved. I sent them a photo just in case he didn't use his real name, and they're going to get back to me."

You hope, I thought, but I didn't say it. "I thought Adriana was doing that," I said.

Adriana looked away from me and said nothing. Bernie shook his head slightly.

I wondered what that was all about. *Things that make you go, "Hmmm."*

"What about Marian, David, and Jeffrey?" I asked. "Did they all get to where they were going?"

"I talked to Marian this morning at her daughter's house," Bernie said. "She's alive and well. I couldn't reach David, but the hotel informed me that the Lord family had checked in and had gone out on an excursion. I couldn't reach Jeffrey."

"Hmm. I was afraid of that. Oh well, maybe Robbie won't be able to find him either."

Melinda Roper had no petechiae in her conjunctivae or on her oral mucosa, as one would have expected from someone who had been asphyxiated. Her tongue was not swollen, blue, or protruding from her mouth. There was a ligature mark that extended up behind her left ear, but there was no associated bruising. It was obvious her hanging had been postmortem, as I pointed out to Adriana, who merely nodded but wouldn't come close enough to see.

Postmortem lividity had turned her legs, arms, and lower abdomen deep purple. There was also a good deal of skin slippage.

Natalie and I went about removing the brain and excising the pithing site. Natalie photographed the scrambled brainstem, and I put the whole shebang in a bucket of formalin.

I found a black hair at the pithing site and called Bernie over to look at it.

140

"So what?" he asked. "She has black hair too. It's probably hers."

"Bernie," I said reprovingly, "this is a black woman. Her hair is frizzy and not this long. You'll need some of her hair for exemplars." We went through the evidence-bag dance, as I'd done with Pete.

When Natalie began the Y-shaped incision, the all-too-familiar odor of decomposition became apparent.

"How long had she been hanging there?" I asked Rollie.

"I don't know," he said.

"I talked to her neighbors and the people who work at her shop," Bernie said. "Her neighbors saw her picking up her mail and newspaper Wednesday morning. Her assistant said she was at work Wednesday also but not since then, which is three days. This was corroborated by the presence of at least three days' worth of mail crammed into her mailbox and three newspapers on her doorstep."

"Three days," I said, "and then she was at your place, Rollie, for—"

"Just overnight," Rollie said. "Then I brought her over here yesterday."

"So four and a half to five days. No wonder she smells so bad. Let's get those respirators on."

"I assume she was pithed," Bernie said.

"She was."

"The reason I assume that is because whoever hung her body up made the mistake of removing whatever it was he had stood on to reach the rafters. And now if you'll excuse me, I think I'll leave you to it."

He was out the door before I could object, but if he'd stayed, we would have had to get a fifth respirator, so his leaving saved us the trouble.

Rollie said, "Anything you can tell me?"

"So far, I can tell you that her larynx and the hyoid bone are fractured, but there's no hemorrhage of the associated soft tissues, which means the fractures were postmortem."

With respirators on, Natalie and I were able to work at a normal pace to dissect the organ block and get everything either into formalin or back inside the body, and Rollie and Adriana could watch in relative comfort.

But Adriana seemed really uncomfortable. I encouraged her several times to come closer so I could show her something, but she just shook her head. She didn't seem to want to look me in the eyes.

While Natalie sewed up the incision, I tried to talk to her. "Adriana, is something bothering you?"

She shook her head vehemently. "No. Nothing is bothering me. I wish people would just leave me alone!" She rushed from the room.

I looked at Rollie. He shrugged. I shrugged back and started washing the instruments.

My plan had been to talk to Piper Briscoe before I left. I knew from the jury list that she was a radiologic technician. But even after I'd discarded my protective gear, I knew I smelled too nasty to encounter anybody in the hospital without showering, washing my hair, and changing my clothes.

I only hoped I could get into the house and upstairs to my bathroom without everybody, particularly Mum, smelling me.

So I went straight from the morgue to the underground parking without checking in with Mike or Brian. To do that, I had to pass through the hallways of the diagnostic imaging department, where I could possibly encounter Piper Briscoe if she was working that day.

But that was not whom I encountered.

"Dr. Day!"

I turned to see Ryan Trowbridge coming up behind me. His big brown parka was unzipped, and a pair of brown leather gloves protruded from one of the pockets.

"Mr. Trowbridge. Fancy meeting you here."

By then, he was close enough to smell me, because he wrinkled his nose and sniffed. "Did you just do an autopsy?"

No use denying it, I thought, *not smelling like this.* "Yes."

"Was it Melinda Roper?"

"Yes. How did you know?"

"I have my methods. Was she pithed?"

"Yes."

"What else did you find?"

"She'd been dead for five days. Her hyoid and her larynx were fractured, but there was no evidence of hemorrhage."

"So they were postmortem. Anything else?"

"Nothing that would interest you."

"Everything interests me, Dr. Day."

Ew. "Okay, nothing pertinent to her demise."

By then, we were at the door to the parking garage. I pushed the door open, and Ryan Trowbridge followed me out.

"Brrr!" he said. "I think it's gotten colder, if that's even possible." He zipped up his parka and pulled his gloves out of his pocket. Something fell to the concrete floor with a dull clang.

An ice pick.

For a nanosecond, I was paralyzed with fear. All I could think was *Oh my freakin' Lord, I am so dead.*

Then I realized that (a) showing fear might not be the smartest thing to do, and (b) there might be an altogether different reason he was carrying an ice pick around, although in my present mental state, I couldn't think of a single one. So I asked.

"Why do you have an ice pick in your pocket?"

He bent over and picked it up, and I involuntarily took a step back, ready to bolt to my car and lock myself in.

He straightened up with the dratted thing in his hand, and I tensed. Then he gave a self-deprecating chuckle and put it back in his pocket. "I was using it to chip ice out of my chest freezer in the garage, and I guess I forgot to put it back in the kitchen."

Oh. Imagine that. He was actually using it to chip ice. Who'da thunk it?

"To defrost it, you mean?"

"Yeah. So there'd be room for my elk meat."

Well, all righty then. "Oh, you got your elk. Congratulations. Well, I gotta go. Enjoy the rest of your day!" Without waiting for a reply, I turned and headed for my car on unsteady legs, hoping that I'd get there before my knees gave way on me and that he wouldn't come after me and pith me before I got there.

"See you around!" he called after me, but by that time, I had already reached my car. With shaking hands, I locked myself in and carefully drove myself home.

Hal met me at the kitchen door, took one look at my face, and went right to the bar and poured me a shot of scotch. "Drink that," he said. "Then you can tell me all about it."

I downed it and handed the shot glass back to him. When I could actually speak again, I said, "Call Pete, and tell him to go to the hospital to check on Piper Briscoe."

"Why?"

"I'll tell you later. Right now, I have to shower and change before I do one more thing."

He must have caught a whiff of me, because he didn't try to stop me from charging past him and up the stairs without even a word to Mum and Nigel. Killer and Geraldine followed me, having caught the scent.

The scotch burned its way down my esophagus before

blooming out into a comforting ball of warmth in my stomach. By the time I'd showered and washed my hair, I felt almost normal. I threw everything I'd been wearing into the laundry hamper, although I briefly considered burning the clothing instead; put on my old black sweats; and went back downstairs.

"Kitten," Mum said with a concerned look on her face, "are you all right?"

"That must have been quite an autopsy," Nigel said.

"Oh, it wasn't the autopsy," I said. "Although she was quite decomposed, and I had to get the smell off me." At that, Mum made a face, but I wasn't through. "What did Pete say?"

"He's on his way over," Hal said. "You can't expect him to go charging over to the hospital without more information than that."

"I may have met the killer," I said.

Mum gasped. "Robbie?"

"No," I said, but just then, Pete came in through the kitchen door. "Toni, what's this all about?"

"Did you send somebody to the hospital?"

Pete opened the refrigerator door and snagged a beer. "Hal?"

Hal assented, and Pete grabbed a second one and handed it to him. "No, I had somebody call the hospital and ask for her. She's alive and well. What's up with you?"

I had curled up on the couch and wrapped myself in an afghan, whereupon Geraldine had curled up in my lap like a little furry heating pad. The warmth in my belly had dissipated, and I felt cold and shivery.

Hal said, "Toni thinks she's met the killer."

"You don't say," Nigel said with interest. He got up and went to the bar. "Toni, old dear? A libation?"

"Yes, please."

"Seriously?" Pete asked. "Who is it?"

"Ryan Trowbridge."

"Who is Ryan Trowbridge?"

Nigel brought me my scotch, and I took a sip before answering. "The reporter who writes about the Jury Killer. I encountered him when I was leaving the hospital. He had an ice pick in his pocket."

Mum gasped, and Nigel reached over and patted her hand.

Pete came to attention. "You mean he tried to pith you?"

I had an insane urge to giggle at the shocked expression on everyone's face. "No. When we got out to the parking garage, he pulled out his gloves, and the ice pick fell out of his pocket."

"Okay," Pete said. "Then what?"

"He picked it up and said he was using it to chip ice out of his freezer so he could put in his elk meat."

"Oh, nice save," Hal said.

Pete took out his cell phone and dialed. "Adriana? Get someone to go pick up a reporter named Ryan Trowbridge at the *Clarion* and bring him in for questioning."

CHAPTER 19

A man always has two reasons for what
he does; a good one, and the real one.

—J. Pierpont Morgan

The headline on the front page of Tuesday's *Clarion* was
business as usual, with no mention of ice picks in coat
pockets.

"Jury Killer Claims Eighth Victim" greeted me as Hal and I
sat down to breakfast, under Ryan Trowbridge's byline.

> The frozen body of Melinda Roper was found hanging
> in her garage Saturday, December 10, by her next-door
> neighbor, Sheila Jackson.
>
> Roper is the eighth victim of the Jury Killer. Based
> on information obtained from Ms. Jackson and the
> employees of Ms. Roper's place of business, as well
> as the contents of Ms. Roper's mailbox, she apparently
> had been dead since Wednesday, December 7.
>
> An autopsy performed yesterday by Dr. Toni Day
> showed that the victim had been pithed and that her

hyoid bone had been broken and her larynx fractured postmortem.

Dr. Day, while forthcoming on the subject of postmortem pathology, continues to remain stubbornly silent on the subject of her relationship to Robert Simpson, who kidnapped her husband, Dr. Hal Shapiro, eleven years ago and left him for dead in a crawl space in the dead of winter.

What is she hiding?

I handed the paper back to Hal with a sigh. "Same old, same old."

"I thought you'd be more upset," he said.

"You know what? Now it just makes me tired."

"Then you're going to go in to the hospital like you planned?"

"Yep. I need to cut in some of those autopsies before they bury us all alive."

That was pathology-speak for taking small slices from the chunks of tissue that had been fixing in formalin, so they could be processed and turned into slides I could look at under the microscope.

The brains needed to fix in formalin for two weeks, but the rest of the tissue would be fixed enough.

I went to the hospital right after breakfast so I could have access to the grossing station before the boys would need to start grossing the surgicals. Also, before I could do anything with autopsy tissue, I'd have to rinse the formalin off it under running water for at least ten minutes if I didn't want to permanently destroy my nasal passages.

I went to the morgue to retrieve the buckets holding the tissue samples of Ralph Partridge and Stan Goldman before going into histology. Since Mike and Brian had done the autopsies on Robin

Jones and Penelope Leroux and there was only a brain on George Starling, I left those alone.

As it happened, Brian was doing a frozen section when I went into histology.

I put the buckets down on the counter next to him and rummaged in the cupboard under it for the big strainer I used for rinsing tissue.

Brian looked up from inking the margins of his specimen, an ellipse of skin with a nasty-looking lesion on it that was almost certainly a squamous-cell carcinoma. "Toni! What are you doing here? You're supposed to be on vacation."

"I thought I'd cut in some of these autopsies," I answered. "I'm assuming you guys weren't planning to do that for me, were you?"

"I hadn't even thought about it," he said sheepishly. "I suppose I could."

"Don't be silly," I said. "You asked me to help with autopsies, and that's what I'm doing. Want me to take care of that frozen? I have to rinse this stuff anyway before I can start cutting."

Brian shook his head. "No, I've got this. Go ahead and use the sink; I'm done with it."

He blotted the skin, sectioned it, embedded it in mounting medium, and carried it over to the cryostat to freeze. I took the opportunity to strain the dirty formalin from Ralph Partridge's tissue bucket into another container for disposal and place it under running water with the strainer upended over the top to prevent fatty tissues that floated to the top from going down the drain.

Natalie left her microtome and came over to me. "Want me to label cassettes for you, Dr. Day?"

"No, I can do it. Thanks. You need to get those slides out for the boys." Suiting the action to the words, I grabbed a handful of cassettes and began labeling them with the autopsy case number.

By the time Brian was done with the frozen, Ralph Partridge's tissues were adequately rinsed. While I cut them in, I set Stan Goldman's tissue bucket to rinsing, which could have been problematic because of the smell of putrefaction. The odor was not improved by formalin fixation; rather, the formalin just added another noxious smell to the mix.

Luckily, the ventilation of the new grossing station was far superior to what we'd had at the old hospital. The histotechs working on the other side of the room didn't even appear to notice the smell.

I returned the unused tissue to Ralph Partridge's bucket, put fresh formalin on it, marked it with a big *C* for *cut*, took it back to the morgue, and picked up Jonathan Swann.

I repeated the process with Melinda Roper, and by the time I finished cutting in all four cases, it was eleven o'clock. Natalie came over to me and offered to take the last two buckets back to the morgue for me. "How many did you cut in?" she asked.

"Four," I told her.

Her eyes widened. "We don't have room to put all that in today," she said.

I pointed to the four smaller containers of formalin into which I'd put the tissue cassettes for each case. "You don't have to. Just put in what you can each day until they're all in. There's no rush."

Brian came back just in time to hear my last remark. "Yeah, those guys aren't going anywhere. You done? It's time for the morning gross."

"All yours," I replied, stripping off my gloves. I washed my hands and left. I detoured through diagnostic imaging, as I had the previous day, with the intention of finding Piper Briscoe and talking to her, but a commotion down the hall distracted me. Dr. Mitzi Okamoto dashed past me, and I ran after her.

I'd known Mitzi since I first came to Twin Falls, as she already had been working at Perrine Memorial as a solo radiologist when I started. She was a petite Japanese American who was the personification of inscrutable. We'd bonded over being the only females on the medical staff as well as solo practitioners in our respective specialties.

A doctor in a white lab coat was berating a technician in scrubs. He was tall, slim, and quite possibly the handsomest man I had ever seen, even with his face contorted in anger. Thick, wavy black hair and a dark olive complexion gave him a slightly exotic look, as if perhaps he had a person of color somewhere in his ancestry. He was almost too pretty to be true.

As Mitzi and I approached, he grabbed the tech by the upper arms and began shaking her. She cried out in pain.

I knew a thing or two about what could happen in such a situation, because it had once happened to me, resulting in bilateral compartment syndrome requiring surgical decompression, so while Mitzi demanded to know what the commotion was about, I attacked.

I ducked under the doctor's arms and came up between them, which broke his grip on the hapless tech, after which I slammed him in the chest with both palms hard enough to make him take a step back. His leg buckled under him, and he crashed to the floor on his butt. He screamed in pain.

"What the hell do you think you're doing, you bitch?" he bellowed, his face red with rage. His hair was disheveled, and he glared up at me through slit and unexpectedly bright blue eyes.

"Haven't you heard of compartment syndrome?" I yelled back. "That girl could lose her arms!"

"That girl" was standing next to Mitzi, rubbing her arms and grimacing in pain. Mitzi had her cell phone out and was dialing. I hoped she was calling security.

The doctor struggled to his feet, still yelling. "I'll have you fired! I'll charge you with assault and battery!" He pulled his cell phone out of the pocket of his lab coat. Something fell to the floor, and he quickly bent to retrieve it but not before I saw what it was and stepped on it.

An ice pick.

Sheesh. What's up with everybody carrying ice picks around all of a sudden? They can't all be Jury Killers.

Or can they?

Mitzi came up to me. "I called security. What's that?"

"An ice pick. So I suppose you too are trying to fit an elk into your freezer?" I sarcastically asked the doctor, who I now noticed wasn't wearing a badge. "Who are you? Where's your badge?"

The doctor didn't have a chance to answer because two burly men in uniforms approached. He pushed me, forcing me to step back; grabbed the ice pick; and bolted. He seemed to be hampered by a slight limp, which slowed him down enough for the security guards to catch up with him and pin him between them. "Either of you ladies know who this guy is?" one of the guards asked.

We shook our heads. "He's not wearing a badge," Mitzi said.

"He's got an ice pick," I said.

"An ice pick?" the security guard asked in disbelief.

"The Jury Killer uses an ice pick to pith his victims," I said. "This guy could be the Jury Killer. You should call the police."

"You got it, Doc," said the guard, and with each of them gripping an arm, they muscled the miscreant away down the hall.

The radiologic tech approached me. She was a slender thirtyish woman of medium height with wavy light brown hair to her shoulders. "Thanks for rescuing me, Dr. Day," she said. "You took an awful risk, though."

"You're welcome, uh"—I checked her badge, which said simply Piper, with no last name—"Piper. Piper Briscoe?"

"Yes, how did you know?"

"I was looking for you when I heard all the commotion. What was he yelling at you for?"

Piper shrugged. "I have no idea. He was complaining about some patient he'd ordered a CT on, but we had no record of it, and I was trying to explain that to him, when he started shaking me. Should I press charges?"

"Definitely," I said, "although it would help to know who he is. Dr. Okamoto can help you report it to HR, and I'm going to call my son-in-law to come talk to you."

Piper looked at me quizzically. "Your son-in-law?"

"Yes. He's a detective lieutenant with the Twin Falls Police. He's been working on the Jury Killer case."

"I heard about that," Piper said. "They tried to get me to go to a hotel, but I know two other jurors have been killed in their hotel rooms, so I refused to go. Then they tried to get me to go somewhere out of town, but I can't do that; I have to work."

"Would you consider coming to stay with us?" I asked. "My husband is off for Christmas break at the college, and my parents are visiting, so there's always someone home, and we have two very protective dogs."

"I'll think about it," Piper said. "Thanks for the offer."

Mitzi put a hand on Piper's arm. "Come on. Let's go talk to HR," she said.

After they left, I called Pete. "Piper Briscoe was assaulted by someone posing as a disgruntled physician. He had an ice pick in his pocket."

"Holy shit, Toni!" Pete exclaimed. "Is she all right?"

"Yes, she's fine," I told him. "Dr. Okamoto took her up to HR to report it, and I told the security guards that he might be the Jury Killer and that they needed to call the police."

"So the security guys have him?"

"As far as I know."

"Okay, Toni, thanks. We'll take it from here."

"Has anyone talked to Ryan Trowbridge yet?" I asked, but Pete had hung up.

So I went home.

At least that was my intention.

CHAPTER 20

The motions of his spirit are dull as night,
And his affections dark as Erebus.
Let no such man be trusted.
—Shakespeare, *The Merchant of Venice*

Ryan Trowbridge waylaid me in the parking garage and fell into step with me as I headed to my car. "So, Dr. Day, I hear you had a bit of difficulty with one of your medical staff just now. Want to tell me about it?"

I stopped. "Want to tell me how you know about it already?"

Trowbridge turned his palms up. "Doctor, please. I'm not trying to trap you. I just happened to be at the end of the hallway, and I saw the whole thing. Where'd you learn that move?"

The hair rose on the back of my neck. "You just happened to be at the end of the hall? Mr. Trowbridge, are you following me? Because that's really creepy."

Trowbridge shrugged and looked sheepish. "I'm a reporter, Doctor, and a pretty good one at that. I go where the stories are, and right now, that's wherever you are."

I threw up my hands. "Fine! So I suppose there's no harm

in telling you I'm not at all sure that guy was a member of the medical staff. I've never seen him before, and he wasn't wearing a hospital badge. I can also tell you that he had an ice pick in his lab coat pocket, and the security guards took him away. I called the police."

"When you say you called the police, don't you really mean your son-in-law?"

"Yes. So what?"

"So you don't mind if I interview him?"

I shrugged. "He's a grown man. I don't need to give anybody permission to interview him." That reminded me that Pete had asked Adriana to have Trowbridge brought in for questioning, and I thought about asking him about it, but on second thought, I decided that might not be such a good idea down there in the deserted underground parking garage, in case he still had the ice pick in his coat pocket.

"I also plan to interview Dr. Okamoto about the young lady he was assaulting when you rescued her."

"Knock yourself out." I turned to go, and an unwelcome thought occurred to me. "Don't you dare follow me home."

He smiled, and it made my blood run cold. "No need. I already know where you live."

"Don't follow me to my car either," I warned. "Or are you going to tell me you already know which one it is?"

He turned his palms up again. "Doctor, really, what do you think?"

Of course he knows my car. He knows where I live. What's left? I gave one last attempt to remain in control, even though I was pretty sure it was a losing battle. "Please have the courtesy to leave my husband and my parents alone," I said.

He touched his forehead in a gesture of farewell and turned to go. I continued on to my car and drove myself home.

When I got home, my mother said, "Kitten, have you been at the hospital all this time? Hal was getting quite worried. He thought something had happened to you."

"Where is he?" I asked.

"He's gone to the hospital, dear."

Channeling my husband, I threw my hands up and shouted, "Oy gevalt!" to the ceiling.

Mum jumped to her feet and took me by the shoulders. "Antoinette, darling, please do calm down. You'll do yourself a mischief."

I'd heard her say the exact same thing to Hal so many times that I had to laugh.

Nigel put aside the newspaper he was reading and joined the conversation. "Toni, old dear, would you care for a libation?"

Oh, would I! "I might, but it's a little too early, don't you think?"

"Nonsense, my girl. It's just past elevenses." He got up and went to the bar. I decided not to argue and accepted the libation, which relaxed me enough for me to realize that chasing after my husband was unnecessary because he'd come home once he figured out I was no longer at the hospital.

Of course, there was always the possibility he'd run into Ryan Trowbridge. I shuddered to think what kind of a mood he'd be in when he returned, since he would already be mad at me for making him worry, and being buttonholed by a reporter certainly wouldn't improve matters.

Why the hell didn't he just call me? I wondered, and then I remembered that I'd left my purse in my car, and my cell phone was in it. Maybe he had called me, and I'd missed it.

I pulled my cell phone out of my purse and checked it. Sure enough, I'd missed two calls from Hal. I called him back.

He didn't answer, but a few seconds later, I heard his car pull into the driveway. I ran out through the garage to meet him as he got out of the Jeep. "I'm so sorry!" I said, and then I noticed there was someone else in the car.

Piper Briscoe climbed out on the passenger side and came around to join Hal and me. "Dr. Day, your husband insisted. I hope you don't mind."

"Of course not," I said. "Come in, and meet my parents."

"Pete insisted too," Hal said as he pulled a small duffel bag out of the backseat.

"Oh, was Pete there already?" I asked. "That was fast."

"He got there about the same time I did," Hal said, "and he said he was on his way to interview Piper and anybody else who was involved."

"So you were there when he interviewed her?"

"Yes, and also when he interviewed Mitzi. So I've heard all about your deed of derring-do."

"Good," I said. "Let's get inside out of the cold, shall we?"

We went inside. I introduced Piper to Mum and Nigel and then took her upstairs to the other guest bedroom to let her get settled in.

When I came back downstairs, Pete was there. He toasted me with his beer. "Hail the conquering heroine!"

I bowed and channeled Elvis. "Thank you. Thank you very much."

"I thought you might like to know who it was you assaulted," Pete said. "He wants to have you charged."

"I only assaulted him because he was assaulting Piper," I said. "I was trying to get him to let go of her arms so she wouldn't get compartment syndrome and end up like me."

"Kitten," my mother said, "what on earth are you talking about?"

"I haven't had time to tell them about it yet," Pete said.

"You may as well tell them," Hal said.

Out of the corner of my eye, I saw Piper come down the stairs. "Why don't we let Piper tell them?"

"Tell them what?" Piper asked. "About this afternoon, you mean?"

"Yes," I said. "It started with you, after all."

Piper sat down on the couch. "Okay," she said. "I was coming out of the CT control room into the hallway, when this doctor came up to me and started yelling at me about a CT he'd ordered that hadn't been done yet, and he wanted to know why. So I offered to go back inside the control room to look the patient up and see what had happened, but he insisted I stay right there and tell him the truth, because he wasn't going to let me go back in there, where he couldn't talk to me. So I said okay, but if I couldn't get to a computer, I wasn't going to be able to get the information he wanted, and then I noticed he wasn't wearing a badge, and I asked him who he was and why he didn't have a badge. That's when he grabbed my arms and started shaking me." Reflexively, she rubbed her left upper arm. "It still hurts."

"Why, that's just like what happened to you, kitten," my mother said.

Piper looked at me, her eyes wide. They were green like Mum's and mine. "What happened to you?"

"It was an administrator who did that to me," I said, "about five years ago. I developed compartment syndrome and had to have surgery."

"Did you press charges?" she asked.

"I certainly did," I said, "and they put him in jail, but he got out on bail. Then somebody put cyanide in his lemonade at the hospital picnic, and he died."

"Who did it? Do you know?"

"His brother's ex-wife," I said. "It's a long story. Anyway, that's where Mitzi and I came in. I ducked under the guy's arms and knocked his arms up so he had to let go of her, and then I pushed him really hard in the chest so she could get away."

Mum gasped. Nigel patted her hand.

"And she yelled at him about compartment syndrome and told him I could have lost both my arms," Piper said. "Is that really true? I could lose my arms?"

"Not if you don't develop compartment syndrome," I told her. "But if you do, the same docs who did my surgery are still here. You won't lose your arms if I have anything to say about it."

Mum got up and headed for the kitchen. "I'm going to prepare some ice packs for you," she said. "The sooner you get some ice on those the better."

"Blimey, what a perfectly rippin' story," Nigel said. "What did the bloke do then?"

"He yelled at me, called me a bitch, and threatened to get me fired and charged with assault. He took his cell phone out of his lab coat pocket, and you'll never guess what fell out onto the floor."

Hal put his hand over his eyes in a theatrical gesture. "Don't tell me. Let me guess. An ice pick."

"Got it in one," I said. "Then the security guys came and took him away. I told them he had an ice pick and that he could be the Jury Killer and they should call the police."

"Then you called me," Pete said.

"Oh, and there's something else," I said. "When I pushed him, he fell on his butt and screamed in pain. Then, when he was running from the security guys, he was limping."

"So?"

"So Killer bit the guy who was in our yard Saturday night. Do you suppose it could have been this guy?"

"Huh," Pete said. "I'll have to check that out."

"He's going to need a tetanus shot," I added.

"So don't keep us in suspense," Nigel said. "Who was he?"

"His name is Lorenzo Collins, and he was recently paroled after doing two years for involuntary manslaughter. His rap sheet's full of assault and battery charges. He's got anger-management issues. He keeps getting in bar fights, and finally, he punched a guy so hard it killed him."

"Was he in prison with Robbie?" I asked.

"He was," Pete said, "but claims he doesn't know him."

"Is he in jail now?" Piper asked.

"He is for now," Pete said. "Do you want to press charges?"

"I don't know. Should I?" she asked me.

"Yes, you should," I told her. "I'm going to have Elliott come over to talk to you. He's our next-door neighbor and a very good lawyer. He'll take good care of you."

Pete drained his beer and stood up. "Well, if that's all, I guess I'll be going. I haven't seen much of my girls lately."

"Wait!" I suddenly remembered something. "Ryan Trowbridge says he wants to interview you."

"Ryan who?"

"The reporter with the ice pick," I said.

"Oh, right. It's mutual," he said. "Adriana was supposed to have him brought in for questioning. It completely slipped my mind until you said that."

"You mean she didn't do it?"

He sighed. "Not to my knowledge."

"You don't have to tell me if you don't want to," I said, "but I'm getting the idea that Adriana is dragging her heels on this investigation."

"I think so too," he said, "but I have no idea why."

"I think she's hiding something," I said. "You don't suppose she's *involved*, do you?"

"God, I hope not," he said. "That's all we need."

CHAPTER 21

O, beware, my lord, of jealousy!
It is the green-eyed monster which doth mock
The meat it feeds on.
—Shakespeare, *Othello*

I called Elliott as soon as Pete left, and Jodi answered. She told me Elliott had a full day in court the next day. Then I told her Mum and Nigel were visiting, and she said they'd be right over.

Not ten minutes later, they were stamping snow off their boots in the garage. While Nigel was preparing libations at the bar, I introduced them to Piper.

While she repeated her story to Elliott and he took notes, I curled up on the couch with Geraldine and my scotch. When she had finished, I told Elliott what Pete had told us about Lorenzo Collins and his anger issues.

"Where is he now?" Elliott asked.

"He's in custody," I said. "He had an ice pick on him. He could be the Jury Killer."

Elliott gave me an eye roll. "Lots of people carry ice picks at this time of year, you know. It doesn't make them the Jury Killer."

"What happens now?" Piper asked.

"Now," Elliott said, "we go to the police station. You'll have to tell them your story, sign some papers, and let them take pictures of your arms."

"How long will that take?" Hal asked.

"At least an hour," Elliott said. "Maybe more."

Hal took out his cell phone. "I'll let Pete know you're coming."

"Have you guys eaten yet?" Jodi asked.

"Not yet," I said.

"I'll order pizza when you get back," she said. "Okay?"

"More than okay," Hal said. "Fiona? Nigel?"

Mum and Nigel assented.

"Order it now," Elliott said. "We won't be gone that long. You want to ride with me, Piper, or come with Toni?"

"I'll go with you," Piper said.

"Toni, you want to come with me or drive yourself?"

"I'll come with you too," I said. "I've already had a scotch."

"Good call," Elliott said. "Let's go!"

Pete met us at the station and took us into a conference room, where a court reporter waited. She transcribed both Piper's and my statements about the incident and printed them out, and Pete had us sign them. A police photographer took pictures of Piper's arms for the record.

"What happens now?" Piper asked.

"Now," Elliott said, "there'll be an arraignment."

"What's that?"

"We go to court, and they decide whether a crime was committed and if it should be decided in county court or remanded to district court, and they set bail."

"Do we have to testify?" Piper asked.

"Not unless we're subpoenaed," I said. "They've got our statements, right, Elliott?"

Elliott nodded. "They'll also set a court date and let us know."

"So he'll stay in jail, right?" Piper asked.

Elliott shrugged. "Unless someone bails him out."

Piper shivered.

Pizza was waiting when we got home. The others were already eating.

"How'd it go?" Hal asked.

I glanced at Piper. She still looked as spooked as she had at the police station, in spite of our conversation in the car. "It went," I said, "as well as could be expected."

"What the hell does that mean?" Hal asked. "What happened?"

"Calm down, Shapiro," Elliott said. "They gave their statements and signed them, and that was all there was to it."

"Then why does Piper look so scared?" Jodi asked.

Mum said, "Piper, dear, come sit by me."

Piper went over to the couch and sat down, and Mum put an arm around her and spoke to her in tones so low that I couldn't make out any words.

I said, "There's going to be an arraignment—we don't know when—at which a trial date will be set, and bail will also be set. Piper is scared to death that someone will bail this guy out, and she'll be in danger again."

"Why would anyone want to bail out such an unsavory person?" Mum asked in a normal tone.

I looked over at her. She still had her arm around Piper, who looked marginally less funereal.

"The worst people can have somebody who loves them," Nigel said, "more's the pity. Even Jeffrey Dahmer had a mother."

"This guy probably has a wife or a girlfriend," I said. "Or

a lot of girlfriends. He's gorgeous." I went on to describe what Lorenzo Collins looked like.

"A wolf in sheep's clothing," Jodi said.

"Hey, I just had a thought," I said. "I wonder if this guy's hair would match the black hairs I've been finding at the autopsies."

"You haven't mentioned that, sweetie," Hal said. "You found one on Penelope Leroux, as I recall."

"I also found them on Jonathan Swann and Melinda Roper."

"You can ask Pete about that next time you see him."

"I intend to."

"Well," Mum said, "as I was just telling Piper, whoever he is, he's going to have to get through all of us first."

"And Killer. He's the same guy who was in the backyard Saturday night, or at least if he's not, it would be the biggest coincidence on the planet," I said, remembering that the commander, now retired, always had said there were no coincidences when it came to murder. "Pete checked. Killer really did a number on him."

Piper suddenly smiled. "No wonder he screamed like a girl when he fell on his butt."

We all laughed, and the tension was broken. We helped ourselves to pizza, and nobody spoke while we munched away. Elliott was the first to break the silence.

"There's something else I need to tell you."

We all stopped chewing.

"Do tell, old boy," Nigel said, as Elliott seemed to hesitate.

"After we looked up Robbie's jury the other night, I did some more research," Elliott said. "I found out why Robbie got out after only eleven years."

Hal swallowed and took a swig of beer. "And you're just now telling us?"

"Not on purpose," Elliott said. "Do you want to hear this or not?"

"Please," I said. "Do continue."

"I found out that Robbie appealed his own sentence and got the charge of attempted murder dropped."

"How could he do that?" Hal demanded. "I very nearly died. How is that not attempted murder?"

Elliott continued, unperturbed. "That left the charge of kidnapping."

"Surely that's a life sentence at the very least," Mum said.

"Ah, but in Idaho, any kidnapping not associated with a demand for ransom is considered second-degree kidnapping."

"I didn't know kidnapping had degrees," I said.

"It doesn't in England," Nigel said.

"It does in Idaho," Elliott said. "According to Idaho code, every kidnapping that is not for ransom is considered kidnapping in the second degree, and the sentence can be anywhere between one and twenty-five years. Robbie's sentence was commuted to twenty years."

"How come we didn't hear about that?" I asked. "It had to have been in the paper."

"It was in the Boise papers," Elliott said, "but not the *Clarion*."

"So that's why Robbie got out on parole after eleven years," I said. "But Hal's kidnapping was for ransom, you know."

"How do you figure, dear?" asked Mum. "No money changed hands."

"Think about it. What did Robbie want?" I asked.

"She's right," Hal said. "She was the ransom."

"Oh dear," Mum said.

At that juncture, the sound of boots stamping off snow in the garage announced Pete's arrival. He snagged a beer from the fridge and came into the living room. "Oh boy, pizza!"

This was getting to be a habit.

Pete grabbed a slice and sat down on the couch next to me. "I questioned your buddy Ryan Trowbridge this afternoon."

"Is Adriana in trouble?" I asked.

"She got a reprimand from Bernie."

"So what about Trowbridge?"

"He came in willingly and was very forthcoming. He described how he happened upon the Jury Killer story and how excited he was, because if he continues to get the exclusive on it and follows it to the end, he might get a Pulitzer."

"That makes sense," I said. "Far be it from me to screw that up. Maybe I should be more forthcoming as well. What about the ice pick?"

"He told me the same thing he told you, and he didn't have it with him today. He said he put it back in the kitchen, where it belonged."

"So you don't think he's been committing those murders so he can be first on the scene to cover them?"

Hal snorted. "Only you, Toni. Only you would even think of that."

"What was I supposed to think?" I said. "Here's this big, burly guy following me around with an ice pick in his pocket. It's creepy."

"He explained that too," Pete said. "The editor of the *Clarion* speaks quite highly of him. Said they were lucky to get him."

"How long has he been at the *Clarion*? Where did he come from?"

"He came here from the *LA Times* a year ago."

I frowned. "Really? Why would he want to do that?"

"Sweetie," Hal said, "we did the same thing, remember? We wanted to get out of Southern California and go someplace more rural, slower-paced, and less crowded."

"See there?" Pete said. "And before you ask, we checked with the *LA Times*. So far, Ryan Trowbridge seems to be exactly who he says he is: a small-town newspaper reporter in pursuit of a Pulitzer."

"Did you and she question him together?"

"Yes, although he asked questions too, mostly about you."

"Oh, so you just now finished with him," Hal said.

"Yes. Adriana volunteered to drive him back to the *Clarion* to get his car, and I came straight here."

A red light began flickering in my brain. "Have you told her about me and Robbie yet?"

"Certainly. I did that Friday. You told me I could, so I did." He sounded defensive. "I told her in confidence and said that it was not to go any further."

"Okay," I said, endeavoring not to sound upset.

"You're not mad at me, are you?"

"No, of course not."

"Adriana will keep her word."

"I'm sure she will."

But I wasn't.

CHAPTER 22

Every woman should marry … and no man.
—Benjamin Disraeli

Ryan Trowbridge didn't disappoint me. "Potential Ninth Victim of Jury Killer Attacked" jumped off the front page at me before I even had my first cup of coffee Wednesday morning.

Hal shoved the *Clarion* over to me as he got up to refill his coffee.

> Piper Briscoe, an employee at Cascade Perrine Regional Medical Center, was assaulted yesterday afternoon at her place of employment by a man posing as a disgruntled physician.
>
> Ms. Briscoe was saved from significant bodily injury by the quick response of Drs. Toni Day and Mitzi Okamoto, who were in the vicinity. A physical altercation between Dr. Day and the assailant resulted in his apprehension by hospital security guards (names given).
>
> Ms. Briscoe was a member of the jury that sent

Robert Simpson to prison in 2005. Eight other members of that jury have been murdered.

The assailant was subsequently arrested for assault and battery by Detective Lieutenant Pete Vincent of the Twin Falls Police and was later identified as Lorenzo Collins, who was recently released from the Idaho State Penitentiary after serving a two-year sentence for involuntary manslaughter.

Collins, himself a physician, had his license to practice medicine revoked by the Idaho State Board of Medicine due to his record of violent behavior after having been convicted of assault and battery of a man in a bar three years ago. The victim subsequently died of his injuries, and the charge was changed to involuntary manslaughter.

Collins will remain in custody until his arraignment, which is scheduled for Friday, December 17.

"Well, I'll be damned," I said, handing the paper back to Hal. "He really was a doctor! I wonder if he was ever on our hospital staff."

"You should know," Hal said. "You work there too."

"Not necessarily," I said. "There are an awful lot of doctors on our staff that I don't know. Some I've never even heard of."

"Well, one thing's for sure," said my husband. "He'd know how to pith people."

"Who would?"

I turned to see Piper descending the stairs in her pajamas. "Good morning," I said as she joined us at the table. "Did you sleep well?"

"Pretty well," she replied. "The ice packs helped, but my arms still hurt."

"Let me see," I said.

She pushed up her sleeves. Her arms were swollen and showed visible bruising—not as bad as mine had but still significant. I took her hands in mine. They were cool but not cold. "Do you have any numbness?" I asked.

"I don't think so," she said. "That's good, isn't it?"

"It is. You need to watch for that. Do you have to work today?"

"No, I have the rest of the week off. Is there anything interesting in the paper?"

Hal handed her the *Clarion*. "There sure is," he said. "Turns out the guy who attacked you really is a doctor."

"No kidding," she said with interest. "Imagine that."

"Want some coffee?" Hal asked.

"Yes, please."

He poured her a cup and brought it over to the table with his own. "What's on the docket for today?" he asked as he sat down.

"I might have some slides to look at," I said.

In my office, two trays of autopsy slides awaited me. I opened the folder for Ralph Partridge and noticed that the date of the autopsy had been December 2. It was now December 16, which meant the brain had fixed in formalin for two weeks and was ready to cut.

I went to the morgue, retrieved the brain, and put it to rinse in the sink while I looked at the slides and dictated the microscopic.

When that was done, I went back to the morgue and cut the brain. The only pathology I saw was the damage to the brainstem caused by pithing. I saved representative tissue from the various parts of the brain in the bucket with the other tissues, put sections from the brainstem in a urine cup, and discarded the remainder of the brain.

I took the brainstem sections to histology, put them in tissue cassettes, and stuck them into the rack of cassettes that would go into the tissue processor at the end of the day.

When I went back to my office to dictate the gross description of the brain, a thought occurred to me.

Now that we had our fancy new computer system, it was possible to access material from all the other hospitals in the system. I went to the medical staff section and looked up Lorenzo Collins.

He wasn't there. Of course he wasn't there; the medical staff roster was updated every month. Lorenzo had been in prison for two years.

So I googled him, and I hit pay dirt.

Two years ago, he'd been on the staff of Cascade Boise Regional Medical Center. He had been an orthopedic surgeon.

He'd know right where to stick the ice pick, by golly, which was what I told my family when I got home.

Nigel went to the bar and began fiddling with bottles. "Libations all around?" he asked.

We all assented, and no sooner had we spoken than Pete came into the kitchen from the garage. "I see I came just in time for happy hour." He snagged a beer from the fridge, by which I deduced he was off duty for the day.

"Get me one too while you're at it," Hal said.

"Where's Piper?" Pete asked. "Is she still here?"

Nigel handed me my scotch and Mum a glass of wine. "She's napping," he said.

"She said her arms were really hurting," Mum said with a worried expression. "I made her some new ice packs; I hope they help."

Pete and I joined her on the couch.

"Did she say anything about numbness?" I asked.

"No, dear," Mum replied.

"Good," I said. "Pete, have you tried to match Lorenzo Collins's hair to the black hairs we found on the victims?"

"Not yet,' he said. "We have, however, established that they do not belong to the victims."

Nigel relaxed in my recliner with his scotch and silently toasted us with his glass. "Any joy?" he asked Pete.

"Not much," Pete said. "We did get information in that Robbie got on a flight to Fort Lauderdale three days ago and then disappeared."

"What!" I exclaimed. "How is that possible?"

Pete shrugged. "He had a one-way ticket and no connecting flight. So either he's somewhere in Fort Lauderdale, or he went somewhere else by car, bus, or boat."

"Or private plane," I said.

"He could be anywhere by now," Nigel said. "Possibly somewhere that doesn't have an extradition treaty with the US."

"You know who else is in Fort Lauderdale?" I said. "David Lord and his family."

"Oh dear," said my mother.

Pete sighed. "Let me call Bernie," he said, taking out his cell phone. "Bernie? Someone needs to check on the Lords in Fort Lauderdale. Why? Because Robbie flew to Fort Lauderdale three days ago, and nobody knows where he went from there. Adriana? No, I don't want to involve her in this anymore. Thanks, buddy. I owe you one."

He disconnected and looked around at all of us staring at him. "What are you all looking at me like that for?"

"What you said about not involving Adriana anymore," I said.

Pete turned his palms up. "She hasn't done anything we've asked her to do, and now she's going home sick with migraines all the time. You were right, Toni; she is dragging her heels, and I've had enough."

"Isn't there anything you can do about that?" Hal asked.

"She's already had one reprimand," Pete said. "She'll probably get another one for this, and if she gets a third one, she'll be on probation, and then if she gets another one, she'll be fired, and I'll be right back where I was, doing everything myself. I'm even beginning to regret having told her about you and Robbie."

Shit, I thought. *If Pete's regretting that, I'll probably be regretting it too.*

CHAPTER 23

We are not amused.

—Queen Victoria

I had no idea how much I was going to regret that until I saw Ryan Trowbridge's article in the *Clarion* Thursday morning, which had an eerily familiar headline.

Hal poured himself a cup of coffee, sat down at the kitchen table, and opened the morning paper, as usual. I stirred some sweetener into my coffee and took a sip but nearly spit it out when Hal slapped the newspaper back down on the table. "No," he said emphatically. "No way. No fucking way!"

"What on earth?" I said.

He shoved it over to me. "That fucking asshole Trowbridge—that's what. Where the hell did he get this stuff anyway?"

I looked at the headline: "Local Pathologist's Love Affair with Jury Killer Revealed!"

My heart sank. I felt sick.

"You might as well read it," Hal said resignedly. "Everybody else will."

So I did.

Thanks to a recent interview with a pair of Twin Falls police detectives, Lieutenant Pete Vincent and Sergeant Adriana Sinclair, the mystery surrounding the Jury Killer and the pathologist is now solved!

Interestingly, Lieutenant Vincent is Dr. Toni Day's son-in-law, married to her husband's daughter. Sergeant Sinclair is a recent transplant from Boise, having been hired when Vincent's former partner, Lieutenant Bernard Kincaid, became captain.

As a family member, Vincent knows Day's family history and her relationship to Robert Simpson, now suspected of being the Jury Killer. She grew up in Long Beach, California, and attended California State College, Long Beach; did a medical technology internship at the Long Beach Veterans Hospital; and then attended medical school at the University of California, Irvine, while simultaneously working as a medical technologist to pay her way.

Day and Simpson were high school sweethearts, and the relationship continued well into college, even though Simpson went to Harvard University while Day remained in Long Beach. One of her college professors was Dr. Hal Shapiro, and that was when the unexpected happened.

They fell in love.

At that point, the unfortunate Robert Simpson returned, having graduated from Harvard with honors and been accepted into Harvard Law School, only to find that the love of his life no longer loved him.

Rather than withdraw gracefully, Simpson attacked Day and raped her. She declined to press charges.

That was the end for her but not for him. He continued to stalk her until she and Dr. Shapiro were married during her first year of pathology residency at St. Mary's Hospital in Long Beach.

The Shapiros moved to Twin Falls when Day finished her residency and accepted a position at what was then Perrine Memorial Hospital.

Simpson next entered Day's life in 2005, when he came to Twin Falls at the invitation of a law school classmate and discovered that his classmate knew Day and that she lived in Twin Falls.

The stalking began again as if the intervening years had never passed, and it culminated in the kidnapping of Dr. Shapiro, who was left to freeze to death in the classmate's crawl space in the dead of winter.

Shapiro was rescued from the crawl space after forty-eight hours but then nearly died of hantavirus pneumonia.

Simpson was convicted of kidnapping and attempted murder and sentenced to life in prison. He was paroled after serving eleven years. The body of Ralph Partridge was found two days later.

Partridge was a member of the jury that put Simpson in prison and the subject of the first of the grisly Christmas cards sent to Day, who astutely made the connection that led to the hunt for the elusive Jury Killer.

Unfortunately, the cards did not reach Day until the victims were already dead, and so far, eight members of that jury have died. A ninth was attacked but survived. The three remaining jurors have all left town for the Christmas break.

Meanwhile, Robert Simpson violated his parole and has not been seen for several days. Will he continue his killing spree after the holidays?

Only time will tell.

I put the paper down and looked up at Hal.

"Well?" he said.

"Well what? Didn't I tell you? You said I was being silly. How silly am I now?"

"If I said that, I'm sorry. Who told him about Robbie?"

Mum came into the kitchen and put the kettle on for her morning tea. "Who told who about Robbie?" she asked.

I handed her the newspaper. She took it and sat down to read it. When she looked up, her face was like a thundercloud. "I'm extremely disappointed in Pete," she said. "How could he do this? He knows perfectly well Antoinette doesn't want this to become common knowledge."

"I don't think Pete told Ryan Trowbridge any of this," I said.

"Well then, who did?" she demanded.

"Adriana."

"Adriana?"

"Pete asked me if it was okay to tell her about me and Robbie because she needed to know everything about the case that he did, and he wanted to keep her in the loop."

"I know, but when would she have told the reporter?"

"Tuesday," I said. "Pete and Adriana brought him in for questioning, and then Adriana drove him back to his car, and Pete came here. I think she volunteered to do that so she could spill the beans without Pete interfering, because he would have stopped her."

"But, kitten, why? Why would she want to do that to you?"

"I don't know. I mean, I don't think she likes me very much, but I don't really know her, do I?"

"I suppose not," she said.

"There's something else weird about her," I said. "Pete asked her to bring Ryan Trowbridge in for questioning, but she didn't do it, and Pete had to. She got a reprimand from Bernie for that. And then Pete asked her to check with the airlines to see if Robbie had gotten on a flight, and she didn't do that either."

Nigel appeared. "She might get another reprimand for that," he said. "Ready for your tea, Fiona? The kettle's boiling."

"Yes, love, thank you."

I was on a roll. "And then yesterday, Pete asked Bernie to do it for him and said he didn't want to involve Adriana anymore, because he was tired of her dragging her heels on this case."

"Do tell," Nigel said, bearing two steaming teacups, one for Mum and one for himself. "What are you getting at, Toni, old girl?"

"What if there's some kind of connection between Adriana and the Jury Killer?"

"Oh, surely not," Mum said. "Why, she's a police officer. She took an oath."

I shrugged. "Lorenzo Collins took one too, the Hippocratic oath. He swore to do no harm. How does that square with what he did to Piper?"

"He probably figured he didn't have to abide by that anymore," Hal said, "now that he's lost his license."

"What I'm getting at is that under the right set of circumstances, having taken an oath might not matter any longer."

"What kind of relationship would she have with a guy who's been in prison for the last two years?" Hal asked.

"They could be related," I said. "He could be her brother or a cousin or her childhood best friend or—"

"Or a lover," Nigel said.

"Right! Or he could be her husband," I said. "She wouldn't want that to be made public, would she?"

"Give the girl some credit," Nigel said. "He's probably her ex-husband. Why would she stay married to a guy who goes to prison?"

"People do," I said, "especially if there are kids involved. Does Adriana have any children?"

"How would we know that?" Hal asked.

"Pete would know if anybody would," I said.

"Not if she hasn't told him," Mum said.

"In any case, it's given us lots of ideas of what she might be hiding," I said. "I think I'll give Pete a call."

Hal simply gave me an eye roll without saying anything, no doubt because he knew it would do no good.

I took out my cell phone and called Pete's cell. It rang several times before he picked up.

"Toni, what's up?"

I came right to the point. "Does Adriana have any children?"

"Not that I know of," he said. "Why?"

"I'm just wondering if there's any connection between her and Lorenzo Collins."

Pete sighed. "We talked about this before, Toni. Why are we talking about it again?"

"Have you seen today's paper?"

"Not yet. Why?"

"Because Adriana spilled everything you told her about me and Robbie to Ryan Trowbridge when she drove him back to the *Clarion* Tuesday—that's why. You told her in confidence, you said, so why would she do that?"

"Jesus, Toni, are you sure it was Adriana?"

"It was either Adriana or you. It certainly wasn't Hal or me."

"Well, it wasn't me." He sounded hurt.

I hastened to remedy that. "Sorry. I know perfectly well it couldn't have been you. Is she there today? Does she know Lorenzo Collins is in jail?"

"She is, and she must. I mean, everybody's talking about it around here, and besides that, it's been in the paper."

"She went home sick with a migraine yesterday, and maybe she doesn't read the paper," I said.

"Okay, so maybe she doesn't know," he said. "What's your point?"

"Even if she knows about him, he certainly doesn't know about her. She didn't go with you to arrest him, did she?"

"No, she didn't."

"It might be interesting to bring them together. Bring him in for questioning or something."

"He was questioned right after he was arrested," Pete said. "Why would we do it again?"

"Okay, so maybe that won't work," I said, "but maybe there's some other way to bring them together."

"What would be the point?"

"What I'm saying is that even if she knows he's there, he doesn't know she's here. I mean, she could pretend not to know him, but if he recognizes her, then you'll know."

CHAPTER 24

The vow that binds too strictly snaps itself.
—Alfred, Lord Tennyson

Lorenzo Collins's arraignment was scheduled for ten o'clock Friday morning. Hal stayed home with Mum and Nigel, but Elliott and I were in attendance.

Elliott had taken a deposition from Piper because her arms were still swollen and painful, and she didn't want to go anywhere.

Elliott and I sat in the front row on the left side of the courtroom, and Pete, as the arresting officer, sat on the other side. To my surprise, Adriana sat next to him, on the aisle.

"All rise!" the bailiff called. "His Honor Judge Robert Welch presiding."

We all stood as the judge entered and took his place behind the stand. Judge Robert Welch was a slightly plump white-haired man with wire-rimmed glasses. He looked like someone's kindly old grandpa, and probably was, but Elliott told me not to be deceived, because Judge Welch was nobody's fool and could be tough.

The judge banged his gavel. "This court is now in session,"

he proclaimed, and we all resumed our seats. "First on the docket today is the matter of City of Twin Falls versus one Lorenzo Collins. The defendant will please rise."

Collins stood up, along with his defense attorney. He was wearing a blue suit with a white shirt and possibly a tie, but I couldn't see that from my vantage point.

The attorney for the defense was none other than my old nemesis Clark Dane of the law firm of Cohen, Klein, Rabinowitz, and Dane of Boise. I wondered if Dane had defended Collins in his previous trial, and if so, why hadn't Collins gotten a different lawyer this time?

Clark Dane had taken a deposition from me a few years back when I was accused of wrongful death of a patient. Elliott and I had built my deposition around grisly photographs of autopsy tissue, which had not only cleared me of that charge but also made Clark sick and unable to continue. The case had been dropped.

I wondered if he would recognize me.

Of course, the more important question was whether Lorenzo Collins would recognize Adriana, and I wondered what pretext Pete had used to get her there without mentioning that.

"Mr. Collins, you have been charged with assault and battery upon one Piper Briscoe," the judge said. "Is Ms. Briscoe present in the courtroom?"

Elliott stood up. "Elliott Maynard, Your Honor, attorney for Ms. Briscoe, who is recovering from injuries inflicted on her by the defendant. I have her deposition here and request it be entered into evidence."

Collins turned, presumably to see who was talking, but instead paused to stare intently at someone on the other side of the courtroom. I hoped it was Adriana, but there was no way to tell. Adriana herself seemed unperturbed. Either she didn't recognize Collins, or she was doing a dandy job of pretending she didn't.

I also noticed Ryan Trowbridge in the back row. Our eyes met, and he nodded almost imperceptibly.

"You may come forward, Mr. Maynard," the judge said.

Elliott did so, and he handed the deposition to the judge, who said, "Let the record show that the deposition of Ms. Piper Briscoe is entered into evidence as exhibit A," and he handed it to the bailiff, who handed it to the court recorder. "Thank you, Mr. Maynard. You may be seated. Mr. Collins, how do you plead?"

"It's Dr. Collins, if you don't mind," the defendant said.

"It's my understanding that you lost your license some time ago, Mr. Collins," the judge said, "and if there are any more outbursts like that, you'll be held in contempt of court. Now, I ask you again: How do you plead?"

"Not guilty."

"You may be seated."

The defendant plopped into his chair and slouched with his arms folded defiantly.

The judge folded his hands in front of him and leaned forward. "Very good. This case will remain in municipal court. Since you have an attorney, there is no need for this court to assign one. Trial will be in two weeks. Bail will be set at one hundred thousand dollars." The judge banged his gavel. "And now, Bailiff, please take the defendant into custody."

The bailiff came over and took Collins by the arm. "Come with me, please, sir," he said quietly.

Collins rose and turned to face the other side of the courtroom, where Adriana and Pete sat. As they were on the aisle, he had to walk right by them. He stopped and shook off the bailiff's hand. "Adriana! It is you!"

Adriana turned away and buried her face in Pete's shoulder.

Collins made a motion as if to reach out and touch her but was restrained by the bailiff. He began to struggle. "Adriana! Please! Help me!"

Judge Welch banged his gavel. "Mr. Collins, you are now in contempt of court. Do you care to go for another count?"

"That's my wife, goddammit!" Collins shouted.

"Mr. Collins, you now have two counts of contempt of court," Judge Welch said. "Bailiff, get him out of here!"

By then, Adriana was sobbing. Pete put his arm around her. As Elliott and I passed by them, she looked up at me with naked hatred in her gray eyes. "Damn you," she hissed. "I'll get you for this."

Pete looked up at me over the top of Adriana's head, and his eyes were sad. "I did what you asked, Toni, and I hope you're satisfied."

CHAPTER 25

Thus grief still treads upon the heels of pleasure;
Married in haste, we may repent at leisure.
—William Congreve

*W*ell? *Are you satisfied?* I asked myself on the way home in Elliott's car, and then I answered myself: *Not really.*

I felt terrible.

Not only was Adriana mad at me, but Pete was too. He hadn't wanted to do it in the first place.

It hadn't helped matters that the estimable—and squeamish—Clark Dane had recognized me.

"Well, well, if it isn't the illustrious Dr. Toni Day," he'd said. "Up to your old tricks, I see."

"Nice to see you too," I'd replied, unable to think of a snappy comeback.

I wondered how the hell a defrocked physician just out of prison could afford the likes of Clark Dane. Last I'd heard, he charged $500 an hour.

Elliott glanced over at me. "You're awfully quiet over there. What are you thinking?"

"I was thinking we've got our connection between Adriana and Lorenzo Collins, and I'm not as happy about it as I thought I'd be. Everybody's mad at me."

"Well, you can't blame Adriana for being upset," he said, "but Pete will get over it."

"You think?"

"For the last couple days, he's been mad at her for not following up on things like she was supposed to. This is a freakin' temporary aberration."

"What's going to happen to Collins?"

Elliott pulled over to the curb in front of my house. "Well, first he has to serve some jail time for two counts of contempt of court, and after that, it depends on whether he can raise bail."

"Don't you think a hundred thousand dollars is a little high?" I said.

"The judge set it high on purpose because Collins represents a threat to Ms. Briscoe," he said. "But she should be safe for another week or so, because that's about how long he'll serve for the two counts after all the formalities are concluded."

"Formalities?"

"Oh yes, he'll have to have another freakin' hearing, trial, and sentencing for that too. Why, he could be in jail right up until the trial for assaulting Ms. Briscoe. And now I've got to get back to the office."

"Oh, of course you do," I said. "Thanks for the lift." I got out of the car and waved as he drove away.

When I walked into the house, Hal, Mum, and Nigel descended upon me with questions about how the trial had gone.

I flopped onto the couch and sighed. "I don't want to talk about it. And it wasn't a trial; it was a preliminary hearing."

Instantly, Mum was concerned. She sat down on the couch next to me "What is it, kitten? Are you sick?"

"No," I said, "I'm not sick. Well, maybe I am—sick at heart."

"What the devil happened?" Nigel asked. "Did that bloke attack you?"

Obviously, not wanting to talk about it wasn't going to get me out of talking about it. "Okay. Do you remember me calling Pete yesterday and asking him to find a way to get Adriana and Lorenzo Collins together to see if he recognized her?"

"Yes," Hal said. "I couldn't stop you. Did he?"

"He did," I said. "Pete took Adriana with him to the hearing. They sat right in front on the aisle, across from Elliott and me. When the bailiff took Collins out of the courtroom, he had to walk right by them, and he did recognize her."

"Isn't that what you wanted, kitten?" Mum asked.

"Oh yes," I said, "but it was bad. She tried to ignore him, but he was calling her name and begging her to help him. The judge gave him one count of contempt of court and asked if he wanted to go for two, and he yelled, 'That's my wife!' and the judge gave him another count. Adriana was crying, and Pete was trying to comfort her, and he told me he hoped I was satisfied. They're both mad at me, and I feel awful."

"Oh, kitten," Mum said, putting her arms around me. I put my head on her shoulder and let the tears come. Holding them back was giving me a headache.

Hal got out of his recliner, came over, and sat down on the other side of me. "Sweetie," he said, "don't worry about Pete. He's a professional, and he'll be okay."

"That's what Elliott said," I sniffled. "He said it was a 'freakin' temporary aberration.'"

Hal chuckled.

Nigel got up and headed for the bar. "I think they're both right, and I also think you could use a libation, old girl."

I sat up, wiped my eyes, and blew my nose. "I'll take it."

Without asking, Nigel prepared drinks for all of us. "Just in time for our elevenses," he said when he brought them over to us. "Cheers!"

"Cheers, lovey," Mum said as she clinked her glass against Nigel's.

I clinked my glass against both of theirs, took a sip, and felt the scotch tingle its way down my esophagus until it bloomed out into a nice, comforting ball of warmth in my stomach, and I instantly felt better.

Then I fell asleep on the couch and knew nothing more until Pete came over at five o'clock.

"Toni!" Someone was shaking my shoulder. "Toni! Wake up!"

I opened one eye and squinted against the light. "Pete?"

"Finally!" he said. "You must have been pretty deep. I've been shaking you for the last five minutes."

I opened the other eye, sat up, and tried to focus. "Seriously?"

"More like fifteen seconds," Hal said.

Pete's face swam into view, but I couldn't see his expression. "Pete? Are you still mad at me?"

He sat down on the couch. "No, I was never mad at you. But you've got to admit that was a pretty bad scene."

"It worked, though."

"Better than we could ever have imagined," he said. "And that wasn't the half of it."

"How so?" asked Nigel, picking up my scotch glass, which was still almost full with all the ice cubes melted.

"When I got her back to the station, she told me the whole

sordid story," Pete said. "They met about ten years ago, when she was working as a ward clerk at Cascade Boise. He was an orthopedic surgeon."

"Oh, I knew that," I said.

Pete frowned. "How?"

"I googled him."

"Toni googles everybody," Hal said.

Piper came downstairs and sat on the couch next to Pete. She was wearing sweatpants and a tank top, and her upper arms were diffusely purple and swollen to at least twice their normal size.

"She said it was love at first sight for both of them," Pete said. "She said he swept her off her feet. They were married within a month."

"Uh-oh. I think I know what's coming next," I said.

"Toni, let the poor man talk," said my long-suffering husband.

"Who are you talking about?" Piper asked.

"Lorenzo Collins," I said. "The guy who did that to you. Your arms look terrible. How do they feel?"

"Better, I think," she said. "Still no numbness."

"Good," I said.

"It's the same old story," Pete said. "Boy meets girl, he sweeps her off her feet, they get married, and then he turns into Bruiser the Abuser. She shows up at work with bruises, a shiner, a limp, or a cast on her arm and says she ran into a door or tripped and fell down the stairs, until he either kills her or she leaves him. In Adriana's case, she left him after two years and filed for divorce, but he nearly killed her first."

"Oh dear," Mum said.

"He beat her up and ruptured her spleen," Pete said. "He called the ambulance and told the paramedics she had fallen down the stairs. She corroborated his story, but the doctors didn't believe it."

"Wow," Piper said. "I got off easy, didn't I?"

Nobody answered her.

"It turns out," Pete said, "that he did the same thing with his first wife, who divorced him after six months."

"Oh," I said. "So Adriana wasn't his first wife."

"No, she wasn't. His first wife wouldn't file charges, and Adriana wouldn't either. Adriana left her job at the hospital and became a cop. She worked her way up and developed a reputation for being strictly by the book and showing no emotion whatsoever. At the station, they called her the Iron Maiden."

"I can see that," I said. "That's how she acts at autopsies—totally disinterested."

"Eventually, she passed the sergeant's exam," Pete said, "but since they had no vacancy for a detective sergeant in Boise, she came here."

"Did she divorce him?" Mum asked.

"She filed, but he wouldn't sign the papers," Pete said. "He claims he's still in love with her."

"Obviously, the feeling isn't mutual," I said, remembering how Adriana had cringed away from Collins in the courtroom.

"So it would appear," Pete said.

"Is there any chance she's still in love with him and pretending not to be?"

"If so, she's one hell of an actress," Pete said.

"Then why was she crying?"

Pete threw his hands up in the air the way Hal did when he shouted, "Oy gevalt!" to the ceiling. "How the hell should I know? She was probably embarrassed."

Pete didn't think she was still in love with her husband, but I wasn't so sure. Collins was a remarkably attractive man. Men like that attracted women like flies—and usually treated them badly, in my experience.

Adriana had been attracted enough to marry the guy and had stuck with him for two years, even though he was abusive.

He probably stepped out on her too, I thought grumpily. *Doctors seem to do that all the time, even those who aren't so physically attractive.* Women were attracted to doctors because they made a lot of money, but a large percentage of male doctors didn't finish their careers with the same wife they'd started with.

"What happens to a cop who gets involved with a case to the degree that Adriana has?" I asked. "A man suspected of being either the Jury Killer or an accomplice of the Jury Killer turns out to be her ex-husband?"

"Her husband," Nigel said, correcting me. "Technically, they're still married."

"I don't know," Pete said. "We've never encountered anything like this before, and none of the seminars we've had to attend have ever dealt with anything this sordid. Bernie put her on administrative leave until this case is closed."

"Then what?" I asked.

"Then," Pete said, "I guess we'll see what happens."

CHAPTER 26

There's husbandry in heaven;
Their candles are all out.

—Shakespeare, *Macbeth*

After Pete left, I found myself in such a grumpy mood that I went upstairs to the office and fired up the computer while Mum and Hal fixed dinner.

Bernie had found out that Robbie had boarded a flight to Fort Lauderdale using a one-way ticket December 12. Was that because he wasn't planning to come back anytime soon? Or maybe he wanted to leave the trip open-ended for some other reason.

To find and kill David Lord, for instance?

And what about Marian Chandler? She was in Miami. How far was that from Fort Lauderdale? Could Robbie rent a car and drive there? Or take an Uber?

A quick Google search told me it was twenty-five miles from Miami to Fort Lauderdale. Robbie could easily go to Miami and kill Marian.

David Lord's cruise didn't leave until December 20. Until

then, he and his family would be at a hotel. We already knew that the victim's being at a hotel wasn't an obstacle to the Jury Killer.

It was December 16. He'd have to hurry, unless he was planning to stow away on the cruise ship.

And how would he know which cruise ship the Lords would be on? Pete had mentioned it was a Disney cruise, but how would Robbie know? Would there be more than one of those in port at the same time? I didn't think so, but what did I know? All he'd have to do was find a ship with a figurehead of Mickey Mouse or Goofy, and it probably would be the right ship.

Would he be able to find out which hotel they were at? David Lord was an accountant and had his own office, which would be in the phone book. It might even have a website. His office staff would probably have contact information and possibly an itinerary, but would they give that information out to a complete stranger?

It would probably be a hotel close to the docks. He could just call around and ask for David Lord, and the hotel would put the call through to his room, and that was how he'd know which hotel it was. Then he could pull the food-service stunt.

The only problem was, there would be the matter of a wife and kids to contend with. He surely wouldn't want to kill them all, but he'd have to if they saw him.

But how would he know where to find Marian Chandler? Would he have had the chutzpah to go to the hospital and ask around? Would her coworkers even know her daughter's address in Miami?

Supposing Robbie succeeds in killing both Marian and David, how is he going to locate Jeffrey Drummond in Mexico? Where in Baja is he fishing? How do we find out?

Jeffrey Drummond repaired computers. He might have an employee or two who had contact information. But again, they wouldn't want to give that out to a stranger.

They would, however, give that information to the police.

So should I call Pete and suggest that he check on all three of them? He'd probably argue because Adriana wouldn't be there to help, but she wasn't helping much anyway, and now we knew why.

Or maybe I could do some digging on my own.

I googled Marian Chandler and found her Facebook page. She had posted multiple pictures of herself with her daughter and grandchildren, many of them in front of a house, which I presumed was her daughter's. She also posted frequent updates about what she and her family were doing each day.

Marian's daughter's house was on a corner, and was that a street sign? It was too far away to read, so I saved the picture to my own picture library and opened it in Adobe Photoshop. That way, I could enlarge it. But the resolution was too low, and the enlargement was too pixelated to read.

I fetched a magnifying glass, which didn't help much. I then changed the picture to black and white and increased the contrast, and lo and behold, with the magnifying glass, I could read not only the street name but also the number of the block it was on.

If I could do that, Robbie could too.

I did the same with David Lord. He wasn't on Facebook, but he had an office website. On it was a picture of him with his wife and kids, including their names.

His wife was on Facebook, and she had posted about how excited they all were about their upcoming cruise. In her posts, she had mentioned the name of the ship and the name of the hotel they were in.

Robbie could get all that information too.

It never failed to amaze me how many people posted in real time while they were traveling, not realizing they were issuing an open invitation for anyone so inclined to go to their empty houses and rob them blind.

Hal and I were on Facebook too, but we never posted anything until we were back home again.

I called Pete. Predictably, he demurred. "Toni, we already checked on them. Why do we have to do it again?"

"Because Robbie is in Fort Lauderdale, and it's only twenty-five miles to Miami, and the Lords sail the day after tomorrow. There's no time to lose!"

"I'll call Bernie and see what he says" was all he would say, and I hung up in frustration. I knew perfectly well that Bernie wouldn't want to call them again either.

I went back to Google and found Jeffrey Drummond's office website. There were no family pictures on it, just an office address and phone number and a notice that it would be closed until the end of December. There was, however, a picture of an attractive white house with tall trees behind it, which looked vaguely familiar. He wasn't on Facebook, Twitter, Pinterest, or Instagram.

I shut down the computer and went back downstairs in a worse mood than before I had gone upstairs.

Mum and Hal had prepared dinner, and it was almost ready. I offered to set the table and help carry the food into the dining area.

As I ate, I began to feel much better.

"What were you doing up there all this time, kitten?" Mum asked.

"Some research on the computer," I said, and I told them about my Google and Facebook searches. "If I can find all that information, Robbie can too. I'm worried he may try to kill Marian Chandler and David Lord. Fort Lauderdale and Miami are only twenty-five miles apart. He could do both of them in one day."

"Does Pete know about that?" Hal asked.

"He does now. I called him."

"Is he going to check up on them?" Nigel asked.

"He said he wanted to run it by Bernie first," I said.

Hal did an eye roll. "That would be a no," he said sourly. "Bernie never wants to do anything Toni suggests."

Nigel helped himself to more mashed potatoes. "P'r'aps it would be better coming from another officer of the law," he said. "Do you have Captain Kincaid's number?"

"It's on my cell," I said.

"I'll call him after dinner."

Nigel was as good as his word. He got Bernie to agree to call both parties in the morning. Would he be in time, or would it be too late?

CHAPTER 27

Surgeons must be very careful
When they take the knife
Underneath their fine incisions
Stirs the culprit … life!

—Emily Dickinson

The weekend passed uneventfully. Mum and Hal cooked breakfast Saturday morning, and Hal and I did some Christmas shopping. We managed to procure a standing rib roast for Christmas dinner, which Mum would cook and serve with Yorkshire pudding.

Pete called with the news that he had talked to both Marian Chandler and David Lord, and both were still alive and well. He had been unable to reach Jeffrey Drummond.

Pete and Bambi invited us to dinner at their house Saturday night. No prowlers disturbed our peaceful family gathering.

On Sunday morning, I went to Jim Bob's and brought home a dozen doughnuts. Hal and Nigel watched football. Mum read a book. I went upstairs to catch up on email and pay some bills.

Piper continued to spend most of her time sleeping. Mum

kept her supplied with ice packs, but her arms continued to swell.

Lorenzo's trial for contempt of court was scheduled for Monday morning. Elliott had said he planned to attend, but I didn't have to.

While we were eating breakfast, Piper came downstairs crying.

Mum bustled around the kitchen table. "Piper, darling, what's wrong?"

"Is it your arms?" I asked.

"They hurt more than ever," she sobbed, "and my hands are numb."

"Here," I said. "Let me see."

She held them out. I took one in each of my hands. Her fingers were ice cold. In the early morning light, they looked blue. I ran a fingernail down the center of her palm, first on one hand and then on the other. "Feel that?"

She shook her head.

"Okay," I said. "Get dressed. We're going to the emergency room."

While Piper dressed, I called the hospital.

Mum said, "Kitten, what's wrong?"

I told her.

"Oh dear," she said. "Didn't the ice packs help?"

"They did but not enough," I said. "She's got compartment syndrome."

"Then you'd better get a move on, hadn't you?"

Russ Jensen and Rod Alexander met us in the emergency room. They were the surgeons who had operated on my compartment syndrome back in 2010.

"Well, well, what have we here?" Russ asked. He was a couple years older than I, with a shock of salt-and-pepper hair, deep-set brown eyes under heavy black brows, and a comfortable, slightly rumpled appearance reminiscent of the good ole country doc of yesteryear. Rod, on the other hand, was young, tall, and thin, with blond hair and gray eyes, and reminded me of a human icicle.

"A case of compartment syndrome," I said. "A guy posing as a disgruntled physician assaulted her at work a few days ago by grabbing her arms and shaking her."

"He really hurt me," Piper said. "I cried out, but he just grabbed me harder."

Russ shook his head in commiseration. "I heard about that. I hope somebody arrested the bastard."

"Everybody's heard about it," Rod said. "It's all over the hospital. Was the guy really a doctor?"

"So they say," I said. "He just got out of prison after serving two years for involuntary manslaughter."

"I hope he lost his license," Russ said.

While we were talking, Rod was assembling the paraphernalia to measure Piper's compartment pressures and explaining the procedure to her.

Russ then explained the surgical procedure and had her sign a consent form. Apparently, the laparoscopic procedure done on me that had been experimental back in 2010 was routine now in 2016.

Piper was admitted, and I went to diagnostic imaging to notify Mitzi that Piper wouldn't be back to work anytime soon.

Then I went to my office to figure out what work I still needed to do on the various autopsies I'd done.

The brain sections I'd put in on Ralph Partridge were sitting in a slide tray on my desk.

I checked the folders on the other pending cases. George

Starling's autopsy had been done on December 5, Jonathan
Swann's on December 6, and Melinda Roper's on December
12. It was December 19. George's and Jonathan's brains would
be ready to cut, so I went to the morgue and retrieved them. I put
them to rinse in the sink while I read out and dictated Ralph's
brain microscopic and signed out the case.

Then I went back to the morgue and sectioned the two brains.
As with Ralph Partridge, the only pathology I saw was the
mangled brainstem in each, so I followed the same procedure
on the other two brains that I had with his brain.

When I went into histology to put the sections into tissue
cassettes, Mike was doing the morning gross. He looked up in
surprise when I greeted him.

"Hey! You're a sight for sore eyes!" he exclaimed. "How's
it going? You wouldn't want to come back to work, would you?
We're crazy busy, I tell you what. Why, we might go over thirteen
thousand surgical cases before the end of the year."

I shook my head. "No, thanks. There's quite enough going
on in my life right now."

"Like what?" he asked. "We haven't had any more autopsies
since that last one you did."

"I know," I said. "Three of the jurors have gone out of town
for Christmas break, and Piper Briscoe just got admitted with
compartment syndrome. She's probably in surgery right now."

His eyes grew wide. "No shit. Hey, wasn't she the one who
was attacked by a doctor in radiology? I heard about that."

"He was a guy who used to be a doctor," I said, "but he lost
his license when he went to prison for involuntary manslaughter."

"I hope he went to prison for this too."

"He's in jail, but he has yet to be tried and sentenced," I said.
"Piper's been staying with us since it happened."

"And your parents are here too, right?"

"Right," I said. "Here—want to stick these cassettes in the basket for me?"

"No prob." He suited the action to the words.

Before I went home, I checked on Piper, who was in recovery, or, as they called it nowadays, PACU, or postanesthesia care unit. Russ told me she was doing fine and should be able to go home in two or three more days.

I explained to him that Piper had been a member of the jury the Jury Killer was targeting and had been staying with me and Hal for her own safety.

Russ raised his eyebrows. "Should she have a police guard?"

"I'm going to call Pete right now and arrange that," I told him.

Pete was on duty when I called the station, and he was startled to hear that Piper was in the hospital. "This sounds like déjà vu all over again," he said. "This is the same thing that happened to you, right?"

"The very same," I said. "She's out of surgery now and should get to come home, or to my house, in two or three more days."

"Well, Collins will probably have to stay in jail for three or four more days, so she shouldn't need a guard until after that," he said.

"That would be true if we could be sure there isn't another accomplice," I said.

Pete had no response for that, so we rang off. I went out to the parking garage, where once again, I was intercepted by Ryan Trowbridge.

"How's Piper doing?" he asked.

"She's out of surgery and doing fine," I said.

He looked startled. "Surgery? What surgery?"

"She developed compartment syndrome," I said. "It required surgical decompression."

Trowbridge looked mystified. "What's compartment syndrome?"

I explained, "When a muscle is injured badly enough, it hemorrhages and swells, and the fascia that contains it doesn't stretch to accommodate it, and the pressure within the compartment causes necrosis of the muscle and compromises blood vessels and nerves. It can result in loss of a limb and can cause death because of the myoglobinemia and hyperkalemia—"

"Wait," he said. "What's that in plain English?"

"The dying muscle releases myoglobin and potassium into the bloodstream. The myoglobin can plug up the kidneys and cause renal failure, and the potassium can get high enough to stop the heart."

He wiped a hand over his face. "Jesus, I had no idea. Is all this because that guy squeezed her arms so hard?"

"Yes."

He looked narrowly at me. "You seem to know an awful lot about it."

"That's because the same thing happened to me about five years ago," I told him. He opened his mouth to ask another question, but I stopped him. "Someday I'll tell you all about it. But for now, would you please not put anything in the paper about Piper being in the hospital? For her privacy and her safety?"

He nodded. "You got it, Doc."

"Where's Piper?" Hal asked when I got home.

"She's been admitted," I told him. "She went straight to surgery, and now she's out and in recovery, and Russ said she did just fine and should get to come home in two or three days, which would be Friday or Saturday."

"Oh, that's good news, kitten," my mother said.

"It's a good job she was here with a medical professional

instead of in her own place by herself," Nigel said. "She could have died."

"In which case the Jury Killer would have had another murder to his credit," Hal said.

"Assuming that guy really is the Jury Killer," I said.

My phone rang, and I answered it. "Just an FYI," Elliott said. "Lorenzo Collins was sentenced to two days per count of contempt, counting today, so he'll remain in jail until Friday."

"Oh, good," I said with relief.

That meant Piper would be safe in the hospital and not need a police guard at all.

Or so I thought.

CHAPTER 28

The Moving Finger writes, and having writ,
Moves on: nor all your Piety nor Wit
Shall lure it back to cancel half a Line,
Nor all your tears wash out a word of it.

—Edward FitzGerald

Tuesday we all went about our business, getting ready for Christmas. Lorenzo Collins remained in jail. Piper remained in the hospital. Mum and I visited her every day.

I called Pete and suggested he contact Marian and David again just to be on the safe side. It had been almost two weeks since Robbie had flown to Fort Lauderdale, more than enough time to kill two people. Pete said he'd run it by Bernie, and again, Bernie nixed it. Nigel called Bernie too, but to no avail.

When Hal went out to get the mail Wednesday, there was a surprise: two familiar holly-and-ivy-decorated envelopes among the bills and catalogs.

Possibly they were about Marian and David, but we decided we'd wait for Pete to open them and see. Hal called the station, and Pete said he'd be over after five, when he went off duty.

He arrived at five fifteen, grabbed a beer out of the fridge, pulled two evidence bags and a pair of nitrile gloves out of his pockets, and went to work.

The first card he opened showed a crude drawing of a male stick figure choking a female stick figure. The verse inside read,

> On the eighth day of Christmas, my true
> love gave to me one maid a-choking.

The second card showed a male stick figure sitting inside a pill bottle. The verse inside read,

> On the tenth day of Christmas, my true
> love gave to me one Lord a-sleeping.

"After all this time, I actually began to think these two were going to be all right," I said. "I guess we know where Robbie is now, don't we?"

"Actually," Nigel said, pulling at his mustache, "we know where he was two days ago."

"I don't want to be anywhere around Bernie when he finds out about this," Pete said.

"Don't tell him," Hal said.

"Yeah, right," Pete said grimly. "He'd find out anyway, and my ass would be grass."

Pete was right. Bernie would have found out the minute he picked up Thursday's *Clarion* and read the story on the front page. "Jury Killer Claims Two More Victims" was the headline in question.

> Two more members of the jury targeted by the Jury
> Killer have turned up dead. Marian Chandler, 61, of
> Twin Falls was found dead at Virginia Key Beach in
> Miami, according to an obituary in the *Miami Herald*.

Ms. Chandler was visiting her daughter (name given) of Miami during the Christmas holidays. The family was visiting Virginia Key Beach on Saturday, December 17, when Ms. Chandler went missing. Despite the presence of numerous lifeguard towers, no one saw her go into the water.

Ms. Chandler's body was found washed up on the beach early Tuesday morning, an apparent victim of drowning. An autopsy is pending.

David Lord, 56, also of Twin Falls, was found dead Tuesday, December 20, in his room at the Embassy Suites Hotel on Seventeenth Street in Fort Lauderdale, where he and his family were staying, according to an obituary in the *Fort Lauderdale Sun-Sentinel*. An autopsy is pending.

Ironically, both Chandler and Lord had left town for their own safety.

Robert Simpson, the presumed Jury Killer, violated his parole by flying to Fort Lauderdale, Florida, on Monday, December 12, using a one-way ticket, according to Captain Bernard Kincaid of the Twin Falls Police. His present whereabouts are unknown.

Interestingly, Lorenzo Collins, who was arrested December 14 for assaulting Piper Briscoe, also a member of that jury, was found to be carrying an ice pick on his person at the time of his arrest.

The first eight victims were found to have been pithed with an ice pick or something like it. No information is yet available as to whether these two new victims were pithed as well.

Collins was arraigned December 17 on a charge of assault and battery. The case will remain in municipal court, and trial is set for December 30. Bail was set at $100,000. Collins was also tried for two counts of contempt of court on Monday, December 19, and will remain in custody without bail until that sentence has been served.

Collins also turns out to be married to Detective Sergeant Adriana Sinclair, who has been placed on administrative leave until the case is closed.

The question remains: Are we dealing with more than one Jury Killer? And what, if anything, does Detective Sergeant Sinclair have to do with it?

"Well," I said, "at least he's off my case."

"I wonder if Pete has seen this," my mother said.

"More to the point, has Bernie seen it?" Hal said. "And how does he feel now?"

We didn't have to wait long to find out. My cell phone rang, and it was Pete. I put it on speaker so everybody could hear.

"Have you guys seen the paper this morning?" he said without preamble.

"Yes, just now."

"Toni, I don't know what to say. None of us here had any inkling that those people were in danger, but you did."

"Don't beat yourself up, Pete. When you called them, they were still okay."

Pete said, "That's the point. We should have notified the Fort Lauderdale police and asked them to keep Robbie under surveillance."

"They might not have agreed to it," Nigel said. "Besides, what evidence is there that Robbie killed them? People drown and are found dead in bed every day. Both deaths could be coincidence."

"Maybe, but I don't believe it," Pete said. "Remember what the commander used to say?"

"There are no coincidences when it comes to murder," I said. "How's Bernie taking it?"

"He's tearing his hair out," Pete said. "You know how Bernie gets when he's wrong and you're right."

I did know. "So what are we going to do about Jeffrey Drummond?" I asked.

"What *we*, white man?" Pete said. "You're not going to do anything. We're going to find out where in Baja he is and whether Robbie got on a plane out of Fort Lauderdale heading in that direction."

"If he did," Nigel said, "he'd be there by now."

"Or Miami," I said. "Maybe you should do that first. If he got on a plane, the final destination might give you a clue."

"We're on it. I'll keep you posted."

"One more thing," I said. "Can you find out whether either of them was pithed?"

"Seriously? We've got Ice Pick Man in custody."

"So what? Do you have any evidence that Lorenzo actually killed anyone with that ice pick? All we know is that he attacked Piper. And what's to stop Robbie from using an ice pick too?"

"That's where you're wrong," Pete said. "There was blood on Lorenzo's ice pick, and the lab says it's human. Unfortunately, it's too soon to know if the DNA matches any of the victims."

"Can you check and see if there's any blood on Ryan Trowbridge's ice pick?"

"Give us some credit, Toni. We already did that. There was blood on it, but it wasn't human. Any idea what it might have been?"

"Elk?" I said.

"That's what we thought too. Now I really have to go. There's a lot of work to do."

We rang off. I turned to Hal and Nigel. "Do you suppose we've been wrong all along?"

"How so?" Nigel asked.

"We're just assuming that Lorenzo pithed all those victims on the basis that he's a doctor and that he attacked Piper with an ice pick in his pocket and that she just happened to be on that jury. I mean, maybe Robbie pithed them all, and all Lorenzo did was assault Piper."

"Sweetie," Hal said, "you're losing it. They're still gathering evidence."

"Think, old girl," Nigel said. "Why did Lorenzo assault Piper? It wasn't because he ordered a CT and hadn't gotten the results. He doesn't have a license or hospital privileges or, for that matter, patients. The reason to attack Piper was a taradiddle, so there had to be another reason, and the only reason we know about is that she was on that jury."

"There might be another," I said. "Piper said he didn't grab her by the arms until she challenged him because he wasn't wearing a badge. Maybe he just didn't like being challenged by a nonphysician."

"But he was carrying an ice pick with human blood on it," Hal said. "If he hadn't been stopped, chances are he would have overpowered Piper and pithed her."

"Also, we're just guessing that Robbie and Lorenzo are accomplices," I said. "Actually, all we really know is that they were in the same prison at the same time. We don't know if they even knew each other."

"But we do know that Robbie was paroled for good behavior," Mum said. "Elliott said he'd been helping other prisoners with their appeals. Maybe Lorenzo was one of the ones he helped."

"And he's paying Robbie back by helping him kill a jury?" I said skeptically. "Why? So they both end up back in prison? For life?"

"Or some other reason," Nigel said reasonably. "These things can be easily checked, you know."

"What other reason could there be?" I asked. "Why else would Lorenzo want to kill Robbie's jury?"

"Blackmail?" Hal suggested. "What if Robbie has something on Lorenzo that he doesn't want made public?"

"Or how about revenge?" Mum said. "If they knew each other in prison, maybe Robbie double-crossed Lorenzo somehow, so he killed the jury and made it look like Robbie did it."

"Well, we know for a fact that Lorenzo didn't kill Marian and David," I said, "because he's right here in jail, and he'll be there until Friday."

"And Piper comes home from the hospital Friday," Hal said. "At least she'll be safe."

But we reckoned without Adriana.

CHAPTER 29

Steep'd amid honey'd morphine, my windpipe
Throttled in fakes of death.

—Walt Whitman

Mum had a hair appointment at Jodi's salon Friday afternoon, so I went to visit Piper without her.

Piper appeared to be asleep when I went into her room. Both her arms were nestled in gauze fluffs, making her look like a Madame Alexander doll, and I was about to leave without waking her, when I noticed something terribly wrong with her IV.

A huge air bubble that ran the length of the tubing was inching inexorably toward her, and the leading end of it was about to disappear under her fluffs. I couldn't see exactly where the tubing ended, but it wasn't in either of the backs of her hands or her arms. When I'd had that same surgery, they had put a central line in one of my subclavian veins.

"Shit!" I said, and I quickly pinched the tubing just below the bubble.

Piper woke up. "Ouch! What are you—oh, Toni. What's going on here?"

I didn't answer her. I was too busy pushing the call button. Nobody was answering, so I hollered, "Nurse!" at the top of my lungs.

After approximately a century, or maybe a minute and a half, a nurse came rushing in.

"What's going on in here?"

"That's what I said," Piper said. "Toni, whatever you're doing is pulling on my IV."

The nurse looked at me and said, "Aren't you Dr. Day, the pathologist?"

"Yes," I said. "Would you mind taking a look at this IV tubing and telling me what you see?"

The nurse looked and gasped. "Oh my God!" She reached for my hand, but I stopped her.

"If you make me let go of this tubing, that air bubble will go right to her heart," I said. "Got a hemostat on you?"

She pulled one out of her pocket and handed it to me. I clamped the tubing below the bubble and let go.

She started to remove the tape holding the tubing in place, but again, I stopped her.

"Wait. I want to take a picture of this. Who was in her room just now?"

"A doctor. At least I think he was a doctor. I didn't recognize him, but he was wearing a white coat."

I pulled my cell phone out of my purse. "Did he have wavy black hair and dark skin?"

"Yes," she said.

"And was he really good looking?"

The nurse frowned. "I didn't notice. Do you know who he might have been?"

"I have my suspicions," I told her. "You need to call security and the police."

Her eyes went wide, but she didn't move.

"Now!"

She went.

Piper's eyes were stretched wide too. "Toni, what is all this about?"

"I just saved your life," I said. "Another second, and that big air bubble would have killed you."

Piper gasped. "But how did it get there?"

"Somebody injected it into your IV line," I said as I took pictures of her IV tubing.

"Who would do that? I don't remember anybody being in here!"

"You were asleep when I got here," I said. "You probably slept right through it. You would have never known what hit you."

I decided to call Pete myself and not wait for the nurse, and I was just doing that, when a burly security guard came in. "You the one who called for security?"

"Yes," I said. "Somebody came in here and injected an air bubble into this IV. I came in and stopped it before it killed her. The nurse described him as having black hair and dark skin and wearing a white coat. He can't have gone far. Can you detain him until the police get here?"

"I can try," he said. He unhooked the radio from his belt and started talking into it as he left the room. I called Pete.

"What's up, Toni?"

"Is Lorenzo Collins still in jail?"

"No. Apparently, he made bail this morning."

"Someone matching his description was just here and tried to kill Piper."

"How?"

"By injecting a big air bubble into her IV. Can you come?" I gave him the room number.

"Be right there."

The nurse returned. "Can I change this tubing now?"

"Can you wait until the police get here? I want them to see it."

"Well, maybe. I hate to leave it like that, though."

"It might be safer if you could clamp it above the bubble too," I said.

"Oh, good idea." She took out another hemostat and did so.

"I'll be right here," I told her. "I'm waiting for the police."

She left.

Pete arrived approximately five minutes later. He took a look at the IV tubing with its air bubble framed between two hemostats. "Jesus, Toni. Good thing you got here when you did. You think Lorenzo did this?"

"The nurse described someone matching his description. But you'll be talking to her too."

"I will. Do you suppose we can take this IV setup just as it is for evidence?"

"I should think so. But you'll have to get the nurse to change out the tubing."

"I'm supposed to go home tomorrow," Piper said. "Maybe I don't need an IV anymore."

Pete left and then came back with the nurse. She disconnected the tubing from the bag and from Piper's port. "Do you want to take this with you?" she asked Pete.

"No, just lock it up somewhere safe, and I'll send a CSI after it."

"I'll just put it in here," she said. She opened a drawer in Piper's bedside table, put the tubing in it, and locked it. She put the key in her pocket. Then she produced new tubing and proceeded to attach it, first to the bag hanging from an IV stand, and then, after the tubing was filled with solution, she plugged it into Piper's subclavian port, using sterile technique.

"Can you stay with Piper while I go talk to the security guys?" Pete asked me. "I'll be right back."

"Sure."

He left. I made myself comfortable in one of the visitors' chairs and played a game on my phone while I waited for Pete. Piper went back to sleep.

Pete came back after about fifteen minutes. "They couldn't find the guy. He must have left the hospital right after he did the dirty deed."

"If he's on the loose, she's not safe," I said.

"Not to worry," Pete said. "I already arranged for a police guard. He should be here any minute. I'll stay until he gets here."

I heaved a sigh of relief. "Thank you."

"Any idea where he might have gone?"

"I don't know. How about Adriana's house?"

"Huh," Pete said. "There's a thought. Let me call Bernie and run that past him."

"Tell him it was your idea," I said. "If he knows it was mine, he won't go there. I'll see you later, okay?"

I had to walk past the nurses' station to get to the elevator, and as I did so, I saw a familiar figure standing there. He looked up as I walked by.

"Dr. Day! Fancy meeting you here."

"Mr. Trowbridge. Have you been following me again?"

"I follow where the story takes me," he said reprovingly. "I told you that before, Doctor."

"And the story always seems to take you wherever I happen to be."

He nodded. "Today the story was that there was a bit of excitement about Piper Briscoe, and here you are."

"Imagine that."

"Want to tell me about it?"

"I don't know. I'm thinking it might be better if I don't."

"And why not, pray tell?"

"Someone made an attempt on Piper's life this afternoon. He tried to give her an air embolus by injecting air into her IV line."

"And that would kill her?"

"Yes. It was a pretty big bubble."

"You said *he*. Do you know for a fact it was a male?"

"The nurse said the last person in Piper's room was a man with dark hair and dark skin, wearing a white coat. She thought he was a doctor but didn't recognize him. Here she is now; you can ask her yourself."

The nurse shook her head. "I have charting to do before I go off duty," she said. "I don't have time to talk to reporters."

"When do you go off duty?" he asked her.

"Three thirty."

Trowbridge looked at his watch. "I'll wait."

"Suit yourself." She went into an alcove off to the side and sat down at a computer terminal.

"Lieutenant Vincent is in Piper's room," I told him. "He's waiting for a police guard. You can kill some of that time talking to him."

"First, tell me—why don't you want to tell me what happened?"

"It occurred to me that if the suspect knows Piper is still alive, he may try again."

"If she has a police guard, she should be safe," he said.

"Even police guards have to go to the bathroom once in a while," I argued. "He could watch and strike when that happens."

"Doctor, are you suggesting I should file a false report?"

"You can run that by Lieutenant Vincent when you talk to him. She's due to be discharged tomorrow, and she'll be staying at my house, where she won't have a police guard. I'm just saying."

217

"Are you going home now?"

"No, I've got some work to do in my office first."

"Then I'll talk to you later." He touched his forehead in a gesture of farewell and headed toward Piper's room.

I headed to the elevator and rode down to the basement level, where our offices were. The slides from the two brains I had cut were in a slide tray on my desk. Thus, I was able to complete and sign out two more autopsies. All that was left was Melinda Roper's brain, and I could deal with that Monday, which was after Christmas.

I looked at my watch and noted with a start that it was nearly five o'clock. *Damn!* Traffic at five o'clock on the Friday before Christmas would be a nightmare.

But it was the only way home. With a shrug of resignation, I headed for the parking garage.

Ryan Trowbridge intercepted me just as I was about to open the door. "I looked for you in your office, and they said you'd just left. Why didn't you tell me that Lorenzo Collins had made bail? And that you saved that girl's life?"

"Because I knew Pete would," I said.

"So is he your suspect?"

"The description fits," I said, "and he is at large."

"Not anymore," Trowbridge said with a note of triumph in his voice.

"They found him?"

"They went to his wife's house, as you suggested."

"He was there?"

"Well, she told them he wasn't, but there was a white doctor's coat slung over a chair in the bedroom, and he was hiding in the closet. He's back in jail; only now the charge is attempted murder."

"Very neat," I said, reaching for the bar that would open the door.

Trowbridge pushed it open and held it for me. I stepped out into the parking garage—and stopped short.

Someone was standing by my car.

A tall, slender someone with long auburn hair.

Adriana.

CHAPTER 30

The female of the species is more
deadly than the male.

—Rudyard Kipling

I grabbed Trowbridge by the sleeve. "Where are you parked?"

"Somewhere out in front of the hospital. Why?"

"Let me give you a lift."

"You're kidding. You're going to let me get into your car? My, how the mighty have fallen."

"Quit kidding around," I hissed. "She won't harm me if there's a witness."

"You're serious, aren't you?"

"As a heart attack. Come on!"

We walked together to my car. "Adriana!" I said. "What a surprise. What are you doing here?"

"I had a doctor's appointment, if you must know."

"And you're parked in doctors' parking? My goodness. You'd better get your car out of here before security finds you and gives you a ticket."

She glared at me. "You think you're pretty smart, don't you?"

"I'm just saying." I unlocked my car with my key fob, and Trowbridge gallantly opened my door for me. I thanked him and got in. He lumbered around to the other side and got in. I locked the doors and looked around.

Adriana had disappeared.

I fastened my seat belt. Luckily, nobody was parked in front of me, so I could just pull through and drive out.

"I hope she's not armed," I said as I got to the top of the driveway, where the gate opened automatically to let me out into the regular parking lot.

Trowbridge turned to look at me. "You're really scared, aren't you?"

"It did occur to me that she might shoot me," I said. "Where's your car?"

He directed me to it. I dropped him off and headed for home.

Delectable smells emanated from pots on the stove. But in the living room, a storm was brewing.

Hal was mad. Mum was frantic. Pete and Nigel were trying to calm them down without noticeable success. When I walked into the living room, all eyes turned to me.

"What's going on?" I asked innocently.

"Where the hell have you been?" Hal demanded.

"At the hospital," I said.

"All this time?" Mum asked. "We were so worried, kitten."

I looked at Pete. "Didn't you tell them what happened?"

"I just got here," Pete said. "I haven't had time."

"All righty then," I said. "To make a long story short, Lorenzo tried to kill Piper and got arrested."

"What Toni isn't telling you," Pete said, "is that she saved Piper's life."

His words were met with a chorus of "What!" and "Oh my God!"

"Not only that," Pete said, "but she told us where to find him."

"I daresay," Nigel drawled, "that you're going to have to give us the long version, old girl."

I folded my arms. "I'm not saying another word until I have a scotch in my hand."

Nigel jumped to his feet with alacrity. "I'm on it, dear girl. Libations all around?"

A chorus of assents ensued. While Nigel fiddled with bottles and glasses, I took off my coat and boots and put them away in the closet.

Soon I was on the couch, ensconced in an afghan with Geraldine in my lap and a scotch in my hand. "Okay," I said. "While you were at Jodi's, Mum, I went to visit Piper. When I got to her room, I noticed a huge air bubble in her IV line."

Mum gasped.

"That's called an air embolus," Hal said with all the assurance of one married to a medical professional.

"Well, it would have been if it had actually gotten into her vein, but I pinched the tubing with my fingers and hollered for a nurse, who gave me a hemostat to clamp it with."

"Quick thinking, sweetie," Hal said.

"Thank you. The nurse said a man had been in Piper's room and left just before I got there. The description sounded like Lorenzo, so I called Pete, and he told me Lorenzo had made bail."

"Oh no," Mum said with her fingers to her mouth. "Who on earth bailed him out?"

"I don't know," Pete said.

"But I have an idea," I said. "Anyway, the nurse called security, and they talked to me. I gave them the description the nurse gave me. But when Pete talked to them, they told him they hadn't been able to find the suspect anywhere in the hospital or on the grounds."

"Toni said to look at Adriana's house but not to tell Bernie it was her idea," Pete said.

"That was smart," Hal said.

"And that's where he was," I said. "Adriana said he wasn't there, but there was a white lab coat in the bedroom."

"I say," Nigel said, "that wasn't too smart, was it?"

"Not by half," I said. "Lorenzo was hiding in the closet. So now he's back in jail."

"Thank goodness," Mum said, fanning herself.

"Wait," Pete said. "How did you know all that, Toni? You didn't hear it from me."

"Ryan Trowbridge," I said. "I ran into him upstairs in the hospital before he talked to you, and then I went to my office and did a little work on the autopsies. Then, when I went to leave, I ran into him again, and that's when he told me."

"I might have known," Hal said sourly. "I think that man is stalking you."

"He's stalking a story," I said. "I just happen to be in it."

"Why are you defending him all of a sudden?" Hal asked. "You usually just complain about him."

"Because today he just might have saved my life."

"What?" said Mum.

"How?" Pete asked.

"When we went out into the parking garage, I saw Adriana standing by my car."

"Why?" asked Hal.

"Your guess is as good as mine, but it creeped me out. So I asked Trowbridge to let me give him a lift to wherever his car was parked, because I figured she wouldn't harm me if there was a witness."

"Brilliant," Nigel said approvingly.

"You took an awful chance, kitten," Mum said. "What if she'd put a bomb under your car?"

"Oh jeez, I never thought of that," I said ruefully. "Oh well, she probably didn't, because I'm here, aren't I?"

"So you drove out of the parking garage with Trowbridge," Pete said. "Where did Adriana go?"

"I don't know," I said. "She disappeared before I'd even started the engine."

"Smart if she'd planted a bomb," Nigel said, "but since she didn't, where would she have gone?"

"Back in through the door you came out of," suggested Mum.

"Not without a hospital badge," I said. "But there are other doors open to the public—like the cafeteria, for instance. And the elevator is right there that goes directly to the inpatient floors. But why would she—oh no."

"What?" Pete said. "What are you thinking?"

"What if she was going to finish what Lorenzo started?"

CHAPTER 31

It may seem a strange principle to enunciate
as the very first requirement in a Hospital
that it should do the sick no harm.

—Florence Nightingale

"You mean you think she's going to try to kill Piper?" Pete asked. "I wish her luck. She's got to get past the police guard first."

"He's got to go to the bathroom sometime," I said. "It wouldn't take that long to shoot more air into her IV. We've got to go see if she's all right."

"Not so fast," Hal said. "Why don't you call and ask how she is?"

"I suppose that makes more sense." I took out my cell phone and dialed the surgical floor nurses' station. When someone finally answered, I identified myself and asked how Piper was.

"She's fine," the nurse told me. "I just took her vitals. And she has a policeman sitting outside her door."

"Has anyone come to see her since I left?"

"Just one. A tall lady with long red hair was here a little while ago. The cop didn't let her in."

I thanked her and disconnected.

"She's had a visitor," I said. "The description matches Adriana."

"I hope the guard didn't let her into the room," Mum said.

"He didn't. But like I said, he has to go to the bathroom sometime."

"Enough with the bathroom already," Hal said. "Let's eat."

Pete went home, saying he'd see us Sunday, which was Christmas.

We ate dinner and spent a pleasant evening watching Christmas movies and being blissfully unaware of whatever might have been happening at the hospital.

On Saturday morning, I called to check on Piper and find out what time she would be discharged. I was unprepared for what I heard.

"I'm sorry to have to tell you this, Doctor, but Ms. Briscoe passed away during the night."

"You're kidding! How?"

"Nobody knows. When the night nurse went in to take her vitals, she was dead."

"Oh my God!"

"What is it?" Hal asked, standing so close that I was surprised he couldn't hear the nurse's end of the conversation.

"Piper's dead," I said sotto voce but evidently not so sotto that Mum couldn't hear me.

"Kitten! Did I hear you right?"

I nodded while asking, "Is that nurse still there?"

"She's gone off shift, but she usually eats breakfast in the cafeteria before she goes home. You might be able to catch her there if you hurry. Her name's Sharon."

I thanked her and disconnected.

"I've got to go," I said. "Can I take the Jeep?"

"Why?" Hal asked.

"In case there's a bomb under my car that goes off when I hit a certain speed I didn't hit yesterday."

Hal threw his hands up and shouted to the ceiling, "Oy gevalt!" But he gave me the keys.

"Call Pete, and tell him to meet me in the hospital cafeteria," I said as I put my coat and boots on.

That early on a Saturday morning, there was practically no traffic, and I reached the hospital in record time. The cafeteria was almost deserted, but a couple nurses in scrubs were eating together. I went over to them and asked if one of them was Sharon.

The older of the two said, "I'm Sharon. Can I help you?"

I identified myself and asked if I could talk to her about Piper.

Sharon's expression grew wary. "I'm not in trouble, am I?"

"I don't think so," I said. "May I sit down?"

"Sure."

I pulled a chair over from one of the other tables and sat. "Tell me exactly what happened."

"I went into her room to take her vitals at midnight. I couldn't feel a pulse, so I listened to her chest, and there was no heartbeat. She wasn't breathing either. I shined a light in her eyes, and her pupils were fixed and dilated. So I called the hospitalist on duty, and he pronounced her dead."

"Had rigor mortis set in?"

"Not that I could tell. She was still warm, so she couldn't have been dead long."

"Was the police guard there?"

"Yes, right outside the door. I think he was a little weirded out to learn he'd been guarding a dead person."

"Did she have any visitors on your shift?"

"No, but there was one odd thing."

"What was that?"

"When I told the cop I was there to take her vitals, he said, 'Again?' I asked him what he meant, and he said another nurse had taken her vitals just a few minutes earlier."

"Did he describe her?"

"I asked him who she was, and he said he didn't know, but she was tall."

"With red hair?"

"He said she was wearing a cap, and he couldn't see her hair."

"Are you going to do the autopsy?" the other nurse asked.

"Most likely."

The cafeteria door swished open, and I looked up to see Pete coming toward me. I waved at him. "This is my son-in-law, Detective Lieutenant Pete Vincent. Will you tell him what you just told me?"

"Sure."

"Good morning, ladies," Pete said. "Sharon? Could I have your last name?"

"Olson."

"Thank you. Now, Sharon, please tell me what you just told Toni."

She complied.

Afterward, Pete turned to me. "Are you thinking what I'm thinking?"

"Probably. I think you need to question the police guard who was here last night."

"I will," he said. "Will you be available for the autopsy?"

"I will if I can do it today. I don't want to have to do it on Christmas."

Pete shuddered. "Christmas Eve is bad enough."

I had a flashback to another autopsy I'd done on Christmas

Eve years ago, during which Rollie had told me about the other body in the embalming room, discreetly hidden under a sheet. The man had shot himself upstairs in the bathroom while his wife was wrapping presents downstairs. That one had creeped me out.

I stood up. "Does Rollie know about this?"

"He does. He picked the body up last night. He should be calling you any time now."

As if Rollie had heard Pete say that, my cell phone rang.

"Good morning, young lady," he said. "I've got a case for you."

"I know," I said. "When can you get her over to us?"

"She's already here," he said. "I'm calling from your morgue. When can you do the autopsy?"

"Anytime, if I can get Natalie to assist. I'll call you back in a few minutes. I'm in the cafeteria right now."

"Okay," he said.

I disconnected. "Rollie's in the morgue with the body," I told Pete, "if you want to go keep him company."

I called Hal and told him I was going to do an autopsy. Then I went to the lab to consult the call list and called Natalie. She was available. "Might as well work," she said. "Dale is working today too. Didn't you see him in the lab?"

I hadn't, but then I hadn't really looked. "How soon can you get here?"

"I'm on my way. It's not another stinker, is it?"

"No," I told her. "This one's still warm."

Piper Briscoe, at age forty-three, would probably have little, if any, pathology. The body lying on my autopsy table was just as it had been in bed, complete with a subclavian port, a Foley catheter, a hospital gown, and fluffs around her arms, wrapped in the bottom sheet from her hospital bed. We had to remove all that before I could even do an external gross examination.

Pete and Rollie helped me remove the sheet from around the body, but we left it under her on the table to catch any debris from the removal of her fluffs and hospital gown.

The surgical incisions were beginning to heal, and drains were in place in both arms to allow drainage. The fluffs showed little drainage, however, which would have been a good sign if she had not been dead.

"Hey, look at this," I said as I noticed a couple black hairs clinging to the neck of the hospital gown, contrasting with Piper's light brown hair. "These must be Lorenzo's."

Pete fetched an evidence bag from his cooler. "Put 'em in here," he said.

I did so, and then I examined the area more closely. "I don't see any red ones here, do you?"

Pete scanned the area with a flashlight. "Nope. Don't see any. Do you, Rollie?"

The stout mortician shook his head.

After the external gross was complete, Natalie helped me examine the back of her neck for evidence of pithing, and there wasn't any. We removed the brain, and the brainstem was intact.

Before opening the body, I drew blood from the heart for toxicology—that was, I tried to. All I got was air.

I turned to Rollie and Pete. "I could stop right now. I know the cause of death."

"But—"

"Don't worry, Rollie. I'm going to finish it, but I know what I'm going to find."

When we opened the body, everything looked perfectly normal, which made a stunning backdrop for the pale, bloodless, distended subclavian veins, superior vena cava, and right atrium.

Further exploration revealed distended pulmonary arteries as well.

"Okay, fellas," I said. "I want each of you to put a glove on and feel these."

They did so. Pete said, "Wow. They're hard as rocks."

"They feel like blown-up balloons," Rollie said.

"That's essentially what they are," I said.

Natalie, without being told, busily snapped pictures.

"She must have shot the air right in through the subclavian port," I said. "Piper would have died instantly."

"She who?" asked Rollie.

"A nurse," Pete said. "Supposedly."

The rest of the autopsy was anticlimactic. Natalie and I pulled out the organ block, took samples of perfectly normal tissue, put what we didn't want back in the body cavity, and closed it up. Pete and Rollie left, and Rollie took the body with him. Natalie washed down the autopsy table while I washed instruments.

"This isn't one of the Jury Killer victims, is it?" Natalie asked me. "She wasn't pithed."

"She is one of them," I said. "Somebody shot air in through her subclavian port and killed her instantly. No need to pith her."

Natalie looked mystified. "I thought the pithing was the Jury Killer's signature."

"I think there's more than one Jury Killer," I said. "I think there are at least two and possibly three. Two more members of that jury were killed in Florida a few days ago, and we don't yet know if they were pithed or not."

"So how many are left?"

"Only one."

CHAPTER 32

Marriage resembles a pair of shears,
so joined that they cannot be separated;
often moving in opposite directions,
yet always punishing anyone who
comes between them.

—Sir Walter Scott

I went to my office, not expecting to find Ryan Trowbridge there on Christmas Eve, but there he was.

He stood up when I came in. "I won't take too much of your time, Doctor, seeing as it's Christmas Eve. I'll keep it short."

I kept it shorter. "Cause of death was air embolism. She was not pithed."

He looked startled. "She wasn't? Does that mean she wasn't killed by the same guy?"

"From what the nurse on duty told Pete and me, the nurse went into the patient's room to take her vitals at midnight and found her dead."

"Didn't she have a police guard?"

"That was what was weird. When the nurse told the guard

she was going to take Piper's vitals, he said another nurse had just taken them a few minutes before."

"Was there a description?"

"Not much of one. Pete said he was going to interview the guard about that."

"Hmm. I suppose I can go with that."

"You'll have to, unless you want to track Pete down and talk to him."

After Trowbridge left, I dictated the gross and provisional diagnoses—or, rather, diagnosis, because there was only one: air embolism.

When I got home, the mail had come, and so had Pete.

The Christmas card was already in an evidence bag. On the front was a crude drawing of a male stick figure smothering a female stick figure in a hospital bed with a pillow. The verse inside read,

> On the eleventh day of Christmas, my true
> love gave to me one Piper gasping.

Killer and Geraldine both left their respective posts to greet me at the door. Spook didn't move. Nigel went straight to the bar and prepared my scotch on the rocks without asking.

The card had clearly been mailed before Piper was killed, which was a departure from the routine followed by the first eight, in which the victims had been dead for two days before I received the corresponding cards. I was not sure what that meant, if anything more than counting chickens before they hatched.

I gathered that Pete had already told them about what we had been doing all morning.

While I hung up my coat and kicked off my boots, I told him, "Ryan Trowbridge is looking for you."

"Where'd you run into him?"

"In my office. I told him you were going to interview the police guard and get a description."

"I did that. You know how you kept saying he had to go to the bathroom sometime?"

"Yes. So?"

"Well, he did. Around eleven fifteen. The nurses were doing change of shift, so there wasn't anybody around. When he got back, there was a tall nurse doing something to the IV tubing."

"How did he know she was a nurse? Was she wearing a uniform?"

"She was wearing scrubs, sneakers, a surgical cap, and a stethoscope around her neck, and she wore glasses. I asked him if it was the same one who had visited earlier, and he said he couldn't be sure. And before I forget, I had one of our bomb guys go over your car this morning, and he didn't find anything."

"Oh, that's a relief. Thank you."

Nigel handed me my scotch. I thanked him and sat down on the couch next to Pete. Geraldine jumped into my lap.

"Didn't you tell me that Adriana used to work as a ward clerk at Cascade Boise?" I asked.

"Yes, she did."

"Then she'd have a pretty good idea of where everything is kept, wouldn't she?"

"I guess. It was a different hospital, though."

"But it's in the Cascade system. The hospitals are all built the same. Everything here would look the same as it would at Cascade Boise. So she'd know where to find things, such as scrubs, stethoscopes, and syringes, and since the other nurses were busy doing report, nobody would have seen her."

"I guess so," Pete said. "And here's another thing. We got

copies of the autopsy reports on Marian Chandler and David Lord. Neither of them was pithed."

"That's interesting," Nigel said. "That points to there being two killers."

"At least," I said. "We've got Robbie, someone who looks like Lorenzo, and someone who looks like Adriana."

"Well, we know Robbie went to Fort Lauderdale," Hal said.

"We also know Lorenzo got caught trying to kill Piper," Pete said, "and is back in jail. And we know that a tall nurse was seen doing something to Piper's IV. So Robbie would have to have killed Marian and David."

"So what did the autopsies on Marian and David show as cause of death?" I asked.

"Marian drowned. She had salt water in her lungs," Pete said. "And David died of a barbiturate overdose."

"Did anybody interview the families? Were there any police reports?" I asked.

"We haven't gotten any so far," Pete said, and just as he said that, his phone rang. "Or maybe we do now," he said as he checked his phone. "Bernie, what's up?"

Bernie must have been talking nonstop, because Pete said nothing, except for making sounds like "Huh" and "Hmm," for quite a long time. When he finally disconnected, his face was grim.

"Well, now we have police reports, and this changes everything."

"How?" Mum asked.

"Marian's daughter said that when they were at Virginia Key, the kids wanted to go to the amusement park across the street, and Marian didn't want to go. Her daughter didn't want to leave her alone, so she asked the lady next to them on the beach if she would keep an eye on her, and she said she'd be glad to."

"And now you're going to tell us that she was a tall redhead," I said.

"Toni," Hal said, "let the poor man talk."

"So Marian and this lady went off down the beach to look for shells, and that's the last she saw of her mother," Pete said, "and yes, the lady was a tall redhead."

"Does this tall redhead have a name?" Nigel asked.

"Yes, she gave it to the police when she reported that Marian had disappeared, but there turned out to be no such person. It was obviously a fake name."

"That figures," I said. "What about David?"

"David and his family were eating breakfast at the hotel, when a tall lady with long red hair and a Bloody Mary in her hand walked by their table and pretended to recognize David. She said that when she'd lived in Boise, he'd helped her with her taxes. Turns out he did live in Boise at that time, so it all fit. So then he invited her to join them, and when she sat down, she managed to knock over his Bloody Mary."

"Uh-oh," I said. "I think I know what's coming."

Hal quelled me with a look.

"So anyway, she apologized all over the place and said, 'Here—take mine. I haven't touched it. I'll go get another one,' and she ran off to the bar and did that. Then she came back to the table and ate breakfast with them, and when they were finished, David said he was feeling too tired to go on the excursion they'd planned, and he decided to go back to bed."

"And when they got back from the excursion, they found him dead in bed," Hal said.

"She spiked her own drink and gave it to him, obviously," Mum said.

"We seem to be awash in tall redheads," I said. "Is there any possibility Adriana went to Florida?"

"She could have," Pete said. "She was on administrative leave." He picked up his phone and dialed. "Bernie? Can you check with the airlines and find out if Adriana Sinclair was on any flights to Miami or Fort Lauderdale?" He listened for a moment and then said, "It would be any time after you put her on admin leave and before Marian and David were killed. Thanks, and merry Christmas!" He then winced and held the phone away from his ear. "Bernie needs a little Christmas right this very minute."

"Candles in the windows. Carols on the spinet," I sang.

"And I need a little angel sitting on my shoulder," sang Mum.

"We need a little Christmas now!" sang Hal and Nigel.

Then we all yelled, "Merry Christmas, Bernie!" and collapsed in laughter. Spook hissed and jumped down from the back of the couch. Killer started barking. Hal shushed him.

Pete put his phone back in his pocket. "Sorry, guys. He hung up."

"You're a mean one, Mr. Grinch," I sang.

Hal said repressively, "None of the rest of us know that one."

"Sorry. I got carried away with all this unaccustomed jocularity," I said. "I bet little Toni and Shawna know it."

"They do," Pete said, "and so does Bambi. And speaking of that, I need to get home. I have the duty tomorrow, so the girls get to open their presents tonight."

Mum got up and went over to the tree. "Then you may as well take ours with you."

I got up too and said, "I'll get a sack for you to put them in."

Once Pete and the presents had departed, there were precious few left under the tree. Nigel surveyed the scene with dismay. "Fiona, love, I think we may have rather overdone it with the children's gifts."

Mum sighed. "It's a shame Pete has to work tomorrow. I had hoped they could all come over here for Christmas."

"That's why I did that autopsy today," I said, "so I wouldn't have to work on Christmas."

"Let's stop talking about it," Hal said, "and eat dinner and watch *It's a Wonderful Life*. We need a little Christmas too."

CHAPTER 33

Heaven has no rage like love to hatred turned,
Nor hell a fury like a woman scorned.
—William Congreve

We woke up early on Christmas morning, even though we didn't need to, as there were no children in the house. Mum and Nigel were already up and enjoying their morning tea when Hal and I came downstairs.

Hal went into the kitchen to start preparing breakfast, while I went out to get the morning paper, followed by the dogs. The headline "Jury Killer Claims Eleventh Victim" was splashed across the front page.

"Ryan Trowbridge strikes again!" I sang as I came back inside.

Hal came out of the kitchen with mimosas for Mum and Nigel and a Bloody Mary for me, as I'd never much cared for mimosas. "There's a surprise," he said. "I think I'll have a heart attack and die from that surprise."

"Shall I read it aloud?" I asked.

"Sure, why not?" Hal answered. "Just a minute." He went

back into the kitchen and then reemerged with another mimosa. "Shoot."

> The Jury Killer has taken the life of Piper Briscoe, 43, after two previous attempts failed.
>
> Briscoe was a member of the jury that put Robert Simpson in prison in 2005.
>
> Briscoe was found dead in her hospital bed at midnight Friday when a nurse came to take her vital signs. Briscoe was recovering from surgery to relieve the compartment syndrome resulting from being attacked by one Lorenzo Collins posing as a disgruntled physician on December 13.
>
> Collins was charged with assault and battery and held in Twin Falls County Jail until making bail Friday morning.
>
> A man matching Collins's description made a second attempt on Briscoe's life yesterday afternoon by injecting air into her IV line but was foiled by the quick action of Dr. Toni Day, who pinched the IV line below the air bubble, preventing it from entering Briscoe's veins.
>
> Collins was arrested at the home of his wife, Adriana Sinclair, now on administrative leave from the Twin Falls Police Department. Collins is back in jail, now charged with attempted murder.
>
> An autopsy performed by Dr. Toni Day showed the cause of death to be air embolism. Unlike the other Jury Killer victims, Briscoe was not pithed.
>
> Could it be that there are two Jury Killers?

"Obviously, he didn't manage to catch up with Pete yesterday," Hal said after I finished reading.

"I guess not," I said. "There's nothing about the autopsy

reports on Marian and David and nothing about tall ladies of any description."

"I rather think," Mum said, "that he'll get all that today from Pete at the station."

"Might I have a look at that article when you're done?" Nigel asked.

"Sure," I said, handing it to him.

"This seems to be all about you," he said. "First you save her life, and then you do the autopsy." He handed it back to me.

Hal drained his mimosa and stood up. "When you put it that way, it doesn't say much for Toni's lifesaving skills, does it?"

"Not much," I said. "Holler when you're ready for me to come do the toast."

"Okay," he said, and he went back into the kitchen just as Pete opened the door from the garage. He was carrying the same sack I'd given him last night to carry presents home in. Both dogs rushed to greet him, and he patted their heads.

"Oh my God, that all smells so good!" he exclaimed. "Too bad I don't have time to stay and eat, but I've got to get to work." He handed Hal the sack. "These are our presents for you."

"Tell Ryan Trowbridge I said hi when you see him," I called out as he turned to go.

He stopped. "What makes you think I'm going to see him?"

"This." I held up the front page of the *Clarion*. "There's a lot of missing detail. Depend on it—you'll see him."

"Whoopee."

"I'm just saying."

The sound of the door closing behind him was the only answer I got.

"Sweetie," Hal called out, "could you do something with these presents?"

"Okay." I retrieved the sack and dumped out its contents under the tree.

"Antoinette, really," Mum said. "Could you possibly arrange those a little more neatly?"

"Aw, Mum, we're just going to open them and make an even worse mess."

But even as I said it, I knew it was useless to argue with my mother on such matters and was already rearranging the presents and shooing Spook away from them. He gave up and resumed his post on the back of the couch.

Hal appeared in the doorway. "Time to make toast."

He had prepared cheesy scrambled eggs and quantities of both bacon and sausage. All I did was make toast—and eat.

After breakfast, we opened the presents I had arranged tastefully, and we made an even worse mess. Spook rolled around in the discarded wrapping paper, biting off the corners and playing with the ribbons, over Mum's objections.

Once the wrappings and other detritus were cleared away, we settled down to the real purpose of the day.

Mum stretched out on the couch with a book, Hal and Nigel watched football, and I went upstairs to check email and pay some bills. All of us were just marking time until we could enjoy Mum's standing rib roast with Yorkshire pudding, which she only prepared on Christmas Day.

Pete called me late in the afternoon to tell me that Adriana had been on a flight to Miami on December 17 and had flown back to Twin Falls on December 22. "That puts her there right when Marian and David were killed," he said. "And by the way, you were right about Trowbridge. He showed up around noon."

"So we'll have another article tomorrow," I said. "You didn't tell him about Adriana, did you?"

"I didn't find out about her until after he left," Pete said, "but why wouldn't I tell him if I knew?"

"Oh, I don't know. It might be a little premature."

"How?"

"Doesn't it strike you as just a little too convenient that both Marian's and David's deaths are linked to a tall redhead?"

"Actually, it hadn't," he said.

"Adriana's a cop," I said. "Don't you think that if she was going to commit a crime in plain sight, she'd at least change the color of her hair or cover it up?"

"So you think the tall redheads are red herrings?"

"Well, couldn't they be?"

"I guess so. How's Christmas so far?"

"Fine." I thanked him for the presents. "Mum's busy getting the roast ready for dinner. How about you?"

"Okay. It's been pretty quiet. I'll be heading home soon. Bambi's doing a turkey."

"Oh, yum. Hugs to the girls!"

We disconnected. Hal said, "What was all that about Adriana?"

"Pete says she was on a flight to Miami Saturday and flew back on Thursday."

"And Marian was killed Saturday, and David on Tuesday," Hal said.

"And Lorenzo made bail on Friday," I said. "Wanna bet Adriana bailed him out?"

"Seriously?" Hal said. "That would be ten thousand dollars for a bail bondsman. Where would Adriana get that kind of money?"

I shrugged. "Maybe she has rich parents. Maybe she has a trust fund."

"There's an awful lot we don't know about her," Hal said.

Nigel got up and headed to the bar. "One thing I do know," he said, "is that it's time we all had a little libation. Fiona?"

"There's a nice bottle of cabernet open and breathing on the table," Mum said. "I wouldn't mind a glass of that. Hal, dear, could you please keep those dogs out of here?"

I called them and made Killer lie down next to the couch. Geraldine jumped into my lap.

Hal rummaged in the liquor cabinet and pulled out a bottle of eighteen-year-old Glenlivet. "I got this for Toni," he said to Nigel. "I'm sure she wouldn't mind sharing it with you."

"You could have asked me," I said in mock indignation at Hal's playing fast and loose with my Glenlivet, which I only got on special occasions, especially eighteen-year-old, which was pricey. "Are you going to have some too?"

"Sure, why not?"

While Nigel poured three Glenlivets on the rocks, Hal poured Mum a glass of wine. "Can you take a break from the stove, Fiona?" Hal asked.

Mum took off her apron and blotted her forehead with it. "I'd like nothing better," she said. She sat on the couch, kicked off her shoes, and put her feet up. "What's the subject under discussion, loveys?"

"We were speculating on whether Adriana bailed Lorenzo out," I said.

"Really? Where would she get that kind of money on a policeman's salary?" Mum asked. "Does she have parents in the area?"

"More to the point," Nigel said, "rich parents who would give her ten thousand dollars to bail her no-good abusive husband out of jail."

"That would be like us giving Antoinette money to bail out that awful Robbie," Mum said.

"It would never happen," Nigel said. "And what about Robbie? He's kind of gone off the radar, hasn't he? Last we heard, he was in Fort Lauderdale, and we've not heard anything since. We don't know whether he killed those people or not. All we know is that he didn't pith them."

"He's been there since the twelfth," I said. "Marian was killed on the seventeenth. David was killed on the twentieth. Why would he wait so long to kill them? That's a whole week."

"I suppose it would make more sense that Adriana killed them," Nigel said, "but we have no evidence she did."

"All we know is that she was in Miami at the right time to kill Marian," I said, "but we have no evidence she was in Fort Lauderdale."

"She could have easily rented a car and driven there," Hal said. "It's only twenty-five miles."

"We also know that a tall redhead was involved with both victims around the times of their deaths," Nigel said.

"But we don't know it was Adriana," I said. "Here's something else. If she killed Marian on the seventeenth and David on the twentieth and came home on the twenty-second, what was she doing the rest of the time? You'd think she'd want to hightail it out of there as soon as she could."

"P'r'aps her supposed filthy-rich parents live in Miami or thereabouts," Nigel said, "and she stopped off to borrow ten thousand dollars before she came home."

"Pete could find out," I said.

"Don't you dare bug him about that on Christmas Day," Hal said before I even had a chance to grab my cell phone.

"This business has me flummoxed," Mum said. "First it was Robbie, then there's this Lorenzo person, and now Pete's partner."

"Adriana," I said.

"Are we now talking about three killers?"

"It's possible," I said. "We know that the first eight victims were killed after Robbie was paroled and before he went to Florida. So either Robbie or Lorenzo could have killed the first eight. Adriana couldn't have, because she was working as a cop."

"Then Robbie went to Florida," Hal said, "but nobody died until Adriana went to Miami, and then two people died."

"So either Robbie or Adriana could have killed them," I said. "Lorenzo couldn't have, because he was here in jail."

"Then she came back," Hal said, "and bailed Lorenzo out of jail, and he tried again to kill Piper and failed and went back to jail."

"And we rather suspect that Adriana finished the job," I said in conclusion. "But there's no evidence except the police guard's description of a tall nurse fooling with the IV."

"But what about the pithing?" Mum asked. "Can you tell who killed whom by the method?"

"We can speculate," I said, "but we don't know for sure. I mean, we know seven of the first eight were pithed, but we don't know about the eighth because she was burned to a crisp. We know Lorenzo had an ice pick on him with human blood on it when he attacked Piper, but we don't know whose blood it was."

"But when he tried to kill Piper in the hospital, he didn't pith her," Hal said.

"Well, that's probably because there was a guard right outside the door," I said. "Pithing would have required turning her to expose the back of her neck. There might have been a scuffle, she might have cried out, and the guard would have come in to investigate, and the game would have been up."

"Wouldn't that have happened if he'd injected air directly into Piper's subclavian line instead of into the IV tubing?" Hal asked.

"Maybe, and that might be the reason he did it that way," I said. "It gave him time to get away before Piper actually died. It was just his bad luck that I came in right after that and stopped the bubble from going any further."

"So why didn't Adriana do the same thing Lorenzo did?" asked Mum.

"Because the guard went to the bathroom," I said. "The nurses were doing report. There was nobody to hear Piper make any kind of noise, and she was dead by the time the guard came back."

A buzzer sounded from the kitchen. Mum sighed and swung her legs down from the couch. "No rest for the wicked," she said, slipping her shoes back on. "That's the roast." She picked up her wineglass and went into the kitchen.

"Can I help with anything?" I asked.

Mum said what she always did: "No, dear, I have it in hand."

I followed her into the kitchen and said what I always did: "You know, you're going to have to teach me how to make Yorkshire pudding sometime."

"I daresay, kitten, but not today. Now, scoot."

"I have to feed the dogs," I said. As if in support, Killer and Geraldine milled around my feet in the doorway.

"You know darn well they're not going to eat dog food when they know they're going to get table scraps!" Hal called out.

I knew when I was beaten. I shrugged and went back to the couch, taking the dogs with me. Then I had an idea.

I went upstairs to the computer and googled Adriana Sinclair.

I found many Adrianas, most of whom were Hispanic. I also found an Adriana Sinclair who was a lecturer in international relations in the School of Political, Social, and International Studies at the University of East Anglia. I did not find a Detective Adriana Sinclair in either the Twin Falls or the Boise police department. Our Adriana Sinclair did not have a Facebook page or a Twitter account and was not on Instagram.

I tried Adriana Collins. I found Facebook pages for three of them, but none of them was our Adriana.

Then I tried searching the Boise Police Department. Other than pictures of Medal of Honor winners, there were no pictures of any officers.

On the TFPD website, there was a picture of the entire SWAT team, but other than that, there were no pictures of any individual officers.

Hal hollered up the stairs. "Toni! Dinner!"

"Coming!" I shouted back as I closed everything I had opened and powered off the computer.

Hal was ceremoniously carving the roast when I arrived at the dinner table. "What were you doing up there?" he asked.

I pulled out a chair and sat down. "Trying to save Pete a phone call."

"What about, kitten?" asked Mum as she passed the mashed potatoes.

"I was Googling Adriana to see if she has filthy-rich parents who live in Florida," I said.

"What did you find?" Nigel asked.

"As you Brits say, no joy."

"Just to be clear," Mum said, "how many of those jurors are left?"

"Just one," I said. "Jeffrey Drummond. And nobody knows where he is."

"He's supposed to be fishing off the coast of Baja California," Hal said.

"Baja California has quite a lot of coast," Nigel said dryly. "When is he supposed to be back?"

"I think Pete said his shop was closed until the end of the year."

"What kind of a shop does he have?" Mum asked.

"Computer repair, I think," I said.

"Does he have employees?"

"I don't know. I guess that's another question for Pete."

Pete dropped in just as we were finishing dinner, but he refused an offer of pumpkin pie. "I've got a turkey dinner waiting at home, and I don't want to spoil my appetite."

"Have you been able to locate Jeffrey Drummond yet?" I asked him.

Pete shook his head. "Not so far."

"Do you know when he's supposed to be back?"

"I think he meant to be gone until the end of the year. At least that's what the sign on his shop says."

"Did Adriana know that?"

"I don't see how," Pete said. "She was supposed to call and check on these people to make sure they were all right, but she didn't do it."

"Do you know anything about her parents?"

"Her parents? No. Should I?"

"I was just wondering where she got the money to bail Lorenzo out."

Pete grinned. "Certainly not from a cop's salary. Maybe she got alimony from Lorenzo."

I shook my head. "They're not divorced. Lorenzo hasn't been able to practice medicine for three years, and he's been in prison for two years, so where would he get that kind of money?"

"Why is that important?"

"I don't know," I said. "Maybe it isn't. It's just a loose end. We know she flew to Miami on the seventeenth. Marian was killed on the seventeenth. David was killed on the twentieth. Adriana flew home on the twenty-second. What did she do on the twenty-first?"

Pete shrugged and turned his palms up. "I don't know. What do you think she did?"

"Go visit her parents and borrow ten thousand dollars?"

"Are her parents in Florida?"

"I don't know. I was hoping you would."

"Sorry. Hey, I gotta go. I just wanted to stop in and say merry Christmas."

"Merry Christmas to you too," Mum said. "Give Bambi and those adorable girls hugs and kisses from all of us."

We exchanged hugs all around, and Pete turned to go, but I detained him. "One more question. Does Jeffrey Drummond have employees? Or a wife?"

"He's divorced," Pete said, "but he does have an assistant—you know, someone to answer the phone while he's working."

I let him go after that, but I was working on another idea. Mum and Hal would hate it, but Nigel might not.

Unfortunately, everything I thought and felt always showed up on my face, so I picked up my plate, took it to the kitchen, and then came back and started clearing the table.

"Kitten, you don't have to do that," Mum said.

"You slaved over a hot stove all afternoon. It's the least I can do."

It also got my face out of sight until the danger passed.

CHAPTER 34

Though this be madness, yet there is method in't.
—Shakespeare, *Hamlet*

On Monday morning, I went in to the hospital. Melinda Roper's brain was now sufficiently fixed to cut, and I also needed to cut in Piper's autopsy tissue, although her brain still needed to fix for another twelve days.

I went directly to the morgue, bypassing my office, to cut the brain. I put sections of the scrambled brainstem in cassettes and representative pieces of the rest of the brain in the bucket with the rest of the autopsy tissue and discarded the remainder of the brain, as I had done with the other brains. Then I retrieved Piper's tissue bucket and took it into histology.

Mike was doing a frozen section when I got there. "Hey," he said, "I know you. Didn't you used to work here?"

"Very funny," I replied. "How are you two coming along with your autopsies?"

"We aren't," he said. "We've been slammed. We're already over thirteen thousand surgicals for the year."

"Wow," I said, "that's a new record." A thought came into my head, and I tried to suppress it. Hal would hate it if I took more time away from him and my parents to—

Mike took the decision out of my hands. He placed the frozen tissue on a metal chuck, put it into the cryostat to freeze, slammed the lid shut, and turned to me. "Toni, would you consider finishing them up for us?"

Damn. Now what? They had given me an extra week of vacation. How could I refuse? I could at least tell Hal it wasn't my idea.

"I will," I said, "on the condition that you have already dictated the gross and provisional diagnoses."

"We have," he said.

"Okay," I said. "Just put their folders on my desk."

He heaved a sigh of relief. "Thanks. That'll be a huge help, I tell you what."

I did feel marginally better upon reflection that each of them had only done one autopsy apiece. I put Melinda Roper's brainstem sections into the basket with the surgicals to go into the tissue processor and set Piper's tissues to rinsing in the sink.

Then I went back to the morgue, retrieved Robin Renee Jones's brain, set it to rinsing in the sink there, and then carried her tissue bucket back to histology. From there, I went to my office.

The only folder on my desk was Melinda Roper's. I fired up the computer and entered Robin's case number. There were the gross description and provisional diagnoses. But when I called up Penelope Leroux, there were no gross description and provisional diagnoses. *Tsk-tsk*, I thought.

I stuck my head into Brian's office. "Hi," I said.

"Toni! What a surprise! Are you here to finish up my autopsy for me?"

"Yes. Mike asked me if I would."

He opened a file drawer and pulled out a folder. "Here you go. Are you going to do Mike's too?"

"As soon as he dictates the gross," I said. "I didn't see it in the computer."

"Uh-oh," he said. "I bet he forgot all about it."

"Let's just hope he didn't forget what he saw, because I can't fake that, especially in a homicide."

I took the folder back to my office and went back to histology, where I cut in Piper's tissues and put the tissue cassettes in a separate container of formalin. Then I set Robin's tissues to rinsing and went back to the morgue, where I cut her brain, and then back to histology, where I cut in her other tissues.

When I got back to my office, I found Penelope Leroux's folder on my desk. I took it back to Mike's office and put it back on his desk.

He looked up. "What's this?"

"You haven't done the gross dictation."

"Yes, I did."

"It's not in the computer."

"You're shitting me." He turned to his computer, where the electronic medical record was already open, and pulled up Penelope's case number. "Damn. You're right. I could have sworn I did that."

"Let me know when you get that done, and I'll come back."

"Okay. Sorry about that."

I went back to my office and shut down my computer. Then I remembered the idea I'd had yesterday, and I called Pete to sound him out on it.

"Toni! What's up?"

"Do you remember when we set a trap for Tyler Cabot back in the day?"

"Yes." His voice sounded guarded, as if he really didn't want to hear what I was going to say. "Why?"

"I was just wondering if we could set one for Adriana."

"Adriana! Why her?"

"Because she went to Florida and murdered Marian and David and then came back and murdered Piper, and now we're down to only one juror."

"Toni, we have no concrete evidence that Adriana killed anybody. It's all circumstantial. No judge in his right mind would issue a warrant for her arrest."

"I know you can't just go to her house and arrest her, but—"

"Toni, stop. I can't get you involved in anything like that. Hal would kill me."

"Pete, listen to me. Just listen. As far as we know, Jeffrey Drummond is still in Mexico. He's not due back until New Year's. We could start a rumor that he's coming back early and stake out his shop or his house to see who shows up. What do you think?"

"I think you're out of your ever-lovin' mind," Pete said.

"We'd be saving Jeffrey Drummond's life," I said.

"What *we*, white man?" Pete said. "I'm not including you in any stakeout. If there's gonna be a stakeout, it's gonna be done by cops, not amateurs."

"So you think it's a good idea, just not with me?"

"I didn't say that."

"You could run it by Bernie. Just don't mention me."

Someone knocked on my office door. I turned to see Ryan Trowbridge standing there. I pointed to the phone and motioned for him to come in.

Pete said, "You better believe I won't mention you."

"So you're going to do it?"

"Damn it, Toni, I didn't say that!"

"Let me know how it goes. I gotta go now. Bye!"

Ryan Trowbridge lowered his considerable bulk into my visitors' chair and said, "Do what? Who was that?"

"That was my son-in-law, and I think I may have talked him into staking out Jeffrey Drummond's shop or house or both."

"To what purpose?" Trowbridge asked. "He's not supposed to be back for another week."

"My idea was to start a rumor that he was coming back early and make sure Adriana knows it and then do the stakeout to see if she shows up."

"Why can't they just arrest her and be done with it?"

"Because the evidence is all circumstantial. They have a record of her flying to Miami and back and a series of tall redhead sightings. Nothing to link her to any of the killings so far."

Trowbridge rubbed his chin. "Hmm. I suppose I could help with the rumor portion of our program."

"Our program?"

"Certainly. You and I could stake out his house. Or his shop. What do you say?" He held out his hand.

I shook it. "I'm in."

He stood up. "How do I get in touch with you?"

I scribbled my cell phone number on a Post-it note and gave it to him. "Don't call me," I said. "I might not be able to talk freely. Text me."

He held out a hand for the Post-it pad. I gave it to him, and he wrote down his cell number and gave it back.

"I'm on it," he said, and he left.

Hal was going to kill me.

My mother would help.

How the hell was I going to keep a straight face under the scrutiny of the two people who knew me better than anybody in the world, one of whom could see right through me?

Had I seriously conspired with a reporter to set a trap for a murderer? A murderer who was also a cop? Would she recognize it for what it was and refuse to fall for it?

Even if she did fall for it and show up, would it even be admissible in court?

What if she showed up with her gun? Would she even be able to keep it while on administrative leave? I googled it and found that officers were most commonly placed on administrative leave after a shooting, so their guns were confiscated as evidence. In some jurisdictions, the officer was issued a replacement gun, and in others, he or she was allowed to carry a personally owned gun only.

Adriana hadn't been involved in a shooting, so she probably did still have her gun. So she could simply shoot me or, worse, Trowbridge.

Then I'd be responsible for his death. I couldn't live with that.

I should probably just cancel the whole thing.

I had to talk to Nigel. Alone.

I shut down my computer and went home.

CHAPTER 35

Where sits our sulky, sullen dame,
Gathering her brows like gathering storm.
Nursing her wrath to keep it warm.

—Robert Burns

When I walked in the door, Mum was fixing roast beef sandwiches for lunch. Killer and Geraldine lurked in the doorway, waiting for fallout. Mum looked up when I came in.

"Kitten! Have you been at the hospital this whole time? You're just in time for lunch. Here—take this tray into the living room for me, would you?"

"Soon as I take my coat off," I said. I hung it in the closet and then took the tray she held out, which was piled with sandwiches cut neatly in quarters.

Hal and Nigel were watching a movie on TV when I came in. "Where do you want this?" I asked.

"Right here on the coffee table," Hal said. "What have you been doing all this time? I thought you just had to cut in one autopsy."

Mum came in right behind me with a pile of napkins in one hand and a relish tray in the other and put them down on the coffee table. "Kitten, would you mind helping me with the tea?"

I accompanied her back to the kitchen, where she fetched four cups and poured tea into them. I grabbed two, and so did she, and we went back to the living room and sat down to eat.

"In answer to your question," I said, "I thought that was all I had to do, but Mike had other ideas." I told them about being asked to help the boys with their autopsies.

"They've got a lot of nerve," Hal said.

"Well, I actually was thinking about offering to do that before they asked," I said. "They're getting hammered by all the surgicals, and they did offer me an extra week of vacation, after all."

"So how many autopsies are we talking about?"

"They only did one each, and I've already cut in one of them," I said, "and two brains."

"Humph."

"Antoinette, really," Mum said. "Could we possibly talk about something else?"

"What is this we're watching?" I asked. "Is that Cary Grant?"

"It's *The Bishop's Wife*," Hal said, "with Loretta Young and David Niven. Cary Grant plays an angel."

"Oh."

Conversation flagged while we ate, and I tried to think of a way to get Nigel alone without having it show on my face, but nothing doing. The four of us sat and watched the rest of *The Bishop's Wife* and then the old black-and-white version of *Miracle on Thirty-Fourth Street* before Pete dropped in.

He snagged a beer from the fridge and came into the living room with a big smile on his face. "Toni! I'm glad you're here."

Where else would I be? I thought uncharitably. *It's my house.* "Have you got news?" I asked politely.

He sat down on the couch. "I ran your idea by Bernie, and he likes it! We're going to stake out Jeff's shop tomorrow night."

"Don't you need to stake out his house as well? Maybe he won't go right to his shop when he gets in."

Hal folded his arms across his chest. "Toni," he said severely, "this was your idea?"

"Yes," I said meekly.

"And Kincaid likes it?"

"He thinks it's my idea," Pete said.

"Ah." Hal managed to get an entire paragraph into that one syllable.

"And in answer to your question, Toni, Jeff lives in the back of his shop. It's in one of those old houses out on Addison."

No wonder the house on Jeff's website looked familiar. I'd probably driven past it countless times and paid no attention, except to wonder what it would be like to live in a house like that.

"Oh. That's handy. And how are you going to make sure Adriana knows about Jeff coming home early?"

Pete put a finger to his lips and looked mysterious. "We have our ways."

"And what time is he supposed to get home tomorrow night?"

"He will come in on the eleven o'clock flight and take an Uber home."

"And who's going to be in the Uber, just in case anybody's watching?"

"A couple of cops."

"One of them being you?"

"No. Adriana knows me. I'll be waiting at the shop to meet them."

"How are you going to get in?"

"I got a key from his assistant."

Okay. Now I knew what to tell Trowbridge.

"Why do you want to know all this stuff?" Pete asked. "You're not planning to be there, are you?"

I looked at Hal. He was glaring. I looked at my mother. She had her fingers to her mouth, and her eyes were wide.

I shook my head. "Nope. It's way past my bedtime."

They both visibly relaxed.

Nigel got up. "Libations?"

"I thought you'd never ask," I said.

After dinner, I went upstairs, ostensibly to check email, and fired up the computer in order to google "Jeffrey Drummond Computer Repair" to find out the exact address on Addison. I wrote it down on a Post-it and stuck it in my pocket.

Then I texted Ryan Trowbridge. I sent the message and immediately deleted it in case Hal got on my phone for any reason.

Tomorrow I'd do a drive-by and a little reconnaissance.

On Tuesday morning, we woke up to snow again.

Most of the snow from the previous storm had melted, and what was left was all black from dirt on passing cars. It needed a new coat of white.

I decided I'd pretty much have to go back to the hospital that day, because I'd need my car to do my snooping around, and the hospital was the only excuse I could think of to drive anywhere without anyone suspecting.

So after breakfast, I did so.

I went to my office first. There by my microscope was a tray of autopsy slides on Robin Renee Jones, as well as brain slides on Melinda Roper, so I did have a reason to be there if anyone asked.

I fired up the computer and got into the EMR. There still was no gross description for Penelope Leroux.

I finished up Melinda Roper's autopsy and signed it out. Then I looked at Robin's slides, not expecting any significant pathology in an outwardly healthy fifty-five-year-old female, and got a surprise.

Robin had chronic hepatitis. She had significant liver damage with fibrosis and had focal areas of cirrhosis. I hadn't noticed that when I cut in the liver samples.

Had she known she was that sick?

I went back to the EMR and looked her up.

Nothing.

I called Natalie. "Do we have any autopsy blood on Robin Renee Jones?"

"Just a minute, Dr. Day. I'll go look and call you back."

She called me back a few minutes later. "We've got one red top tube."

"Good. I need an acute hepatitis panel."

"Okay."

Our acute viral hepatitis panel included hepatitis B surface antigen, hepatitis B surface antibody, hepatitis B core antibody, anti–hepatitis C, and anti–hepatitis A IgM, which would tell me everything I needed to know.

I hoped Brian hadn't cut himself doing that autopsy.

I took the tray into his office and sat down opposite him at his microscope.

"What's this?" he asked.

I put a liver slide on his microscope stage. "Robin Renee Jones. You need to see this."

He took one look and recoiled. "Holy shit!"

"I'm having her tested. You didn't cut yourself, did you?"

"No."

"Good."

"Thanks for letting me know."

"No problem."

I finished dictating the microscopic and shut down the computer. Then I left.

Ryan Trowbridge intercepted me as I opened the door to the parking garage. I wasn't surprised. After all we'd been to each other, I would have been disappointed if he hadn't.

"We have to stop meeting like this," I quipped.

"I got your message, Doc."

"Good. I'm going to do a drive-by. Want to come?"

"Sounds like a good idea. Right now, you mean?"

"Yes, right now."

When we reached my car, he opened the door for me, as before. "You'll bring me back to get my car, right?"

"Of course."

The snow was still falling as we exited the underground parking, and by then, it was two or three inches deep. Luckily, the grounds crew had spread ice-melt around, and the major streets had already been plowed and sanded.

I drove south on Washington and turned left onto Addison, heading east. The house was located on the north side of the street, just a few houses west of Eastland. I made a left turn and drove into the driveway. There were parking spaces off to the side of it. I pulled into one of them, and we got out.

"Are you sure we should do this?" he asked.

"Do what? You mean look around?"

"Park here. They won't be expecting anybody to be parking here while the place is closed, and they might get suspicious."

I looked around. "That's true. But we'll be leaving footprints too. Hopefully the snow will cover them up before tonight. And by the way, we won't be driving in here tonight. We'll park in the grocery store parking lot and walk over."

"Good idea."

"That front door is probably the entrance to the shop, so the living quarters are probably around back."

"You lead the way, Doc."

We made our way around the side of the house, noting that the tall trees sheltered much of the driveway that continued on past the house and ended in a small detached garage in back. At the back of the house was a large enclosed porch accessed through a screen door.

"Oh, this is nice!" I exclaimed. "I wish we had something like this in back of our house. I'll have to bring Hal here so he can see it." I mounted the steps, reached for the screen door, and nearly fell right back down the stairs. Luckily, Trowbridge was right behind me and caught me.

The screen door was open.

I walked right in and tried the back door to the house, which was locked. I stood on tiptoe and saw someone moving around inside.

A tall redhead.

Shit!

I ducked down and got off the porch in record time. Trowbridge followed as I hightailed it down the driveway to my car.

"What?" he panted behind me.

"Adriana's in there," I hissed. "Hurry—get in!"

"She didn't see us, did she?"

"I hope not." I backed rapidly out of the space, headed down the driveway, and barely stopped for oncoming traffic as I got onto Addison and headed back in the direction of the hospital. Again, Trowbridge directed me to where his car was parked, and I let him out.

"Now what?" he asked.

"I'll meet you in the grocery store parking lot at eleven tonight."

"So we're still going to do this?"

"Yes. I'm going to call Pete and let him know about Adriana, and if there's any change, I'll text you."

"Okay."

I drove back into the parking garage, parked, and called Pete.

CHAPTER 36

The pellet with the poison's in the
flagon with the dragon,
The vessel with the pestle has the brew that is true.
—Norman Panama and Melvin Frank

"**Y**ou did what?"

Pete did not sound happy to hear that I'd been snooping around Jeff Drummond's property. I didn't even mention Trowbridge.

"I went up onto the back porch and looked through the window in the back door, and guess who I saw inside?"

"Toni, I don't have time for games."

"Adriana."

"What!"

"What would Adriana be doing inside Jeff Drummond's house?"

"Your guess is as good as mine. I have no idea."

"She would have needed a key. How'd she get a key?"

"I don't know. If she knew Jeff Drummond, I didn't know about it."

Then I had an idea. "You don't suppose she was dating him, do you?"

"How would I know that? She hardly ever talked to me."

"It would be a reason for her to have a key, and she'd have a legitimate reason to be in there. Maybe she was doing some housekeeping to make the house ready for him to come home to."

Pete chuckled. "Maybe she was planning to be there for him to come home to."

"That's going to screw up your stakeout, isn't it?"

"It might. We're going to have to work out something else."

Uh-oh. Now what am I going to tell Trowbridge?

"She might even drive out to the airport to pick him up," I said.

Pete chuckled again. "Then she's gonna be mighty pissed when he doesn't show up."

"Anyway, I thought you needed to know she was there."

"You're right about that, but, Toni, promise me you'll stay away from that place tonight. It could be dangerous if you're caught."

I couldn't make Pete a promise I had no intention of keeping.

"Don't worry," I said instead. "I'll stay safe."

That must have been close enough for Pete because he said, "Okay," and he hung up.

The rest of the day passed like molasses in January. I vacillated between keeping it all to myself and taking Nigel aside and telling him what I was planning to do that night. I had no idea what to tell Trowbridge, because I had no idea what Pete's plan was going to be. So I didn't tell him anything.

I spent most of the afternoon upstairs on the computer, aimlessly surfing the web, letting each website lead me to another, and then another and another, with no goal in sight. The last thing I wanted to do was sit downstairs with Hal, Mum, and Nigel, making aimless conversation about the case, for fear I'd let something slip, or my face would give me away.

After a couple hours of that, I heard heavy footsteps on the stairs. Assuming it was Hal, I hastily switched to a catalog website so he would think I'd been shopping online.

But it was Nigel. He tapped on the doorjamb. "Can I come in?"

"Of course."

He sat in one of the recliners. Naturally, Hal and I both had recliners up there too. Comfort ruled.

"Fiona's wondering if something's wrong," he said. "I volunteered to come up and check."

Here was my chance. "As a matter of fact, I need to talk to you about something I don't want Hal and Mum to know about."

He leaned forward with his elbows on his knees. "Do tell, old girl."

I got up and pulled the door almost but not quite shut. Then I sat down in the desk chair and pulled it close to Nigel so we could converse in tones low enough to prevent being overheard.

I'd no sooner done that than Killer poked his nose in, and I had to let him come in so he wouldn't whine and scratch and attract attention.

"Pete is planning to stake out Jeffrey Drummond's shop tonight," I said. "His shop's in the front, and he lives in the back. He let it slip that Jeff is coming back early and will fly into Twin on the eleven o'clock flight tonight."

"You don't say. I suppose you're planning to be there?"

"Yes. In fact, I did a little recon today, and I saw Adriana inside."

"Blimey!"

"Sh! Not so loud. I got out of there, and I don't think she saw me. Then I called Pete and told him she was there."

"I daresay that's going to bollix up their stakeout, eh, what?"

"Probably. Pete and I were speculating that maybe Adriana has been dating Jeff and has a key to the place, so maybe she's there legitimately."

Nigel nodded. "You do realize, however, that the other more likely reason she's there is to lie in wait to kill Jeffrey."

"Yes, I do. And I'm also aware that she probably still has her gun."

Nigel leaned back in the recliner and gave a heavy sigh. "Toni, old dear, this is an incredibly dangerous thing you're planning to do, and I'm not going to let you do it alone."

"I won't be alone. Ryan Trowbridge will be there too."

"The reporter?"

"Yes. Do you want to come too?"

"I thought you'd never ask."

By then, it was late afternoon, so when Nigel and I came back downstairs, he went straight to the bar to prepare libations, and I went to the kitchen to see if I could help with dinner, but Mum and Hal had it in hand, as the Brits say.

"What were you doing up there all that time?" Mum asked.

"Shopping online," I said.

"What did you buy?"

"Nothing. I didn't see anything I liked enough to pay the prices they were asking, and then with shipping and handling on top of that."

Mum and Hal were both satisfied with that answer, so I retreated to the couch with a book and Geraldine.

Dinner was an ordeal. I didn't dare meet Nigel's eyes, for fear someone would notice and wonder what was going on. It seemed Nigel was no better than I was at keeping his facial expressions under control.

After dinner, while the three of them watched TV, I

surreptitiously rummaged through the bin in the closet where scarves, gloves, and hats were kept, and I found two black balaclavas that Hal and I used for skiing and other outdoor winter sports. I stuffed them into the pockets of my black peacoat and then joined the others in front of the TV and promptly fell asleep on the couch.

When Nigel shook me awake, the TV was off, and so were most of the lights. Hal and Mum had gone to bed. Nigel was already dressed in dark trousers and Hal's dark gray coat. I was already wearing black pants, which nobody would question because I wore black pants a lot.

I silently got off the couch, put on my peacoat, and picked up my car keys and cell phone, and we tiptoed out by way of the front door. Fortunately, Hal always put the Jeep in the garage, and my Subaru stayed outside so that if I got called at night, he wasn't blocking my car. The downside was, of course, that I had to scrape the windows in the winter before I could go anywhere. I had managed to do that earlier in the afternoon, after it had stopped snowing.

Unfortunately, the snow had started again, so I still had to brush it off the windows. Then I started the car, hoping the sound wouldn't wake Hal or Mum, and drove to the grocery store where we were to meet Trowbridge.

Trowbridge was already there. I recognized his car. He'd parked it over to the side of the building, where the lights from the store wouldn't illuminate it. I parked back there too, and we got out.

Trowbridge was wearing his big brown parka with the hood that pretty much concealed his face. I introduced him to Nigel. Then I pulled the balaclavas out of my coat pockets and gave one to Nigel before donning the other.

Before putting gloves on, I directed them to program each other's cell numbers into their phones so we could text each other if necessary, and we made sure our phones were set on vibrate.

Then we walked up the sidewalk to the Drummond house. It wasn't easy going. The snow was lumpy and uneven where people had walked during the day, and it was slippery in places, and snow boots were clumsy at the best of times. I hoped we wouldn't have occasion to try to run in them.

To my surprise, lights were on inside the house. The garage door was open, and the garage was empty and dark. *Adriana must have gone to the airport*, I thought.

Nigel stationed himself in the shadow of the front entrance. Trowbridge and I continued back to the garage, where I hid inside, and Trowbridge hid in the shadow of the back porch.

Nothing much happened for the first maybe five minutes, but then my phone vibrated, and I read a text from Nigel: "Car turning in."

It wasn't necessary, because I could see the headlights, but more importantly, I realized they would light me up like a Christmas tree if I stayed where I was. I ran around the side of the garage and hid in the shadows.

Unfortunately, I wasn't quite fast enough. Adriana saw me. She drove into the garage, jumped out of her car, and ran around the garage after me. I kept moving, but she was faster. The next thing I knew, she had jammed the barrel of her gun into the back of my neck right where, I thought, the ice pick would go if she was going to pith me.

For the second time, all I could think was *Oh my freakin' Lord, I am so dead.*

But she didn't shoot. Instead, she grabbed my arm and turned me so that I faced her, and the gun was pointing right at my heart. "Who the hell are you, and what are you doing here?" She sounded angry, and I remembered she'd been expecting Jeff Drummond at the airport, and he hadn't shown up.

That would have made any girl pissy, even without an

unknown intruder in the backyard, so I kept quiet. With sudden fury, she ripped my balaclava off.

"You!" she hissed. "Why are you always in my way? Do I have to kill you?"

"I don't think so," I said, simultaneously stomping on her instep and slamming the heel of my hand into her nose.

She howled in pain, dropped the gun, and put both hands to her nose, which was pouring blood. Miraculously, she stayed on her feet but not for long.

An arm went around her neck, pulling her backward. She crashed to the ground on top of her assailant, and while they thrashed around on the ground, I picked up the gun and put it in my coat pocket.

"Doc! Are you all right?"

I turned to see Trowbridge crashing toward me through the bushes in back of the garage.

"I am now," I said.

He threw his arms around me. "Thank God! I saw her pull a gun on you, and I thought—"

"No worries," I said, pulling the gun out of my pocket and showing him.

"How the hell did you do that?"

I told him what I'd done. "It seems she couldn't hold a gun and her nose at the same time."

Nigel appeared from the other side of the garage. "Bloody hell," he said. "What's all this?" He grabbed Adriana's assailant, hauled him to his feet, and shone a flashlight into his face. The man was a little heavier, his hair was longer and darker than I remembered, and he had a dark tan, but otherwise, he looked pretty much the same, especially when he smiled.

I stared in astonishment. "Robbie?"

Adriana remained crumpled on the ground.

Headlights lit up the trees surrounding the garage, and a car door slammed. Pete came running around the garage and fetched up behind Nigel. He stopped, staring in fascination at the tableau before him, before he looked at me and said, "Toni, you promised."

I handed him the gun. "Sorry."

I heard another car drive up, and two car doors slammed. Two more police officers came around behind Pete, who stepped aside. "Arrest those two," he said. "Toni, come with me. Your husband and mother are worried about you."

I followed him back out to the driveway, where Hal and Mum stood next to Pete's SUV. *Damn*, I thought, *I am so busted.*

It was a toss-up which one of them would get arms around me first. It was a veritable Toni sandwich until Hal loosened his grip and said, "You've got blood on your hand."

Nigel was hugging Mum. He turned to look and said, "She's lucky that's all she's got."

"It's Adriana's," I said. "I gave her a nosebleed."

"Good for you!" Hal said.

Mum sniffed and said, "Antoinette, really."

CHAPTER 37

The play's the thing, wherein we
catch the conscience of a king.
　　　　　—Shakespeare, *Hamlet, Act II, Sc. 2*

I t figured. Mum was still trying to make a lady out of me and
failing miserably.

We were still standing there, when one of the police officers
came out gripping the arm of a handcuffed Robbie, whose coat
was covered in a mixture of snow, mud, leaves, and twigs. He
did not look at me.

Mum peered at him. "Is that who I think it is?"

"It's Robbie," I said, "and it looks like he's let his hair grow
and dyed it black."

"And what's all that caterwauling back there?" Mum asked.

Apparently, the second police officer was trying to get
Adriana on her feet, and she wasn't having any truck with it.

"I broke her foot," I said. "She probably can't walk."

"Who's back there?" Hal asked.

"Adriana."

The first police officer, having put Robbie in his police car, came back to help his partner. Together they managed to get a filthy and combative Adriana into Pete's car. Her face was covered in blood.

"How are we going to get home?" Mum asked. "We can't ride in a police car surely, not with her."

Adriana was still yelling, mostly epithets aimed at me.

"Well, I'm guessing she's not going to let me borrow her car," I said. "We'll have to walk."

"Walk?" Mum gasped. "In this?"

"I can take you home," I said. "But my car is at the grocery store down the street. Trowbridge's car is there too."

"Trowbridge!" Hal said in disgust. "What's he doing here?"

"Covering the story," I said.

Trowbridge came up behind us. "That's right," he said. "Thanks to the doc here, I got an exclusive."

I introduced him to Mum and Hal. Hal was just short of rude, and Mum looked bewildered. "But Antoinette," she said, "I thought you didn't like him."

"I didn't," I told her, "but he turned out to be a good guy."

"Just a minute," Hal said. "Did you two arrange this together?"

"Three, actually," Nigel said. "We knew there was going to be a stakeout, and we just arranged to be here—that's all."

"Pete told me about it," I said, "but he wouldn't let me come with him."

"I should hope not," Mum sniffed.

Pete came up to us. "We're done here," he said, "but I can't let you go home yet. You're going to have to come to the station to help us untangle this mess."

"Look here," Nigel said, "surely Fiona and Hal can go home. They had nothing to do with this."

"Of course they can," Pete said. "I didn't mean them.

Unfortunately, we seem to be somewhat short of cars at the moment."

"I can walk down and get my car," I said. "Assuming you trust me to come to the station afterward."

"But, kitten," Mum said, "it's not safe."

"I'll go with her," Nigel said.

"Me too," said Trowbridge.

"See?" I said. "I have two big, strong men to protect me."

She kissed me. "Be careful, kitten."

Pete said, "Go ahead. I'll see you later."

We reached the parking lot without incident. Trowbridge went straight to the station, and I drove Nigel back to the Drummond house, picked up Hal and Mum, and took them home. After that, Nigel and I went to the police station.

It was quite a party. I almost expected to find pizza, but no such luck.

Adriana and Robbie were in holding cells, out of sight but not out of earshot. I couldn't make out words, but they were clearly having an argument.

Pete met us at the desk and escorted us to an interrogation room in which Bernie was waiting. He didn't look happy.

"I wish you'd tell me, Toni, just what it is we're supposed to be charging these people with."

"Murder comes to mind," I said.

"Well, that seems to be a problem. We have no proof that either of them committed murder."

"Well, Robbie violated his parole, and I know for a fact that Adriana stuck a gun in the back of my neck. Does that help?"

"Not much. Chief Inspector, what do you have to say about this?"

"Eleven people have been murdered," Nigel said. "All of them were members of a jury that convicted Robert Simpson of kidnapping and attempted murder. That would tend to implicate Robert Simpson, would it not?"

"Robert Simpson maintains that he didn't murder anybody, and we have no concrete evidence that he did."

"Bernie," I said, "I realize that everything we have is circumstantial, but the fact remains that the three people involved are finally all behind bars, and the twelfth juror is still alive."

"Actually," Nigel said, "we don't know that for a fact either because nobody has been able to contact him."

"In fact," Pete said, "the only one of the three we can pin anything on is Lorenzo Collins, who assaulted and attempted to murder Piper Briscoe, and that's because we do have concrete evidence."

"Wait," I said. "Were you able to match the black hairs we found at autopsy to Lorenzo yet?"

"Oh jeez, I forgot all about that," Pete said. "I'll check first thing tomorrow."

"How about the DNA on the ice pick?" I asked. "Does it match any of the victims?"

"We don't have that information yet," Bernie said.

"Could I make a suggestion?" I asked.

"If you must," Bernie said repressively.

"You must have noticed that Adriana and Robbie are having a hell of an argument back there in the holding cells. Might it be possible to record what they're saying?"

"Not without violating their rights," Bernie said. "We'd have to let them know they're being recorded, and then they wouldn't say anything."

"So I suppose the same would apply to putting Robbie and Lorenzo together in an interrogation room and recording what they say?"

"Probably," Bernie said. "Why do you think that would reveal anything useful?"

"Robbie was paroled for good behavior, part of which consisted of giving legal advice to other inmates and helping them with their appeals. Maybe Lorenzo was one of them."

Bernie shook his head. "Sounds like a long shot to me."

"What would it hurt?" Pete murmured.

Bernie shot him a sharp look but did not reply. "Have either of them lawyered up?"

"Not yet," Pete said. "Lorenzo Collins hasn't either."

"He didn't retain Clark Dane again?" I asked.

"Not so far."

Bernie turned his attention back to me and Nigel. "Is there any reason I shouldn't arrest both of you right now for interfering in a police investigation?"

"Yes," I said. "We didn't interfere. We got there before anybody else, and you would never have known we were there if Adriana hadn't pulled a gun on me."

"And that reminds me," Nigel said. "What about that reporter johnnie?"

"He means Ryan Trowbridge," I said. "He was there too. Didn't he come here? He said he was going to."

"We haven't seen him," Pete said. "Maybe that's him now."

A minor commotion ensued out in the main office, which culminated in the arrival of Ryan Trowbridge, escorted by another police officer, who roughly manhandled him into the room with us and slammed the door.

"What the hell was that for?" Trowbridge said. "I haven't done anything."

"What took you so long?" I asked him. "I thought you were going to come straight here."

"I had to file my story," he said, "so that it comes out in tomorrow's paper."

Bernie threw up his hands and rolled his eyes much like Hal did when he yelled, "Oy gevalt!" to the ceiling. "This is turning into a goddamn circus. We're gonna have to split you up."

He went out of the room and came back with two other policemen. He assigned one to Nigel and one to Trowbridge and sent them to two other interrogation rooms. Then he said, "Toni, you stay here. I'm going to interrogate you myself."

Oh goody. My heart sank to my toes.

"I'm going to record this," he said. "I assume that's all right with you?"

"Am I in trouble?" I asked. "Do I need a lawyer?"

"That's entirely up to you," he said.

"Then I'm going to call Elliott," I said, and I took my cell phone out of my coat pocket.

Bernie stood up. "Then I'll leave you to it. Open the door when you're done." He went out, closing the door behind him.

I called Elliott. Predictably, he was not pleased to be dragged out on a night like that.

"Toni, do you realize what freakin' time it is?"

I looked at my watch. To my astonishment, it was nearly midnight. "I'm at the police station, and I need a lawyer."

"Do you want to tell me about it?"

"Pete arranged a stakeout at Jeffrey Drummond's house tonight. He put it out there that Jeffrey was coming home tonight—to see who would show up to kill him."

"Okay."

"Nigel, Ryan Trowbridge, and I got there before anybody else, hid, and waited. Adriana came back first."

"What was she doing there?"

"I forgot to say that I did a drive-by this afternoon, and I saw her inside the house. I told Pete about it. I don't know what she was doing there."

"Okay. Go on."

"I was hiding in the garage, and I realized she'd see me if I didn't get out of there, so I went and hid in the bushes."

"What did she do?"

"She saw me. She drove into the garage and came after me with a gun."

"Jesus Christ!"

"Actually, I didn't know she had a gun until she stuck it in the back of my neck."

"Then what?"

"She turned me around and ripped my balaclava off, and then she got mad."

"*Then* she got mad?" Elliott echoed.

"She doesn't like me," I said. "She asked me why I was always in her way and if she had to kill me. I said I didn't think so and stomped on her foot and punched her in the nose and gave her a nosebleed."

"Holy shit," he murmured. "Remind me not to get you mad at me."

"She dropped the gun. Then somebody came up behind her and dragged her down, and they were fighting on the ground. I picked up the gun and put it in my pocket. And then Trowbridge came up behind me and asked me if I was all right, and then Nigel came around the other way and yanked the guy up onto his feet, and it turned out to be Robbie."

"No freakin' way!"

"Oh yes. Then Pete arrived with Hal and Mum, and two more cops came after him and arrested Robbie and Adriana."

"What happened to the gun?"

"I gave it to Pete."

"So is that it?"

"Pretty much. I took Mum and Hal home first, and then Nigel and I went to the station."

"Voluntarily?"

"Yes. I mean, Pete wanted us to."

"Did he arrest you?"

"No, but Bernie suggested that *he* might for interfering in a police investigation. And then he split us up, and we're all being interrogated."

"You haven't told him anything, have you?" Elliott asked with a note of alarm.

"No. That's why I wanted to talk to you."

"Good. Don't say anything else until I get there. I'm on my way."

"Thank you," I said with relief, but he had already hung up.

Bernie knocked on the door. I motioned for him to come in. "Are you done?" he asked.

"Yes. Elliott's on his way, and he said for me not to say anything until he gets here."

"Peachy," Bernie said. "You can wait for him in here." He closed the door a little more firmly than seemed necessary. This was clearly the pissed-off Bernie, not the amorous one.

Elliott arrived about ten minutes later. One of the other police officers showed him to the room I was in.

"Are they treating you all right?" he asked.

"More or less," I said. "Bernie seems pissed, but I haven't seen a billy club or a rubber hose yet."

"Good. Is there anything else you need to tell me before you let Kincaid interrogate you?"

"I don't think so."

"Okay. I don't see that there's anything in what you have told me that would get you in any more trouble than you're already in. So let's get Kincaid in here and get it over with."

"Okay."

He went out and returned with Bernie in tow. Bernie sat down and turned on the tape recorder. "This is Captain Bernard Kincaid interrogating Dr. Toni Day, December 28, 2016, at 0045 hours with her consent. Her attorney, Elliott Maynard, is also present. Dr. Day, would you please tell me in your own words what transpired at the home of Jeffrey Drummond on East Addison in Twin Falls, Idaho, tonight?"

As always, I had to bite my tongue so as not to ask whose words he thought I might use instead. I told him the story exactly as I had told it to Elliott.

"Thank you," he said when I had finished. "How did you know there was going to be a stakeout at that address and at that time?"

"Pete and I talked about it. I wanted him to take me with him, but he refused."

"I should think so. Why did Lieutenant Vincent even mention it to you?"

Now we were getting into dangerous territory. I looked at Elliott. He shrugged.

"I suggested to him that we should set a trap for the killer by spreading a rumor that Jeffrey Drummond was coming home early."

"So the whole stakeout was your idea?" He raised his voice and looked angry—that was, angrier than he had looked the whole time I'd been there.

I hesitated. I didn't want to get Pete in trouble, but I also didn't want to lie to the police.

"I suggested it, but I think Pete had already thought of it."

Bernie looked narrowly at me but apparently decided to let it go. He turned off the tape recorder and stood up. "We'll get this typed up and will call you to come in and sign it."

"So I can go?"

"Yes."

"What about Nigel?"

"We were done with him some time ago. He's out in the waiting room, wondering what took you so long."

To me, that sounded like a slam at my decision to get a lawyer, and I lost my temper. "If you hadn't threatened me with arrest, *Captain* Kincaid, I wouldn't have had to get a lawyer, and it wouldn't have taken so long."

Bernie stepped back with his hands raised defensively.

"I'm just saying," I added.

He didn't try to stop us as we walked out the door. In fact, I thought I saw a ghost of a smile before the door closed behind us.

CHAPTER 38

"There's no use trying," said Alice: "one
can't believe impossible things."
"I daresay you haven't had much
practice," said the Queen.
"When I was your age, I always did
it for half-an-hour each day.
Why, sometimes I've believed as many as
six impossible things before breakfast."
—Lewis Carroll

Clearly, Mum and Hal had tried to wait up for us, but sleep had overtaken both of them. Mum, in her pajamas and bathrobe, was curled up on the couch, while Hal, fully dressed, snored in his recliner.

It would have been nice to just tiptoe past them up to bed and not have to hash over the evening's events while exhausted and sleepy, but they would never have forgiven us if we did that.

Plus, we had two dogs who had to wag their tails, whine, and click their toenails on the kitchen floor in greeting.

Mum took the decision out of our hands by waking up. "My goodness," she murmured, "what time is it?"

Nigel went over and kissed her. "It's after two, my love. Shall we go upstairs?"

I watched in amazement as Mum got up and followed Nigel up the stairs without a word. Did I dare just leave Hal sleeping and go up to bed? No, I decided, I'd never hear the end of it.

I went over and kissed him. He came awake with a start. "Holy shit. What the hell time is it?"

I channeled Nigel. "It's after two, my love. Shall we go upstairs?"

He squinted at me. "Who are you, and what have you done with my wife?"

I shrugged. "It worked for Nigel," I told him.

He brought his recliner upright and looked around. "Where are they?"

"They've gone to bed. Shall we do the same?"

"Not so fast. What happened at the station?"

"We all gave statements."

Hal looked at his watch. "For over three hours?"

"Well, Bernie threatened to arrest us for interfering in a police investigation, so I called Elliott."

"Bastard," Hal growled. There was no love lost between Hal and Bernie. Years ago, when Hal and I had been having marital problems, he'd suspected Bernie and I were having an affair. We hadn't been, but the whole thing had left Hal with a bad taste in his mouth.

"He was unsure what he was supposed to charge Robbie and Adriana with exactly, and it made him pissy."

"Are you shittin' me? How about murder of almost an entire jury?"

"Well, that's the problem, you see. All the evidence they have is circumstantial. The only thing concrete is that Lorenzo attacked Piper and then tried to kill her, and that's because there was concrete evidence."

Hal frowned. "So are they in jail or not?"

"They are so far. Robbie violated his parole, and Adriana pulled a gun on me. Robbie attacked her. They're in holding cells, and last I heard, they were having a hell of a fight."

"What were they fighting about?"

"I don't know."

"It might be something the police should know about."

"I mentioned that to Bernie and also suggested he should get Lorenzo and Robbie together in an interrogation room and see what happens. He wasn't interested."

"That figures," Hal said. "Let's get some sleep."

"Good idea."

We all slept late Wednesday morning and were still not quite awake as we sat around the kitchen table, nursing cups of tea or, in Hal's case, coffee. Hal had brought in the paper, taken a cursory glance at the front page, and handed it to me.

"You may as well be the first to read this," he said.

"Why don't you read it aloud, kitten?" Mum said. "I'm too sleepy for newsprint this morning."

So I did.

Two Jury Killer Suspects Arrested

Two suspects in the Jury Killer case were apprehended last night in a police sting operation. Robert Simpson and Adriana Sinclair are now in custody at the Twin Falls County Jail.

The Twin Falls Police carried out a sting operation at the home of Jeffrey Drummond, the remaining member of the jury that convicted Robert Simpson of kidnapping and attempted murder eleven years ago.

By circulating a rumor that Drummond, now

vacationing in Mexico, would be coming home early, police officers were able to stake out Drummond's home and apprehend anyone who might show up to kill him.

Robert Simpson, who was convicted of kidnapping and attempted murder in 2005, was paroled after serving eleven years of a twenty-year sentence. After violating the terms of his parole, he will most likely be returned to Idaho State Penitentiary to serve out the remainder of his sentence.

Adriana Sinclair a detective sergeant in the Twin Falls Police Department, is on administrative leave because she is married to the third suspect, Lorenzo Collins, who is now in custody, charged with the attempted murder of juror Piper Briscoe, who died December 24.

Specific charges against these three suspects have not been filed. Investigations are proceeding as to what part each of the suspects played in the killings of these eleven jurors.

"Huh," I said. "He didn't even mention me."

"That's a first," Hal said. "I wonder why."

"I'm not surprised," Nigel said. "None of us were supposed to be there. If he mentioned any of us, he'd have to mention that he was there too. It would be awkward, you see."

"Not only that," I said, "but when Bernie threatened me with arrest, he was also threatening Nigel. If one of us was interfering in a police investigation, we all were. Bernie doesn't need any more ammunition."

"I'm just curious, kitten," Mum said, "and I hope you won't mind my asking, but had Robbie changed much?"

"Not too much," I said. "He looked a little heavier, and his hair was longer, and it looked as if he'd dyed it black. Plus, he had a really dark tan. In fact, you know, with longer, blacker hair and a dark tan and without glasses on, he might be able to pass for Lorenzo if one didn't look too closely at his face. They're the same height and build."

"Are you suggesting it was Robbie who tried to kill Piper?" Nigel asked.

"If that's true, then Lorenzo doesn't need to stay in jail," Hal said. "But it had to be Adriana who actually killed Piper."

"Maybe not," I said. "If Robbie wore scrubs, a surgical cap, and a stethoscope around his neck, he could pass for Adriana in low light. The guard said the nurse was wearing glasses too."

"The light couldn't have been too good behind the garage, even with a flashlight," Hal said. "Yet you knew it was Robbie."

"It would have been hard not to," I said. "He smiled. I'd know those buck teeth anywhere."

"Toni, old dear, I deduce that you're trying to cast doubt on Adriana and Lorenzo having had anything to do with killing Piper," Nigel said. "But how do you explain Robbie passing as Adriana with her long red hair uncovered in broad daylight?"

"I can't," I said. "So maybe we can't eliminate Adriana. I mean, it's still possible that Lorenzo killed the first eight, Adriana killed the last three, and all Robbie did was make grisly Christmas cards, but I can't figure out why either Lorenzo or Adriana would want to kill off Robbie's jury."

"What I want to know," Hal said, "is how Robbie got hold of the jury list. I mean, Elliott had to use his office computer and still needed a password and a PIN."

"If Robbie was helping other inmates with legal matters," Mum said, "he would have needed access to computers and legal websites, and maybe he had a password and a PIN."

"That's a thought," I said. "That's very likely how he did it."

"But how did he manage to drown Marian and poison David

Lord?" Mum asked. "He could hardly masquerade as a tall woman with long red hair who was most likely wearing beach attire."

"He would have had to be wearing scuba gear to be able to pull someone under and keep her there long enough to drown," I said, "especially if he had to wait for them to walk down the beach and get in the water without being seen. I remember reading about someone who did that in a John D. McDonald mystery."

"And somebody else besides the tall redhead in the bar could have poisoned David Lord's drink," Nigel said.

"Like who?" Hal asked.

"How about the bartender?"

"Pete could check out dive shops in Miami," I said, "especially in the Virginia Key Beach area. He could also send Robbie's picture to the hotel where the Lords were staying and ask if they'd hired a bartender who looked like that around the time Robbie went there."

"He would have had to have a fake ID," Mum said.

"I daresay he had connections from being in prison," Nigel said.

"Then what was Adriana doing in Miami?" Mum asked.

I shrugged. "Maybe she was just visiting her parents. It would be easy enough for Pete to find that out."

"Then what was she doing at the Drummond house last night?" Mum said.

"She's a cop," Hal said. "Maybe she just wanted to be in on it, like some other people I could name." He winked at me.

"Pete and I were speculating about whether or not she was dating Jeffrey Drummond," I said. "I saw her inside the house earlier in the day, so I figured she must have a key, and last night, when we got there, the garage was empty, and she came back right after that, so maybe she went out to the airport to meet him, and then when he didn't show up—no, that won't work. If she went to the airport and he wasn't there, why would she think he'd be at the house?"

"Now we're back at the cop scenario," Hal said. "Why did Robbie attack her?"

"To save me probably," I said. "She was holding a gun on me and threatening to kill me."

"But you broke her nose and made her drop the gun before that happened," Nigel said.

"True," I said, "but she was still on her feet, even though I'd broken one of them."

"Okay, that takes care of Adriana," Hal said, "but what about the ice pick? If Lorenzo didn't kill anyone, why did he have an ice pick with human blood on it in his possession?"

"That's a little trickier," Nigel said. "Maybe Robbie gave it to him to hold until he got back from Florida, although I can't imagine Lorenzo would be stupid enough to take it."

"Still, he was carrying it around when he attacked Piper," I said. "It suggests he was planning to use it on her."

"Why attack her otherwise?" Mum asked.

"Because she challenged him about his badge," I said, "and he has anger-management issues. Maybe that was enough to set him off."

"Why did Robbie come back?" Hal asked. "All this time, we were thinking he'd gone to Fort Lauderdale to get out of the country and go someplace without extradition."

"If he really did kill all the other jurors himself," I said, "he came back because he wasn't finished. Otherwise, I have no idea."

Hal groaned and ran his fingers through his hair until it stood on end. "I've had enough of this. Why don't we stop talking about it and wait for Pete to drop over after work?"

CHAPTER 39

There is less in this than meets the eye.

—Tallulah Bankhead

After breakfast, I called Mike to see if he'd dictated the gross on Penelope Leroux's autopsy yet. He had, so I went to the hospital to cut it in.

The brain was problematic because she had been shot in the head. Her brain was actually in pieces, which made it difficult to section in a way that would accurately show the extent of the damage. Other than that, the cutting-in was pretty routine. She had no other significant pathology.

Natalie brought me the results of Robin Renee Jones's lab work, which showed she had hepatitis C. I showed it to Brian and thought to myself how ironic it would be if Robbie—or Lorenzo—had accidentally stuck himself with the ice pick and died in prison of hepatitis C. It would be as if she'd killed him back, the ultimate revenge.

After that, I did the grocery shopping and then the laundry, so Mum and Nigel would have less of it to do when they went home in four days. It didn't seem possible.

Pete showed up around five o'clock and helped himself to a beer. The four of us descended upon him, peppering him with questions. He held up his hands defensively.

"Whoa, whoa, one at a time! Who do you want to hear about first?"

"Robbie," I said.

"Robbie denies ever having killed anyone," Pete said. "He says he went to Florida to get away from the snow for a few days."

"He violated his parole to 'get away from the snow for a few days'?" I asked in disbelief. "Doesn't he know he's just going to have to go right back to prison?"

Pete shrugged. "That's his story, and he's stickin' to it."

"What about Adriana?" I asked.

"Adriana went to Florida to visit her parents in Miami," Pete said. "You were right about that, Toni. She gave us their phone number, and they confirmed that she was there the whole time."

"She didn't go to Fort Lauderdale?"

"Apparently not."

"Did she go to Virginia Key Beach?"

"No. They went to the beach but not that one."

"Did she bail out Lorenzo?"

"Yes. She got the money from a payday loan place."

I covered my forehead with my hand. "Oh jeez. She's going to get killed on interest."

"Antoinette, dear, could you possibly put that another way?" my mother asked.

Hal and Nigel chuckled.

"Sorry," I said. "So she has an alibi for all the murders?"

"Pretty much."

"Is she going to be able to go back to work as a detective?"

"Yes, but not here," Pete said. "She's already got two reprimands, and Bernie doesn't want her back."

"Oh." I wasn't sure how I felt about that. On the one hand, I didn't much like Adriana, but that sounded like sex discrimination, which made me mad. It was not the time to say that, however. "So is she out of jail?"

"Yes. We let her go this afternoon."

"What about Lorenzo?" Hal asked.

"If we can prove that Robbie made the failed attempt to kill Piper, Lorenzo can be out on bail until his trial, but until then, he'll have to stay where he is."

"Hey," I said, "what about those black hairs from Piper's hospital gown? And the ones from the other autopsies? Do they match Lorenzo?"

"Jeez, I forgot all about that," Pete said. "I'll check on it tomorrow."

"You were going to check on it Wednesday," I said. "And you know what else? You could see if they match Robbie."

"You're right, Toni," Pete said. "I should have thought of that."

"I have a couple suggestions too," I said. "It occurred to me that Robbie could have rented scuba gear and pulled Marian down under the water long enough for her to drown and also that he could have gotten a job as a bartender at the hotel in Fort Lauderdale and poisoned David Lord."

"What you're saying is that the two tall redheads were red herrings."

"Yes. Tall redheaded herrings."

Pete chuckled. "I'll run those ideas by Bernie and not mention you."

"Perfect."

"Any news on the blood on the ice pick?" Nigel asked.

"Not yet. There's a backlog, you know. This isn't television, where they have to get the DNA back within sixty minutes or less."

Pete sounded frustrated, for which I couldn't blame him. Most people didn't understand that science couldn't be rushed, and unfortunately, some of them were physicians.

After Pete left, we finished dinner, and then I retired to the couch with a book, a scotch, and Geraldine. Hal and Nigel watched ESPN. I didn't know or care what was on, because anytime something involved two or more players and a ball, Hal would watch it on TV.

My mystery novel held my attention for a while, until a disquieting thought niggled its way into my subconscious and wouldn't take no for an answer.

What if there was no evidence connecting Robbie to any of the murders? What if they had to let him go, as they had Adriana? What would he do next?

Well, first, I figured, he'd wait for Jeffrey Drummond to come home so he could kill him. Then he'd come after Hal and me.

That was the reason Mum and Nigel had come to visit us early in the first place.

Then we had Lorenzo and Adriana and their possible roles in the murder scheme to think about. If the murders had been committed by either or both of them, that threat was no longer a concern.

But whom would the black hairs match?

I knew our lives might depend on the answer.

CHAPTER 40

The game is afoot.

—Sir Arthur Conan Doyle

On Thursday morning, I went back to the hospital to read out the autopsy slides on Penelope Leroux and sign out the case. That was the last of the autopsies; all were done and signed out before the end of the year.

After I was done, I called Pete.

"Toni, what's up?"

"The hair, Pete. The hair."

"Oh. Well, none of it matches Lorenzo."

"Does that mean he gets out of jail too?"

"He's getting processed as we speak."

"I assume he's going back to Adriana's house?"

"She's here to pick him up. It won't be for long, though, because his trial is tomorrow."

"Are you serious?" I was startled. Even though I knew his trial was scheduled for December 30, it seemed so soon.

"As a heart attack," Pete said. "Oh, and here's something else.

We finally got the DNA report back on the ice pick Lorenzo had. The blood doesn't match any of the victims."

"No! Really? Who does it match?"

"You won't believe it."

"Come on. Who?"

"It matches him."

"It's his own blood?" I asked incredulously.

"Told you you wouldn't believe it."

"So he cut himself with it? What was he doing?"

"Chipping ice out of Adriana's chest freezer. She told us that just now."

"Was there an elk involved?" I asked, because that would have been too coincidental.

Pete chuckled. "No, he just wanted to do her a favor."

"Okay. Does that mean Robbie has an ice pick of his own?"

"Well now, that's another thing. Robbie didn't use an ice pick. He used a shiv, which he made by filing the handle of a toothbrush to a point. We found it in his coat pocket."

"Did it have blood on it?"

"Not so's you'd notice," Pete said. "But we sent it off to the lab anyway."

"When will you know about whether the hair matches Robbie?"

"You'll be the first to know."

That wasn't really true, I knew. He would. I'd be second.

"I'm not trying to be a nag," I said. "It's just that I'm afraid that if he gets out of jail, he'll go kill Jeff Drummond and then come after Hal and me, and Mum and Nigel are here."

"Don't worry, Toni. He's not going anywhere."

I let it go at that. Pete had told me everything he could. All that was left was matching the hairs to Robbie.

If they didn't match, then what?

Would that mean Robbie was innocent?

That in turn would mean Hal and I were safe, and so was Jeff Drummond.

But the police would have to start over from scratch with no suspects in sight.

I turned off my computer and prepared to go home, but a young man standing next to Arlene's desk detained me.

"Are you Dr. Toni Day?"

"Yes."

He handed me an envelope. "You've been served."

I wasn't surprised. I'd known all along that I would have to testify about Lorenzo's attack on Piper Briscoe, in which I'd played a major role by physically defending her. I'd have been surprised if they hadn't subpoenaed me.

I was sure they'd also subpoenaed Mitzi and the two security guards.

Ryan Trowbridge waylaid me just outside the pathology office. He had an envelope suspiciously like the one sticking out of my purse. He pointed his at mine. "You too, huh?"

"Yep."

"Have you heard anything new from your son-in-law?"

I looked up at him coquettishly. "How did you know?"

"I didn't. That was a shot in the dark. I was just on my way over to the police station to talk to him. So you have heard something new?"

"Yes, a couple somethings. The black hairs I found on some of the bodies do not match Lorenzo."

"Do they match Robbie?"

"I don't know yet. Also, the blood on the ice pick Lorenzo was carrying does not match any of the victims."

"Who does it match?"

"It's his own blood," I said. "He cut himself with it while

trying to chip ice out of Adriana's chest freezer—and before you ask, it was not because of an elk."

He chuckled.

"And finally," I said, "Robbie didn't use an ice pick. They found a shiv on him. He'd filed the handle of a toothbrush down to a point."

"That's three somethings," he said.

"I know. Consider it a bonus. But you probably ought to go talk to Pete anyway. Maybe by now he knows if the hairs match Robbie."

Pete called me again after I'd gotten home. "The hairs match Robbie," he said. "You and your family are safe."

"Oh, thank God," I said.

"What did he say?" Hal asked.

I told him.

"I say, that's pretty convincing evidence, eh, what?" Nigel said.

"There's something else," Pete said. "The lab wants the tissue from the pithing sites to see if the puncture wounds match the shiv. Can you do that?"

"Sure."

"The sooner the quicker," he said. "Can you get those to me today?"

I looked at Hal, who was looking back at me with a question in his eyes. "I'll go back to the hospital right now and take care of that," I said.

"Thanks. You're the best."

"Right back at you."

After I hung up, Hal said, "Well?"

I told him.

He shrugged. "Go get it done. A scotch will be waiting for you when you get back."

In the morgue, Natalie helped me collect all the tissue buckets from the autopsies of the eight victims. "What are we doing this for?" she asked.

"They found a shiv on Robbie," I told her. "They want to see if the puncture wounds match it."

"Wow," she said. "That's really cool. It's a good thing you thought to do that."

While I dug around in the formalin to retrieve each of the pithing sites, she labeled plastic baggies for me to put them in. When that was done, she accompanied me back to my office, carrying the eight baggies in a plastic basin.

"We need a chain-of-evidence log," I said, and I found a yellow legal pad in one of my drawers. I wrote the names of all eight victims and then the words "tissue from pithing site back of neck," and Natalie and I both signed it with the date and time. "That should do it," I said. "Thanks for your help. I'll bring that basin back later."

"Don't worry about it," she said. "We have tons of them."

"Wow, that was fast," Pete said when I showed up at the station. "And you did a chain-of-evidence sheet too. I'll just pack these all together in the same box with it—after I make a copy for our records, that is."

I produced an extra baggie. "You'd better put it in here in case anything leaks."

"Oh, good idea. You going home now?"

"Yes. A scotch awaits."

"I'll be along when I'm done here."

Pete showed up just after five, snagged a couple beers out of the fridge, gave Hal one, and settled on the couch. Geraldine jumped up into his lap, fickle female that she was.

"Your buddy Trowbridge showed up right after you left," he said. "He said you told him everything, but he wanted to check with me before he put anything in print."

"I know," I said. "I told him to. And now he knows about Robbie too."

"Things are moving fast," Hal said.

"Not fast enough for me," Mum said. "I won't rest easy at night until they put him away where he'll never again see the light of day."

Pete pointed at my purse, which was sitting on the coffee table with the summons sticking out of it. "Is that what I think it is?"

"Yes. I've been served."

"Me too," he said.

Mum said, "Served? With what?"

"Subpoenas," I said. "We both have to testify tomorrow at Lorenzo's trial."

"That's tomorrow?" she asked in surprise. "Dear me! So much has happened that I forgot all about that. We'll all have to go and give you moral support, kitten. You too, Pete."

"Of course," he said, and he drained his beer. "I'm going to go home now and kiss my girls."

"And get a good night's sleep," I said. "I know I'm going to now that Robbie's no longer a threat."

"Amen," said my mother.

CHAPTER 41

The jury, passing on the prisoner's life
May in the sworn twelve have a thief or two
Guiltier than him they try.
—Shakespeare, *Measure for Measure*

Lorenzo's trial was scheduled for ten o'clock Friday morning. Besides Pete and me, they had also subpoenaed Russ Jensen, Rod Alexander, Mitzi Okamoto, and the two security guards.

Hal, Mum, Nigel, and Jodi were present, seated toward the back of the room. Those of us who had to testify sat in a row along the front, right behind the defendant and his lawyer, my old buddy Clark Dane. Elliott, who was representing Piper, sat alone at the plaintiff's table, because in this case, the plaintiff was dead.

Adriana sat alone in the row behind us, directly behind Pete.

The jury sat along the west wall.

The bailiff announced the judge, and we all stood while Judge Robert Welch ascended to his lofty perch.

"You may be seated," he said.

We all resumed our seats.

Judge Welch swore in the jury and then said, "The defendant will please rise."

Lorenzo and Clark Dane stood up and faced the judge.

"Well, well, Mr. Collins. How nice to see you again."

Lorenzo said nothing. I saw Clark Dane grip his arm, probably to stave off any outburst that might lead to contempt of court.

"I see your manners have improved since I saw you last. Let's see now. You've been charged with assault and battery by Ms. Piper Briscoe. Is Ms. Briscoe present in the courtroom?"

Elliott stood up. "Your Honor, Ms. Briscoe is unable to be here today. You have her statement in evidence."

"Ah yes, Mr. Maynard, I see that. Why is Ms. Briscoe unable to be here today?"

"She's dead, Your Honor."

A gasp spread across the courtroom. I struggled with an insane urge to giggle as I thought of the old song "Miss Otis Regrets She's Unable to Lunch Today," about a lady who shot down her unfaithful lover and was subsequently strung up by an angry mob.

Judge Welch banged his gavel once. "Order in the court, please. Mr. Maynard, are you telling me that Ms. Briscoe has died of her injuries? That would require that the charge be changed to involuntary manslaughter."

In front of me, Lorenzo put his elbows on the table and his head in his hands. I could almost hear what he was thinking: *Oh no, not again!*

"No, Your Honor. Ms. Briscoe was murdered. The suspect is in custody."

"So this defendant will not be charged with her murder?"

"No, Your Honor."

"You may now make your opening statement to the jury."

Elliott did so, and then Clark Dane made his opening

statement, which was basically that the defendant had had no intention of inflicting harm on Piper Briscoe. He couldn't very well say Lorenzo hadn't done it, not with two eyewitnesses, both of whom were doctors.

"Mr. Maynard, do you wish to call any witnesses?"

"Yes, Your Honor, I call Dr. Rodney Alexander to the stand."

Rod stood and made his way to the witness stand, where he placed his right hand on the Bible and swore to tell the truth, the whole truth, and nothing but the truth, so help him God.

"Dr. Alexander, please tell the jury who you are and where you work."

Rod testified that he was a board-certified orthopedic surgeon who practiced at Cascade Perrine Regional Medical Center.

Elliott took him through a detailed description of what compartment syndrome was, what caused it, what could happen if it was not treated, and what the treatment consisted of. Then he turned Rod over to cross-examination.

Clark Dane approached the witness stand.

"Dr. Alexander, is the procedure you performed on Ms. Briscoe the standard of care in Idaho?"

"Yes, sir."

"How many times have you performed this procedure?"

"About fifty, sir."

"And has anybody ever died from this procedure?"

"Not by me, sir."

"So how likely is it that Ms. Briscoe could have died from this procedure?"

"Very unlikely, sir. She was healing up nicely and was due to be discharged the next day."

"No further questions."

Judge Welch dismissed Rod, and Elliott called Russ. He asked Russ the same questions he'd asked Rod, and Russ testified that he agreed with Rod in every particular regarding compartment syndrome.

Clark Dane then asked Russ the same questions he'd asked Rod, and Russ testified that he was a board-certified general surgeon and that he had only assisted with the procedure, and then only about ten times.

"In your opinion, how likely was it that Ms. Briscoe could have died from this procedure?"

"Very unlikely," Russ said. "She was ready to be discharged the next day."

"No further questions, Your Honor."

Russ was dismissed, and Elliott called Mitzi.

"Dr. Okamoto, please tell the jury who you are and where you work."

Mitzi did so.

"Was Ms. Piper Briscoe known to you?"

"Yes, she worked in my department as a CT technician."

"What does CT stand for?"

"Computerized tomography."

"That sounds very specialized," Elliott said. "You must have been very sorry to lose her."

"Yes, we all were. It was a major shock, and we're all in mourning. Piper was well liked."

"Dr. Okamoto, please tell the jury what happened the afternoon of December fourteenth."

"I heard a commotion in the hallway outside the CT control room and went to see what was going on."

"What did you see?"

"I saw Piper being harassed by what I thought was a disgruntled physician. He grabbed her by both upper arms and shook her, and she was crying out in pain."

"What did you do?"

"I ran as fast as I could to intercede and find out what it was all about." A flash of anger crossed Mitzi's normally expressionless face. "I don't like to see my employees being abused."

"Why did you think he was a physician?"

"He was wearing a white coat."

"Was he wearing a hospital badge?"

"No, he wasn't, and he wasn't anybody I recognized."

"Is he present in the courtroom today?"

"Yes. He's the defendant."

"Did anyone else see what happened?"

"Yes. Toni Day was in the hallway, and I passed her as I ran. She came running after me."

"Dr. Toni Day the pathologist?"

"Yes."

"What did she do?"

"She barreled right into them and pushed that doctor so hard that he fell on his butt."

"My goodness. Then what happened?"

"She yelled at him about compartment syndrome, and he called her a bitch and threatened to have her fired and to sue her."

"What did you do then?"

"I called security. They sent two guards, who took him away. Then I took Piper up to HR so she could report the incident."

Elliott had no more questions, and Clark Dane didn't either. Then Elliott called me.

"Dr. Day, please tell the jury who you are and where you work."

I did so.

"Please tell the jury what happened on the afternoon of December fourteenth in the radiology department."

"They call that diagnostic imaging now," I said. "I was walking down the hall, looking for Piper Briscoe."

"You were looking for her? Did you know her?"

"No, I'd never met her before. I was looking for her because she was on the jury that was being targeted by the Jury Killer. I wanted to talk to her."

"Then what happened?"

"I heard a commotion down the hall, and then Mitzi came running past me like a bat out of hell, and I followed her."

"What did you see?"

"I saw Piper being assaulted by what appeared to be a disgruntled physician. I mean, I didn't know she was Piper until afterward, but anyway, he gripped her by the arms, and I knew that could cause compartment syndrome, because the same thing happened to me. It made me mad, so I just charged in there, knocked his arms away from her, and slammed him in the chest. He fell down and yelled at me that he was going to get me fired and sue me. He got back up and took his cell phone out of his coat pocket, and an ice pick fell out."

"My goodness. Then what happened?"

"I stepped on the ice pick before he could pick it up. I asked him who he was and why he wasn't wearing a badge, and then the security guards showed up. He pushed me, grabbed the ice pick, and tried to run, but they caught up with him and took him away. I told them to call the police because he had an ice pick and might be the Jury Killer."

"What did you want to talk to Piper about?"

"Well, the police had been trying to sequester the members of that jury in hotels around town, but two of them got killed anyway, so Piper refused to go to a hotel. I invited her to come stay with us. She said she'd think about it."

"Then what did you do?"

"I called Pete and told him what had happened."

"Pete being your—"

"My son-in-law, Detective Lieutenant Pete Vincent."

"Did Piper ever take you up on your invitation?"

"Hal, my husband, went to the hospital and brought her home."

"And she stayed with you until when?"

"Until she developed compartment syndrome and I took her to the emergency room."

"You said earlier that the same thing happened to you. Can you tell the jury about that?"

Clark Dane said, "Objection. Not pertinent to the case."

"Your Honor, Dr. Day's testimony is relevant in light of the defense's questions about how Ms. Briscoe might have died from the procedure."

"Overruled," the judge said. "I'd like to hear this myself."

I explained, "Compartment syndrome occurs when a muscle is injured and bleeds and swells until the fascia surrounding it cannot stretch to accommodate it. The swelling compromises nerves and blood vessels, cutting off circulation. The muscle can become necrotic, and it could cause loss of a limb if not treated."

"But could such a patient die from it?" Elliott asked.

"Yes," I said. "The dying muscle releases myoglobin and potassium into the bloodstream. The myoglobin can plug up the kidneys and cause renal failure, and the potassium can go high enough to stop the heart."

At that, I heard a few gasps from the jury. They looked around at each other with shocked expressions. A couple of the women had their fingers to their lips.

"What does it feel like?" Elliott asked.

"It hurts," I said. "It hurts more and more every day, even when keeping ice on it, and finally, one's hands become cold and numb."

"Is that what happened to you?"

"That's what happened to me, and that's what happened to Piper. She had the same procedure I had back in 2010, when it was brand new. In fact, I was the first patient Rod Alexander did it on. He'd just come back from a conference where he learned about it."

"So you were a guinea pig," Elliott said.

"Yes, but I didn't mind. See, this procedure is laparoscopic and only requires a couple of small incisions. The old procedure required big, long incisions all up and down the arms." I gestured at my own arms, describing the extent of the incisions required, at which the jury gasped again. "I would have had to lie there with my arms laid open like that for two days with my muscles hanging out there in the air before they could sew them up again. There would have been more blood loss and an increased risk of infection."

Elliott released me for cross-examination, but Clark Dane had his elbow on the table and his hand over his face and merely shook his head when asked if he had any questions.

I had to restrain myself from showing my glee at having done in Clark Dane a second time, this time in open court. I wondered if he'd make a dash for the men's room, but he remained where he was while Elliott called Pete to the stand.

Pete corroborated my phone call and described his interview with Piper and Mitzi. "And then Hal showed up and took Piper home with him," he said.

The two security guards described how they had detained Lorenzo until the police arrived.

Elliott and Clark Dane made their closing statements to the jury, and with that, the trial was over. The judge charged the jury, and they went away to deliberate, while the rest of us went to lunch.

Except for Clark Dane, of course.

The jury was already back when we returned to the courtroom after lunch. They returned a unanimous verdict of guilty.

"Mr. Collins," Judge Welch said, "you have been convicted of one count of assault and battery. The usual sentence for that is six months in county jail or a fine up to one thousand dollars or both."

I heard a sigh of relief from Adriana. But the judge wasn't through.

"However, that's for a first offense. You, Mr. Collins, have recently served a two-year prison sentence for involuntary manslaughter. Therefore, this is your second offense, which carries a sentence of one year in county jail or a fine up to two thousand dollars or both. In light of the severity of your first offense and the severity of Ms. Briscoe's injuries, I sentence you to one year in county jail and a two-thousand-dollar fine. Bailiff, take him away."

The bailiff did so.

"Toni?"

I turned to see who was talking to me. It was Adriana, and she was actually smiling. "Toni, I want to apologize for being so nasty to you. I wish I could have told you what was bothering me that day in the morgue, but I just didn't want to talk about it to anybody."

I put my hand over hers on the back of my seat. "It's okay, Adriana. I get it."

"Lorenzo nearly killed me, and I'm still in love with him."

"Then you're probably angry that he got the maximum sentence."

"Not really," she said. "It's not a good idea for Lorenzo and me to live together, but we've found that we can be friends. He's signed the divorce papers, and I've filed them, and now I can get on with my life. I'm going back to Boise to start over."

"I wish you luck," I said, and I meant it.

EPILOGUE

When you have eliminated the impossible, whatever
remains, however improbable, must be the truth.

—Sir Arthur Conan Doyle

Robbie had killed them all.

The black hairs found on four of the first eight murdered jurors matched him.

He'd made the grisly Christmas cards at the halfway house where he and Lorenzo were staying. He knew Lorenzo from prison, where he'd helped Lorenzo with his appeal. He'd managed to get Lorenzo's ten-year sentence reduced to two years.

He'd mailed the cards as soon as he killed the victims, and because the mail had to go to Boise to be processed, I hadn't gotten them until the victim had been dead for two days, and I never did get the card about Eleanor Morehouse and her house a-burning.

The card for Melinda Roper had been hand delivered by Lorenzo, who, curious to see what the woman Robbie was so obsessed with looked like, had peeped in the windows to get a glimpse of me, until Killer had bitten him on the butt.

Robbie had pithed the first eight and arranged their bodies to look like a hit-and-run, a stabbing, a shooting, a suicide, hypothermia, a car fire, a bathtub drowning, and a hanging. The shiv he'd been carrying matched the puncture wounds from the pithing.

But he had run into an unexpected glitch when he found out that both Marian Chandler and David Lord had gone to Florida.

Using a computer in the Twin Falls Public Library, the same library in which he'd killed Penelope Leroux, he'd googled Marian and David and found the same information I had found.

Using a fake ID he'd obtained in prison, he'd flown to Fort Lauderdale and obtained a job as a bartender at the hotel where the Lords were. The restaurant manager had recognized Robbie's mug shot. "Only his hair was different," the man had told Pete. "It was long and wavy and was always falling in his face and looked a lot darker than this. It looked like he'd dyed it. I told him he'd have to cut it off if he couldn't manage to keep it out of his face. You can't have that in the food business."

On his first day off, he'd driven to Miami and located Marian's daughter's house. He'd hung around and followed them wherever they went, and they had gone to Virginia Key Beach, where the kids could go to the amusement park, and Marian had either fallen asleep in the shade or gone up and down the beach, looking for shells.

He'd spread his towel in a spot right next to her and struck up a conversation. Marian had liked to talk, so he'd had no difficulty in finding out that they were planning to come back to that beach on Saturday, December 17.

Pete had been able to locate the dive shop where Robbie had rented his scuba gear on Friday, December 16. The proprietor had recognized Robbie's mug shot but also commented on the hair being different and the dark tan the fellow had.

Robbie had hung around the neighborhood, waiting for the family to get packed up and head for the beach. He'd followed them, watched where they set up, and then gone into a public restroom and donned his dive gear. He'd gotten into the water, swum out far enough to dive down twenty or thirty feet, and then surfaced and waited.

He'd watched while the mom and children went across the street to the amusement park, after having talked to a tall redheaded lady who had set up next to them, where he had been the week before. He'd watched as the two women struck up a conversation, and when they both had gotten up and walked down the beach, he'd followed them in the water.

Pete had been able to talk to the policeman who had interviewed the redhead when she reported Marian's disappearance. Robbie had gotten his chance when the redhead went into the water and coaxed Marian to join her. "Come on in; the water's fine," she'd called out, and after a few seconds, Marian had gone into the water too. The redhead had swum out almost to the spot where Robbie waited, so Robbie had dived down about fifteen feet. Soon both women had been cavorting about in the water just above him. After a few minutes, the redhead had swum back toward shore, and that was when he'd grabbed Marian by the ankle and pulled her down. When the redhead had reached the beach, there had been no sign of Marian.

The police report from the precinct where the beach was located stated that the redhead had gone to the nearest business to report Marian's disappearance, which had just happened to be the dive shop. The proprietor had called the police, and they'd investigated, but they hadn't found Marian until she washed up on the beach three days later.

Meanwhile, Robbie had returned the rented scuba gear and gone back to Fort Lauderdale.

On the morning of Monday, December 19, he'd spied the Lord family having breakfast in the restaurant. David Lord had ordered a bloody Mary, and Robbie had brought it to him, spiked with the contents of some sleeping pills he had managed to acquire.

David had drunk it all down and ordered another. Robbie had brought it to him and returned to the bar, where he'd prepared a Bloody Mary for a tall redheaded lady in a sarong, who had gone over and sat down with the Lord family and knocked over David's Bloody Mary. Robbie had watched while she gave her drink to David and came back to the bar, where he'd fixed her another, most likely thanking his lucky stars that she'd waited until David drank his first drink before she showed up and spoiled everything.

Pete had checked the airlines and found that Robbie had flown back to Twin on Thursday, December 22, the day before the person we'd assumed was Lorenzo made his failed attempt on Piper's life by tampering with her IV. The nurse who'd seen him hadn't recognized Robbie's mug shot, but she also hadn't recognized Lorenzo's. "I'd remember somebody that yummy," she'd said. "It definitely wasn't him."

The police guard had recognized Robbie's mug shot. "I'd know those buck teeth anywhere," he'd said.

So the evidence piled up. Robbie would most likely be convicted on at least six of the eleven jurors he'd killed, if not all of them.

At his arraignment on Monday, January 2, 2017, Robert Simpson was indicted for eleven counts of first-degree murder. His case was remanded to district court in Boise.

I did not attend. I was working. The way I saw it, Mike and Brian owed me at least six autopsies. At the rate we usually got autopsies, I figured I shouldn't have to do another until at least 2020.

Why, I might even forget how!

Praise for *Murder under the Microscope*

Murder under the Microscope is an exemplary first novel.

——*US Review of Books*

As a winner of an IP Book Award for Excellence, I wasn't the least surprised that this book was selected.

—*GABixler Reviews*

Praise for *Too Much Blood*

Munro's writing is entertaining, believable, and fast-paced. She takes you into the autopsy room, shows the fragility of the characters, and makes the readers feel they are inside the story. Readers will definitely be looking forward to solving more cases with this character.

—*US Review of Books*

Exceptional realism that only comes from personal, hands-on experience. Munro writes with captivating flair, and her story line is believable and realistic.

—Charline Ratcliff, *Rebecca's Reads*

Praise for *Grievous Bodily Harm*

Sassy pathologist Toni Day shines in this modern-day mystery of corporate shenanigans and hospital politics … A smart, enjoyable summer read.

—*Kirkus Reviews*

Munro's story is a roller coaster ride of suspense and intrigue, with twists and turns that will entertain a lover of mysteries and forensic crime novels for hours.

—*US Review of Books*

The author brilliantly shares her expertise in forensic pathology, allowing readers inside the room during the autopsy, and sharing her expertise and knowledge.

—Fran Lewis, BookPleasures.com

Praise for *Death by Autopsy*

A solid mystery far from DOA.

—*Kirkus Reviews*

If this is your first Toni Day novel, you'll want to go back and start the series from the beginning.

—*BlueInk Reviews*

Fans of medical drama and mysteries will be sure to love this fast-paced and fact-laced romp through the world of pathology.

—*US Review of Books*

This book is a fantastic crime thriller. You won't be able to put it down until you finish reading it. I loved it. I gave it 5 stars but it deserved many, many more. I highly recommend this book to everyone especially if you enjoy crime and thriller books. You will love this one. I look for more from Jane Bennett Munro.

—Marjorie Boyd-Springer, *Goodreads*

Praise for *The Body on the Lido Deck*

An entertaining murder mystery to cruise through.

—*Kirkus Reviews*

The Body on the Lido Deck will keep readers guessing until the action-packed end. And when it's all over, the story's satisfying solution will leave them eager to explore Toni Day's other adventures.

—*BlueInk Reviews*

This book offers believable dialogue, a breakneck pace, and a unique story that breathes new life into the literary murder-comedy genre. It's Jessica Fletcher meets *CSI*, with the usual crime-scene gore and droning medical jargon now wrapped up in a charming, entertaining package.

—*Clarion Reviews*

The mystery's nomadic setting—on a cruise ship still on course for its vacation destinations—and the protagonist's go-getter attitude make for an enthralling beach read.

—*US Review of Books*

Praise for *A Deadly Homecoming*

A Deadly Homecoming is an addictive mystery with a clever heroine and enough plot twists and cozy charm to captivate.

—*Foreword Reviews*

With its modern pathology science and its gothic setting, the book makes for a classic haunted-house story with a satisfyingly credible forensic mystery at the heart of it. As with Toni's past adventures, Munro offers a wonderful bit of escapism. An entertaining haunted-house mystery with a few modern twists.

—*Kirkus Reviews*

A Deadly Homecoming, by Jane Bennett Munro is a tightly-packed mystery with lively dialogue, quirky characters, intricate settings, irresistible intrigue, faultless timing and just a hint of bold humor which will topple the staid police mind trying to solve this case like a game of Jenga when the wrong piece is removed.

—*Pacific Book Review*

An exciting and intense story with the unknown paranormal element thrown into the mix for an extra element of fun, this is a mystery that will not only satisfy mystery lovers but will also draw in newcomers to the genre with its energetic and enjoyable characters. Readers will eagerly await the next mystery for Toni Day to solve!

—*US Review of Books*

CPSIA information can be obtained
at www.ICGtesting.com
Printed in the USA
LVHW041011131120
671368LV00002B/97